PARDON MY FRENCH

A Romantic Farce
Written By **Allison McWood**

Annelid Press

FIRST EDITION

Cover design and logo by Wei Lu

Cultural Consultant: Pierre-Yvan Poilbout

ISBN: 978-1-9994377-5-6

For that random taxi driver in Pari

A WORD FROM ALLISON:

Hello Friends!

I feel the need to explain. This book is a romantic farce. If you are hoping for a traditional romantic comedy or a realistic documentary about French culture, then I strongly suggest that you put this book down and walk away. This is not that book. This book is in fact, a lot more fun than that book. As a farceuse, it is my job to point out all the stupid things that humans do to other humans and the ridiculousness that ensues. In this case, I am making fun of the social calamity that results when cultural stereotypes cause predetermined prejudices. People travel the world with their backs up and their minds closed, cheating themselves out of enriching experiences and connections with truly amazing people. Don't panic though. While the undertones of the theme may seem dark, this is in fact, a feel-good story. Trust me.

I could have written this novel about literally any culture, but I chose the French culture because it is one of my favorites. (And because I am a direct descendant of a French King. I know, I know. You're all jealous now) During my travels in Paris I noticed two things. 1) All of the ominous warnings I received regarding Parisians were the opposite of correct. 2) Of all the cities I have visited, I have never witnessed the same level of disrespect and abuse from tourists towards locals as I did in Paris. It was shocking because in my experience, Parisians have always treated me with warmth, enthusiasm, graciousness and respect. So you can understand that I had no choice but to write a book that makes fun of those who have an irrational fear of French people. And to give a shout out to all the incredible people I know from France. (You know who you are)

As with most farces, the characters in this book are archetypes. For example, I took all of my favorite things about Paris and crammed them all into the character of Benoît. (as opposed to Benoît's cousin who represents the many ridiculous stereotypes of French culture – but who is still impossible not to love). So you could say that Benoît is himself a metaphor of Paris, or at least a representation of all the things people love about the city.

Benoît is modelled after a taxi driver I had in Paris, who incidentally is one of my favorite people ever. He was the most rhapsodic person I have ever met and his enthusiasm for Paris was refreshing, contagious and profoundly inspiring. It was funny because so many people warned me not to take a taxi in Paris, saying that Parisian taxi drivers are surly, verbally abusive, aloof, shifty, egomaniacal, Anglophobic, inherently evil and will go to nefarious measures to exploit me in every possible way. Then this effervescent taxi driver - the first person I encountered in Paris – suddenly bounded out of the taxi, excited about showing me around. He was literally the epitome of *joie de vivre*. The Universe has extremely ironic, comedic timing and strangely appreciates my love for juxtapositions. I only knew the taxi driver for about fifteen minutes, but I couldn't wait to write a story about him. I hope I did him justice.

To all my American friends, I love you all. You are beautiful, hospitable, warm, fun, soulful, patriotic, gorgeously tanned and you make really good hushpuppies. The fact that Courtney is American does not reflect my personal views of American culture and she is not modelled after anyone in particular. I simply had to pick a country outside of the EU and America lost the coin toss. I wrote her the way I did to reflect the notion of living in a state of cultural isolation and how that can make us vulnerable to the influence of cultural stereotypes – and also to set up some great opportunities for comedic banter. Likewise, Colby Haven is not a real place but rather a farcical exaggeration of what happens when we polarize ourselves. I am not making any sort of commentary about Wisconsinites either. I just really like the word *Milwaukee*.

Obviously, no culture is perfect, but there is beauty in every culture. My goal is not to convince you that there are no jerks in France or that Paris is some kind of flawless Utopia where everyone rides unicorns and barfs rainbows. I merely wrote this book to highlight the aspects of French culture that are truly special and have resonated with me personally. And if I happen to make a few people laugh their butts off in the process, well that's even better.

Oh, and if you happen to find yourself in a Parisian taxi, please say something to your driver that will make him smile. Maybe one of you will get my driver.

Peace,

Alli

ACKNOWLEDGMENTS

Good grief, where do I start?

I guess it would seem fitting to begin by thanking that random taxi driver who picked me up at the airport in Paris. Wherever you are right now, thank you for your enthusiasm, warmth, humor, graciousness, uninhibited musical stylings and beautiful energy. You probably have no idea that my favorite character is based on you or the profound impact you had on me. I am so lucky to have met you, however briefly. I hope you are continuing to uniquely touch people's lives every day. This book would not exist without you. Keep being amazing.

Thanks to Tai Duncan (Paul Schiff Productions/Zero Gravity Management) for helping me develop the characters in the earlier screenplay version of the story. Without your pointed notes and constructive advice, Courtney Stent would still be an irredeemable twat. Thank you for believing in me, sticking up for me and for your unwavering encouragement.

Loads of thanks to Virginia Disimino for pulling double duty as editor and marketing genius. Thanks also to Annelid Press and Wei Lu for the logo and stunning cover art.

Special thanks to the wonderful Poilbout family from *La Bréhandaise Catering* for giving me a unique place to caffeinate, connect with amazing people and get inspired. Thank you for making me feel so welcome and for bringing a distinct, French vibe to the community. (Everybody go check this place out! Their éclairs are life-changing!) And of course, thank you to Pierre from *La Bréhandaise Catering* for being the world's most excellent cultural consultant. I truly appreciate your support. (and coffee)

Thank you to Professor Derek Cohen & Professor Deanne Williams for believing in me, Peter Karrie for your mentorship, B.W. Powe for your guidance, PG Wodehouse for writing great banter, Bono for being my spirit animal, King Charles IX for giving me a trace of French ancestry, crêpes for being delicious and Freddie Mercury for inspiring me not only to write this novel, but to do so fearlessly and with style.

Most of all I would like to send infinite thanks to Dan for never letting me give up.

For the benefit of my English-speaking readers, all French dialogue will be written in English with italics.

WARNING: This book contains extreme irony, satire & sarcasm. May not be suitable for those who lack a sense of humor. If you have a history of laughter-induced injury, please consult a professional before reading.

CHAPTER ONE

"*Bienvenuuuuuue...,*" Benoît Garnier stopped himself abruptly when he heard a breathless snogging noise. Feeling his face redden like rising mercury, Benoît glanced in his rearview mirror to see who had toppled wordlessly into the backseat of his taxi. Benoît's deep brown eyes widened awkwardly when he found a pair of amorous honeymooners mangled in a passionate mess on the back seat of the cab. Their mouths were attached like a couple of desperate barnacles. Benoît's eyeballs lolled around, not knowing exactly where to look.

"Where are we going today?" Benoît asked after clearing his throat a little too conspicuously. He craned his neck as he pulled out of the queue of taxis outside *Charles de Gaulle* Airport. An impossibly long lineup of tourists was waiting for taxis, but somehow the lascivious ones always seemed to find Benoît.

"Honeymooning I see," Benoît tried again. "You have chosen your destination wisely. Might I recommend some romantic attractions such as the Eiffel Tower or an enchanting cruise along the Seine?"

No reply from the backseat. Only some ravenous noises that can only be described as something you would hear in a barnyard at feeding time. Benoît tried not to look but it was impossible not to see the wild display of sprawling arms and hands and... more hands?

Benoît swallowed hard on a ball of humiliation lodged in his throat. Still, he refused to let his genial charm waver. "Where are you from, my friends? Wait. Do not stop on my account. I will guess. Düsseldorf? Oslo? Cork? Sacramento? Moosejaw, Saskatchewan? Give me a signal if I get it right."

The kissing in the backseat was now making a louder, smacking, slurping noise that made Benoît wince. Nevertheless, the eager cabbie persevered. "Excellent technique, *Monsieur.* The French invented that kiss, you know."

An undergarment suddenly flung through the air and landed on the dash. Benoît pursed his lips, musing on the satire that was transpiring in his taxi. Was this what his life had been reduced to? Would these people in the backseat ever tell him where they wanted to go? Should he toss the undergarment back to them? Was that even sanitary?

* * *

The car was small, rusty and taupe. It made a loud, obnoxious hiccup sound every time the engine turned off, which made it next to impossible for Courtney Stent to arrive home, unnoticed. Add on the sound of gravel from the dirt road spattering the rusty fender and Courtney might as well have had a fanfare of trumpets announcing her arrival. The attempt to close the car door quietly was futile as the rusty hinges shrieked like monkeys. As she teetered towards the front door, her yellow stilettos made their signature crunch on the limestone driveway.

When she saw that the light was still on in the living room, Courtney felt hopelessness wash over her. She took a deep breath as she turned the doorknob, bracing herself. Maybe if she made a beeline towards the basement door…

"I thought you were working the closing shift," Courtney's mother said, not looking up from her knitting.

"I'm tired," Courtney said, trying to cross the room without making eye contact. She was trying to ignore the overpowering smell of gravy, boiling water and leathery chicken skin but the blend of odors lingered in the air of the stuffy house. Most people would find the smell of home cooking comforting but it suffocated Courtney.

"You got fired, didn't you," said Courtney's dad, putting his face in his hands.

Courtney was just about to say something when she found herself suddenly wrapped in her mother's freckled arms. "Oh thank God! I never liked the idea of you working in the city."

"I like the city," Courtney said firmly, prying off her mother's arms. "It's not *here.*"

"You can live in the basement as long as you want," her mom said, ladling gravy onto Courtney's dumplings. "We don't mind."

"I mind a little bit," Courtney said, pushing the plate away.

"I never understood the point of you squandering half your pay check, driving all the way downtown. To work for minimum wage, no less."

"My job was fashion related," Courtney protested.

"Shoe store," Mr. Stent grunted. "Who gets fired from a shoe store?"

True, Courtney had been fired from a meager retail job. While she was shelving shoes, she could not resist the urge to discreetly put a pair of her own shoes on display; a pair that she had designed herself. She had no malicious intentions. She just put them on the shelf to see if they generated any interest. After all, they were quality shoes. Handmade by a local designer. Was it Courtney's fault that her manager was still in high school and had zero appreciation of high fashion? Her manager still had zits, for God's sake. Even as Courtney was in the process of being fired, she fought the urge to pop that grizzly whitehead on the side of her manager's left nostril. And that little twit thought he knew more about footwear than Courtney? Anyhow, there was no way her parents would understand the sacrifice she made for her craft so explaining it to them would be pointless.

Mrs. Stent broke the silence. "The city is overrated. Everything you need is in Colby Haven. Six generations of Stents lived in Colby Haven. It's safe here, Courtney. A relatively attractive young girl like you can't be too careful, you know."

Didn't her mother get it? Courtney wanted OUT of Colby Haven, Wisconsin. She wanted to get as far away from this rural nightmare as she possibly could. The dusty roads were giving her respiratory problems. The nearest mall was almost two hours away. She had nothing in common with the one hundred and twelve people in this town. That funky basement apartment was swallowing her alive with its flickering lights, poor air circulation, green astro turf carpet and sterile walls. Nobody even cared about fashion in Colby Haven. People would wear the same pair of corduroy pants for eleven straight years so long as the crotch didn't rip.

Colby Haven is where dreams go to die.

"You can work at my microbrewery." The finality of her dad's declaration made Courtney wince.

"Dad, no. It's too damn close."

"Don't exaggerate."

"Dad, I'm looking out the window right now and I can see the microbrewery from here."

"Consider the thousands you'll save on gas money. You're welcome."

"My heart wouldn't be in it, Dad."

"So?"

"I don't even like…"

"Craft beer is delicious."

"Not yours."

"What's that supposed to mean?"

"You're cheap, Dad."

"Frugal."

"You order your hops online from a sketchy wholesale factory in Taiwan. All your beers taste exactly the same. Like cat pee."

"It's good business sense."

"How do you expect me to care about your beer when you don't even care enough about it to make the stuff palatable? I can't, Dad. You need to start respecting my choices."

"What about your sister?" Mr. Stent argued. "She worked her way up to senior manager at the brewery. You want independence? Learn from her example."

"Dad, Chastity lives in a bungaloft three blocks away! For that matter, our entire extended family lives within a five mile radius!"

"It's a stable job, Courtney. With perks."

"What about fashion?" Courtney's voice was quavering. "That's all I've ever wanted to do ever since I was little! Remember how cute I was when I thought I invented the color green? You were supportive back then."

"Yes," Mr. Stent's arms were crossed stubbornly, "and we were supportive when you were three and a half and wanted to be a Smurf."

"I don't understand why you can't do some honest work," her mom said with questionable concern, "then you can doodle in your own free time. As a hobby."

"Doodle?" Courtney's teeth were clenched, "Hobby? Mom, this is my whole life! Do you know how many fashion contests I've submitted to...?"

"Oh Honey..."

"...How much time, money, fabric I've invested in? Do you think I WANT to live in that wretched basement? It's like a frigging asylum down there! What more can I possibly do to... Can't you see I'm trying?"

"But you've been trying for such a long time. You're twenty-three years old and still in this holding pattern. Maybe it's time to try something else?"

CHAPTER TWO

A rogue spring was puncturing Courtney's kidney as she lay on her lumpy mattress, staring hopelessly at the popcorn ceiling. The menacing basement walls seemed to be closing in on her. She felt a hot tear rolling off her face and wetting her pillow. The room was filled with yellow; a color Courtney was obsessed with, but right now it was blinding her, taunting her and giving her a migraine. The room was peppered with unfinished garments, draped over seamstress dummies, waiting to be sewn into masterpieces. Her sketchbook was busting with dog-eared pages and open to a page with an innovative sheath dress, etched with meticulous detail and heart.

So much yellow.

A poster of Paris was taped to the wall. Courtney gawked at it with her eyes glazed over like a pair of lifeless donuts. She had always imagined herself launching a fashion career in Paris. Hobnobbing with iconic designers. Overusing the word *Fabulous*. Shopping sprees on *Rue de Passy*. Eating fancy cheese. Sipping wine that she can't pronounce. Sitting provocatively by a fountain somewhere with the Eiffel Tower reflecting off her sunglasses. Coy, European men giving her *The Eyebrow*.

Courtney's phone had the nerve to ring, interrupting her perfectly constructive trance. She answered grudgingly.

"What."

"It's Chastity."

"Not a good time, Chass."

"I heard about your job at the shoe store."

"Can you just freaking not?"

"It's a small down, Courtney. Won't be long before everyone knows."

"I'm in Hell."

"We're all worried about you. It's not healthy to keep living in this delusion..."

"Wait, what?"

"It seems clear to everyone but you that this fashion thing is not going to happen. Mom and Dad have been giving you a free ride for like six years and I think it's time for you to come up with a realistic plan. It was fine to experiment when you were seventeen but at this point you're just frittering around and wasting your life."

Courtney squinted at her phone, wondering if her sister was some kind of trippy nightmare.

"Courtney, I'm not trying to be mean. I'm just trying to help you keep it real. Maybe you're just not special enough, you know? Do you really see yourself fitting in with all those poised *Dolce and Gabbana* types?"

The words *I'm going to Paris, you foul shrew* lingered on Courtney's tongue. But instead of being spoken, the words just sort of mushed in the back of Courtney's throat, choking her.

"Courtney? Are you there?"

Courtney squeezed her eyes shut and did a silent ugly cry.

"There's always a place for you at the microbrewery."

Shrieking like a velociraptor, Courtney hurled her phone across the room. It hit the wall, putting an angry nick in her Paris poster.

***

"I am so excited for you!" Benoît said with his eyes turning into twinkly crescents of joy. "The Eiffel Tower is said to be the most romantic destination in Paris! And your fist time is always the most special. You should see this place lit up at night! It will make all the beautiful love endorphins explode inside your brain!"

The sixteenth pair of infatuated lovers, (Yes, Benoît had been counting) barely noticed Benoît as they had a playful argument regarding who loved whom more. Benoît patiently smiled and nodded, waiting for them to stop smooching and giggling. Thankfully, they remembered to leave a wad of Euros for Benoît as they fumbled out of the cab. Benoît rolled down the window and called, "Please take pictures! And if you think *this* is romantic, you should see *The Wall of I Love You's!*"

Once the lovers disappeared into the swelling crowd around the iconic tower, Benoît let out a cleansing breath and put his head down on the steering wheel, only to be jolted back to reality by the car door opening in the back seat again.

"Take us to the most romantic restaurant in Paris," a well-coiffed man said, winking at Benoît and revealing a hidden ring box in the inner pocket of his jacket. A woman with meticulously tamed, auburn curls wrapped her arms around the man's collar bone and buried her face in his perfect hair.

Benoît mustered one of his most enthusiastic smiles. "Of course, my friends! I will ensure that tonight is your most magical yet!"

***

Nothing is more soul-sucking than being at the *Stent Microbrewery* at 6:30 a.m. Courtney's puce, polyester shirt draped shapelessly over her slight torso, making her armpits itch. She felt like she was trapped inside a burlap potato sack filled with fleas. To make matters more unbearable, Courtney was stiffed with the revolting task of sniffing the contents of every single bottle of beer as it wobbled by on a conveyor belt. She had grown up with this smell. Her dad reeked of cheap craft beer every day of her childhood. The odor seeped into all of his shirts so no amount of scented laundry detergent could exorcise the stench.

It was the smell of anguish.

With each sniff, Courtney felt her stomach rise up into her throat, prompting a gag reflex. If it was possible for a face to turn avocado green, Courtney imagined her face doing just that.

"Paris," Courtney muttered, trying to concentrate on not throwing up. "Just imagine you're in Paris."

"Talking to yourself?"

Courtney's heart sank to her ankles as her supervisor Bruce sauntered in with his thumbs in the pockets of his faded, un-ironed jeans. His smirk curled up into a lecherous dimple as his eyes wandered up and down Courtney.

"Kill me," Courtney grunted.

Bruce circled Courtney like a vulture surveying the carcass of a tantalizing zebra. He seemed to be completely unaware of how slovenly he was as he ran his fingers through his unruly hair. It was not the sexy kind of unruly. He just seemed to be unfamiliar with shampoo and scissors.

Courtney squirmed as though trying to wriggle free from his glare.

"Boss's daughter, huh?"

Courtney looked away, partly from revulsion, partly scouring the room for exit strategies.

Bruce eyeballed a sketchbook that Courtney was trying to stash out of sight. Bruce's hairy hand snatched it.

"What's this? Bruce sneered.

"Don't."

Bruce thumbed through the sketchbook and stifled a chortle as he viewed a few of Courtney's fashion sketches. Courtney grabbed it violently away from him.

"I said DON'T!"

"Feisty," Bruce said smoothly, putting his beefy hand on the small of her back, sliding it down sleazily to her butt.

"Bruce," Courtney said warningly as she abruptly pulled away, "I didn't say you could touch me. And I'm not comfortable with the way you are looking at me. You need to stop."

"This is a very small town," Bruce said, faking puppy dog eyes, "with a very unfair ratio of dudes to chicks. But you happen to be the second hottest girl in Colby Haven, next to Peggy Lambert the meter maid."

"That's inappropriate, Bruce."

"Your dad tells me you're fair game."

"He... he had no right to..."

"My Pinto is parked out back. What do you say the two of us go and..."

"You get away from me!"

"You think you can do better than *this?*" Bruce scoffed as he gestured towards his slithery self. "There's slim pickings around here, sister."

"This town is so ridiculously small, there's a good chance I *am* your sister!"

"I have an open mind," Bruce said, encroaching on Courtney's personal space. His hot breath was giving Courtney hives on the back of her neck.

"I can't wait to get out of here," Courtney stammered.

"And where exactly do you plan to go?" Bruce scoffed.

Courtney spun around and pierced Bruce with a Clint Eastwood glare. Her sea blue eyes were like glistening knives. "Paris," she said, carefully wrapping her lips around the word for effect.

Bruce burst into a sudden cackle. "Paris? Hey that's rich! Are you going to wear one of them tarty French maid numbers?"

As if in slow motion, Courtney watched Bruce's raunchy hand reach for Courtney's lady business. Biting her lower lip in fury, Courtney took a swing at Bruce with both fists.

"Take is easy, Doll," Bruce said, amused.

"I'm not your doll," Courtney said, backing away, pretending she was not on the brink of tears. Her heart was thumping like that of a hunted deer. Courtney dodged out of the way as Bruce tried to lunge at her. Losing her footing, she toppled backwards into a huge vat of beer.

Bruce's mouth gaped stupidly as he watched the ripples and air bubbles where Courtney had just submerged. She suddenly thrashed out of the beer, choking and sputtering.

"You are such a perv!" Courtney shrieked in a squeakier manner than she had intended.

"Is this because I'm your supervisor?" Bruce asked, nonplussed.

CHAPTER THREE

"Palais Garnier!" Benoît bubbled as he dropped off a preoccupied couple wearing matching Paris shirts. "You are in for a treat! This building holds a very special place in my..."

The couple slammed the taxi door, leaving Benoît visibly disappointed. He loved to share his knowledge of the *Palais Garnier*. He looked forward to taking people here every day. Even just driving past the opera house gave him goosebumps. Sometimes during downtime he would explore the building himself, each time as though it was his first. He had roamed those corridors more times than he could count but the marble, the baroque art, the theatrical staircase stirred his spirit in a way that nothing else could.

As he drove through the inching Paris traffic, Benoît mused on the uninhibited enthusiasm this city inspired. He loved Paris. People from all over the world flocked to this city, thinking of it as the world capital of romance. Benoît would not want to live anywhere else but his beautiful Paris. But as cinematic as this place was, Benoît always felt as though he was watching somebody else's movie.

Benoît pursed his lips, noticing how dry they were. His mind meandered as he was bombarded with images of affection and intimacy from every angle. The restaurant patios were peppered with multinational tourists sharing sensuous foods. The people were all so beautiful as though they had absorbed the beauty of the city itself.

Love just erupted everywhere and was accentuated by the classic, French music echoing off each antiquated building. It was like Paris was buzzing with passion. The lights, the sounds, the people, the spirit...

"Merde!" Benoît shouted as a snobbish woman illegally crossed the street with no warning. He screeched his taxi to a halt and clutched his chest, trying to catch his breath. Suddenly, a garish face appeared on the windshield, pounding the glass. Blood colored lips contorted into an angry snarl. The most self-righteous up-do Benoît had ever seen bounced around in fury but strangely stayed in place. Unsightly cleavage was nearly popping out of a skin tight dress as though someone was forcing toothpaste out of a tube. The dress was an even bloodier color than the lipstick. And what was wrong with her eyes?

"You dullard!" the snarling woman shrieked.

"Madame! Are you okay?" Benoît yelped as he ran out of his taxi.

"Do you have any idea who you almost killed?" the woman barked, adjusting her toothpaste tube dress and reinforcing her gaudy earrings. "I am more expensive than Dubai!"

"I did not see you. I beg your forgiveness, *Madame."*

"You don't know who I am, do you? Commoners."

"If you will only let me..."

A shrill noise emitted from the woman when she saw her handbag on the road, scuffed and mutilated. Benoît's eyes widened in fear.

"Someone is going to die!" the woman howled.

Benoît winced.

"Do you have any idea what this used to be?" the woman said as she held the lifeless bag dramatically in her arms. "You recklessly turned my *Louis Vuitton* clutch into mangled roadkill! The only thing in this world that I truly love!"

Benoît's mouth moved a few times before he found words. "My condolences?"

"Perfect," the woman said while cracking her neck in an unladylike fashion. "I have a kink in my swanlike neck. If I need a chiropractor, so help me God!"

"What God might that be? Benoît muttered inaudibly, "The one with the horns?"

"And to think they let you operate a motor vehicle. I'll have your license revoked. Or make you disappear, I haven't decided which. I know people."

"In my defense, you did not use the pedestrian crossing. Perhaps that enormous, yet comely brimmed hat you are wearing obstructed your view of traffic."

The woman unexpectedly took a swig from a flask. "I am numb to your charm, Raoul."

"Benoît."

The woman pierced Benoît with her demonic stare. Seriously, what was wrong with her eyes? "I don't like you," she enunciated way too precisely.

"Because you have not taken time to know me," Benoît said with a jovial shrug. "You will find that I am quite adorable." Benoît smiled with all of his teeth.

"If you ever cross my path again, I will turn your life into Dante's Inferno. You have no idea what I am capable of."

Benoît gaped as the woman farcically adjusted her bosom then pompously trotted away with her pointy nose in the air.

"*Diable*," Benoît shuddered.

***

Drenched in beer, Courtney stormed through the front door of her parents' house. Her blond ponytail was no longer wavy but hopelessly sopping and tangled. She was already dreading the idea of pulling the elastic band out of the matted, sticky mess. Her parents were seated with Courtney's ornery grandmother at the kitchen table, drinking tea. All three were scrutinizing the rivulets of mascara streaking down her cheeks and her oversized, waterlogged work shirt slipping off her left shoulder.

"Oh good," her mother said, nonplussed. "You're home. Gramma's house is being fumigated so…"

"I'm not in the mood," Courtney said, making sloshy noises with her socks as she padded across the linoleum.

"What smells like cat pee?" Gramma complained, scrunching her nose.

"It's craft beer, Gramma."

Mr. Stent exhaled in that special, disappointed way of his.

Courtney stopped sloshing and lolled her head, exasperated. "Dad. You have something to say?"

"I spoke to Bruce."

Courtney parted her lips and squinted her left eye. "... And?"

"He told me what happened."

For a nanosecond, Courtney's eyes glinted with hope.

"Courtney, how could you have let something like this happen?"

"Wait, what?" Courtney was squinting with both eyes now.

"You are taking this opportunity for granted. I know this isn't your dream job but you need to leave your attitude at home, you hear?"

"Dad, what are you trying to..."

"Don't interrupt. Your behavior at work today was reckless. Look at you. This is disgraceful. You've wasted inventory, committed a major health and safety code violation, hindered our productivity, made an utter arse of yourself, assaulted your supervisor..."

"Whoa! Okay? Just Whoa! Bruce assaulted *me!*"

"Bruce is a fine young man," Mr. Stent said, wagging a finger in Courtney's face. "You had no business swinging punches at him just because he gave you a friendly warning about doodling in your little notebook during work hours."

"You've got to be frigging kidding me! Dad, Bruce is a pig! He was trying to do all kinds of unholy things to my sacred temple!"

"He likes you," Mrs. Stent said dotingly as she lifted Courtney's chin. "Couldn't you just give him a chance? He comes from a nice family. His mother is in the quilting guild, don't you know. Sure, he's not the most dashing fella but you shouldn't be so superficial. A girl like you can't be too picky and eventually you're going to have to embrace the fact…"

"What do you mean, *a girl like me?*"

Mrs. Stent looked at Courtney compassionately. I mean condescendingly. "Oh Honey. It's hard not having a lot of options. But someday you'll find a good man who will overlook everything and take care of you."

Gramma muttered something about Courtney and lots of cats.

"I'm saturated in beer. Can we do this another time?"

"I'm worried, dear," her mother persisted. "It's like you've been on a downward spiral ever since Paul…"

"Nope," Courtney said, sloshing towards the basement. The door slammed behind her.

"I slipped your mail under the door!" her mother called after her.

***

Safe in her musty abode, Courtney let the tears fall freely. She couldn't wait to peel these horrible clothes off and burn them. Her baggy shirt pretty much just fell off when she wiggled, but her beer-drenched yoga pants were basically glued to her legs. She lay on her back, trying to pry the pants down her thighs but the spandex clung for its life. She turned her head and spotted an envelope at eye level.

It was post marked from Paris.

Courtney jolted back to life, tearing open the envelope while trying to stand with her yoga pants stuck halfway up her thighs. Her eyeballs rapidly scanned each line of the letter until she uttered a frantic shriek. She ran for the door but fell over herself.

Damn yoga pants.

***

"This happened!" Courtney announced, slapping the letter on the kitchen table.

"What's this?" her dad asked, unimpressed.

"I'm going to Paris!" Courtney squeaked. "They like my designs!"

"It's a scam," Gramma blurted.

"Gramma…"

"There must be some kind of mistake."

"Mom, no. They included notes that are specific to my portfolio. This is a thing. It's really happening. I'm going to Paris!"

"Paris. Pffft. "Gramma snorted. " I don't trust anyone who eats snails."

"Look," Courtney said, pointing to the letter, "I get to spend the summer in Paris. I arrive the beginning of July and I get to stay until Fashion Week. My designs are going to be showcased by top models at a major venue during Fashion Week. Can you believe that?"

"No," Gramma grunted.

Courtney continued, paying no mind to the negativity in the room. "They're setting me up in a snazzy hotel. I get my own, personal driver and luxury vehicle. Like an actual driver who will be like a guide and personal concierge type thing. And the best part? I've been assigned a mentor. Alexandria Fontrose! Snap!"

Everyone gaped stupidly at Courtney.

"She's a renowned designer," Courtney explained. "From New York? From all the magazine covers? Her own fashion channel on cable? Faux Fur? Chime in anytime, guys."

"Let me see that," said Mr. Stent, sliding the letter across the table.

"It's fine, Dad."

"I'm sorry, Courtney. This just seems suspicious to me," her father said, slipping his bifocals down his nose to analyze the letter. "They could be trying to lure you into the country for nefarious reasons."

"They?"

"The French," said Mr. Stent matter-of-factly.

"Dad, that makes no sense. Did it ever occur to you that they chose me because I'm talented?"

Mr. Stent gaped at Courtney, utterly perplexed.

"I'm worried," her mother said in a deathly serious tone.

Courtney rolled her eyes. "Here we go..."

"The thought of you all by yourself," her mother said, shaking her head. "You don't know the language. The customs. You're not up to date on your vaccines. You're going to be taken advantage of. I have a very bad feeling."

"Listen to your mother," her dad muttered.

"I don't believe this," Courtney said, furrowing her brow. "Would it kill you to be supportive?"

"We let you live in the basement," her father growled, "while you do your thing and blow off adult responsibilities. I even offered you a viable career but you screwed that up too. Don't you stand there and tell us that we don't support you."

"I've been running headfirst into a wall over and over again trying to prove to you that I deserve this," Courtney blinked back stinging tears, "but the minute someone tells me I'm good enough..."

"Paris is so worldly," her mother added. "What, with the Red Light District."

"Wrong city, Mom."

"All those communal baths."

"Nope, guess again."

"And there's pickpockets. I saw a documentary."

"Mom, I have a personal driver who will be looking after me. I'll be fine."

"Is he French?" asked Mr. Stent, raising a suspicious eyebrow.

"Dad!" Courtney gasped.

"The French have fewer inhibitions than normal people. I've heard things."

"How would you even know that, Dad? You've never driven further than Wauwatosa!"

"I'm just saying," her dad said, lifting the left hand of rationality, "they are an impulsive people. Am I a bad person for wanting to protect my baby girl from being accosted, mugged, kidnapped or sold as a slave?"

Courtney could not have made a more farcical face at her father, had she been in a production of a Georges Feydeau play. Moments ago, had he not literally referred to the ape who groped her as a *fine young man?*

"How are you going to pay for all this?" her mother worried.

"Everything's paid for," Courtney persisted.

"What about incidentals, Courtney? Food. Personal hygiene products. Floss, for example. Sightseeing..."

"Birth control," Gramma barked.

"Gramma!"

"Those French men are handsy!" the old lady insisted.

"I really don't think you've thought this through, Courtney."

"I'm doing this, okay? By myself! I don't need your approval, I don't need your advice and I definitely don't need your permission!"

25 - Pardon My French

"Will you need a ride to the airport?"

CHAPTER FOUR

In the Stent family's powder blue Buick, Courtney's mom and dad exchanged knowing looks of concern in the front seat.

"I'm not going to disgrace the whole family. Back off, Gramma."

Gramma snorted, seeming to be having an argument with herself next to Courtney in the backseat.

"There's still time to back out, Courtney. Just say the word and your father will turn this car around."

"Mom, no. It's Paris."

"Meh," Gramma interjected. "Paris is overrated."

"Take your pills, Gramma."

"Did I ever tell you I spent the summer of 1953 in Paris?" Gramma gurgled.

"No you didn't. Stop making things up."

"I was an exotic dancer," Gramma continued. "Worst goddam summer of my life. Sweltering heat. More damn people than you could realistically fit into Hell. Bloody cobblestones gave me blisters. Don't get me started about the rude..."

"Gramma, you've never even been to the French cheese aisle at the grocery store. Paris cannot possibly be that bad. Otherwise people wouldn't write so many songs about it."

"You wouldn't say that if you were deflowered by a smirking mime!" Gramma spat. "Last time I feed pigeons outside the Louvre."

"Gramma, you know perfectly well that never happened... did it?"

"Here," Gramma said abruptly, tossing Courtney a book. "It's got everything you need to know. How to tolerate French waiters. How to translate French insults. How to get what you want when you are denied service for being American. There's a whole chapter on how to interpret the various French glares, ogles, scowls and grimaces."

Courtney turned the book over in her hands. A wave of uncertainty suddenly tugged at Courtney's innards. The Buick pulled up in front of the airport and Courtney gaped as her mother started to cry.

"Mom?" Courtney asked nervously.

"Did you pack your rape whistle?" her mother sniffled.

Courtney swallowed hard. This was a journey she had always wanted... always needed to take alone. But she suddenly realized she had never actually done anything alone. What if her family was right? What if she couldn't do this by herself? Or at all?

"I'll be fine."

"This all just seems like such an unnecessary risk."

Courtney closed her eyes and took a deep breath, clutching the handle of her carry-on.

Courtney was halfway out of the car when her dad locked eyes with her. "Be aware of your surroundings. Don't look any of them directly in the eyes. Your pockets must always have zippers. Avoid anyone who looks like an international criminal. Brush your teeth with bottled water and if you see a street caricaturist, *run.*"

Courtney nodded uncertainly.

***

Benoît's apartment was Paris-sized. The tiny kitchen and sitting room were separated by an L-shaped, white leather couch. A double bed took up his entire bedroom which only had a partial wall. His favorite spot was his balcony that sat one comfortably or two cozily. If Benoît angled himself to the left, he could see the Eiffel Tower in the distance. It was usually the darkest time of night by the time Benoît traipsed home after work so he would grab himself a baguette and a glass of wine, admiring the glowing tower from his balcony.

On that particular night, drizzle was pestering the windows and the tower's glow was stifled by a stubborn fog. Benoît hummed absentmindedly as he entered his little home, dropped his car keys on the inch of countertop, slipped off his shoes and plopped onto the couch. He flicked the television on, but every channel seemed to have a *Nespresso* commercial featuring George Clooney. His mind whirred with a mosaic of thoughts which tended to happen when he was alone in the quietness of the night. He loved Paris. He loved his job. He loved interacting and connecting with people. He loved sharing his enthusiasm for his beloved city. But every so often, especially as summer was approaching, when love seems to waft around freely with all the blowing pollen, Benoît felt completely alone.

Benoît exhaled towards the ceiling as he lay on the couch. Tourist high season was coming fast. More honeymoons, marriage proposals, anniversaries, summer flings. The season would be beautiful but it would be intense. Maybe this would be a good time to take vacation and travel. But he could never afford to do that. He was barely scraping by and he was still making payments on this amazing couch. It was the only real luxury of which he had ever treated himself. Benoît pondered how cool his couch was.

The buzz of Benoît's phone startled him.

"Allo?"

"Benoît. Good. You are up."

"I am off duty, François."

"Yes, Yes. But I need your thoughts on something."

"You are the boss."

"Listen, I know you have been feeling a bit down lately."

"It is that obvious? I thought I was hiding it quite well."

"I have known you for over a year, Benoît. I can sense things. Normally you are rhapsodic. Of late, you have been merely peppy."

"Insightful."

"I will not get into your personal business right now. But an opportunity has just come up and I think it would be perfect for you. It might be just what you need."

"I am listening."

"How would you feel about a special assignment?"

Benoît suddenly sat up, his eyes widening with intrigue.

CHAPTER FIVE

Courtney had never been on a plane before. The cabin was much more cramped than she had imagined. After being adequately elbowed and bopped around while trying to find her seat, she found the spot where she would be wedged for the next nine hours and fifty-four minutes. She had the middle seat. A sleek businessman was already seated by the window. He smelled like a chemically infused meadow.

"I think this is me," Courtney said, pointing to her seat. "Mind if I..."

The businessman answered Courtney with a raised eyebrow and immediately put in his ear buds. Courtney nestled her rear end into the seat as a very large, hairy man with pit stains took the aisle seat next to her. Since each man had annexed an armrest, Courtney found herself basically folded between the two.

"Excuse me!" Courtney flagged an apathetic flight attendant. "I was wondering if maybe I could switch seats? I suffer from claustrophobia and I'm starting to feel a bit anxious. Probably because I live in my parents' basement which has no windows or air flow. Small, enclosed, geometrical spaces make me feel a bit existential. Like maybe I'll be stuck forever in..."

"Flight's fully booked," the flight attendant said, licking orangey-red lipstick from her teeth. "Why isn't your seat in the upright position? Is this your first time flying or something?"

As the flight attendant prepared for her bland presentation on seatbelt function, Courtney heard her cell phone. Reaching for her back pocket was an interesting feat, wriggling between Meadow Man and the Sasquatch.

"What's up, Chass?" Courtney finally managed to answer the phone. "I'm on the plane."

"So you're really doing this," Chastity sighed on the phone. "Please, Courtney. Do the family a favor and don't screw this up."

"Remind me again about why this has anything to do with you or the family," Courtney said, massaging her temples. "Because last time I checked, I was a grownup woman with legitimate career goals."

Pretty much everyone on the plane could hear Chastity's heaving sigh from Courtney's cell phone. "Courtney, would you please stop being so sensitive. I'm trying to give you constructive advice here. Don't roll your eyes at me. I know you're rolling your eyes right now. You always do that. Stop. Listen, you can't just waltz into Paris like a common Midwestern country bumpkin. There's going to be people there who actually know what they're doing. If you want to be successful..."

"What, like you?"

"*If you want to be successful* you have to make a good impression. I love you Courtney, but you're a bit naïve. Always keep your back up. People can smell inexperience. It smells like baby powder and old Bandaids. If anyone smells you they'll never take you seriously."

"I don't mean to be a twat-waffle but you work for Dad. Are you really in a position to give me a motivational speech about being successful in a field you know nothing about?"

"Do you really want the Paris fashion scene to know you live in your parents' basement and got fired from a shoe store?"

Courtney slunk into her seat, shading her face from the stares of irritated flyers. "Everyone has to start somewhere. This is my first step, okay? Just let me do this without trying to freak me out."

"Trust no one, Courtney. Don't dish out more information about yourself than you absolutely have to. You're not there to make friends."

"I'm going there to network."

"Those people aren't your friends, Courtney. They don't love you like your family does. They are foreigners in a strange land and do not have your best interest in mind. Keep things professional and impersonal."

"I'm going to Paris. Not Jupiter."

"Remember what Gramma said."

Courtney's stomach dropped suddenly and the plane had not even started moving yet. She caught a glimpse of Gramma's Paris survival manual peeping out of the magazine pocket in the seat in front of her. "The scary sky-waitress is giving me the stink eye. I have to go."

"Courtney, be careful..."

"*I have to go.*"

Courtney quickly shoved her cell phone into her purse, as though it was burning her fingers. She noticed that her heart was racing so she tentatively pulled a small, plush duck from her carry-on. She gave the duck a squeeze, forgetting that the duck squeaks when you squeeze it. Suspicious eyes started peeping over magazines and novels all around her. Aware that she was being judged, she quickly whispered, "Got me a lucky duck. Only good things can happen now."

The plane started to roll down the runway and panic gripped Courtney's midsection. She squeezed the armrests until her knuckles whitened, brushing the stubborn arms of the strangers on either side of her. Her eyeballs scanned the plane for something to focus on other than her angst. She grabbed her Gramma's handbook, clutching it tightly like a miserly old woman with her pearls. Meadow Man did a double take when he saw the title of Courtney's book: ***"An American's Guide to Surviving Paris."***

"Pffft," the man said, shaking his head.

But Courtney was already trying to drown herself in the book. Good thing she had some dense reading material to keep her engrossed for the next nine hours and fifty-four minutes.

***

His delicious, dark blue eyes were so alluring he could beckon customers with a meager wink. His sleek black hair was perfectly coiffed with just enough body to floop foxy locks out of his face by running his fingers through. His coy eyebrows seduced more women than Giacomo Casanova. He had a smile that would make your knees buckle. His body was lean but smoldering. He looked like he just stepped out of a sizzling cologne commercial.

And they called him Étienne.

In the shadow of the magnificent *Sacré Coeur Basilica* was Étienne's modest yet bustling open concept souvenir shop. The merchandise was cheap but the vendor was hot. Was it any wonder that ninety percent of Étienne's cliental was female? Take Darla, for example. She was a dainty little thing with an adorable bob haircut, admiring a selection of felt berets. She blushed at Étienne's suave mannerisms as he recited the selection of colors. How was it even possible for him to be so sensual about hats?

A taxi pulled up in front of the shop and Étienne smiled with recognition. Out of the cab came Benoît, dressed in a black and white shirt, beret and a red kerchief tied around his neck. He was carrying a baguette and had a thin mustache drawn with eye pencil above his upper lip.

"Cousin!" Étienne chimed, *"Right now the most luscious woman I have ever seen is picking out a beret!"* He turned to Darla and spoke in English for her benefit. "Try the red."

Benoît fidgeted with his beret and awkwardly adjusted his quirky attire.

"Benoît, why are you dressed like a deranged cartoon?"

"Special assignment. I am a personal driver. This outfit is mandatory. Apparently tourists want us to look like this."

Étienne raised his legendary eyebrow. *"Personal driver? Anyone famous or exciting?"*

"Exciting people do not ride in taxis."

"You do not seem your sunny and charismatic self."

Benoît shrugged.

"Tell me about this new assignment. Why the sudden change?"

"François thought I would be well suited for this gig. He said of all his drivers I am the most enthusiastic and have the best manners. I am not sure what he meant by that. Anyhow, I think it would do me good to have a change of pace this summer. You know how summers can be."

"Are you okay, Cousin?"

Benoît scuffed his shoe on the sidewalk, forlorn. *"We are entitled to our bouts of melancholy, no?"*

"What is bringing on this change of mood?"

Benoît found a timid smile and did his best to change the tone of the conversation with a playful wink. *"Tourist season. You know how tourists can be."* Benoît pretended that his head was exploding and then half-laughed.

Étienne's penetrating eyes turned to slits of concentration as he looked deep into Benoît's soul. *"Do yourself a favor, Benoît. Get laid. Take a few of my ladies out for a test drive. I do not mind. We are family."*

After a brief beat, Benoît burst into an explosive laugh. *"Étienne, mon dieu. You are too much sometimes."*

"I am being serious!"

"That is a bit personal, Étienne."

"Why are you holding back?"

Benoît stopped laughing for a moment, remembering.

"Cousin?"

"It was around this time last year..."

"Get over yourself, Benoît. You have not kissed a woman in over a year. Me? I enjoyed four women last night, not including Bernice. Four women, Benoît. Where is your passion, dear cousin? Where is your joie de vivre?"

Benoît took a breath. *"Why can tourists not occasionally choose a different city as a romantic destination? It is hard sometimes..."*

"Paris is peppered with comely women who are waiting eagerly for you to disrobe them with your teeth like an untamed, Eurasian lynx."

"Étienne..."

"You are a smoldering Frenchman, my dear cousin. If I was a woman I would do things to you that would blow your mind!"

"I cannot, okay?"

"Because of..."

"Not now, Étienne," Benoît said, making his way back to his taxi.

"But Cousin..."

"Good talk," Benoît said out the window as he drove down the narrow street.

CHAPTER SIX:
(DAY 1 IN PARIS)

Why did Courtney's cell phone always ring at the most inopportune of times? She was brisk-walking through *Charles de Gaulle* Airport at 7:45 a.m. awkwardly lugging her suitcases and carry-on, having no idea where she was going and trying to keep up with the rapid flow of foot traffic.

Courtney managed to position her cell phone between her shoulder and her cheek. "Yeah, hello."

"It's Chastity. Did you land? Has anyone tried to accost you?"

"I'm fine," Courtney said as her stiletto heels clacked with a steady beat. "But that red eye flight was a very bad idea. I didn't sleep at all. I smell. I don't know what's going on with my neck right now. I'm starving and I have a ponytail headache."

"Did you read Gramma's book?"

"What else did I have to do for nine hours? I don't know how people are able to sleep on airplanes. I should have brought pills or something."

Courtney squinted at various signs. "French," she sighed.

"What?"

"French signs. French people. French... hats."

"Courtney, are you in some kind of trouble?"

"I just have no idea where I'm going."

"Hold your head up, Courtney. Don't let anyone know you're way in over your head. Those Parisians will eat you for breakfast. It's a cultural thing."

"Shush," Courtney said, still brisk walking. "My driver is supposed to be waiting for me."

"Check his references, Courtney. You don't want to be trapped in a car with some kind of French predator."

"For the luvva... I told you a million times, this whole thing is legit. I have a personal driver who happens to be a professional. And he will be collecting me in a luxury vehicle with champagne, no doubt and..."

Courtney spotted Benoît standing outside by his taxi, holding a sign that said, **STENT.**

"Oh hell no," Courtney said hollowly as she dropped her phone.

***

Courtney's heels clacked outside as she dropped her luggage with a dejected thud. She was not prepared for the sight she beheld. There stood Benoît, decked out in the most cliché attire imaginable and leaning against a taxi. Not a limousine. Not a Bentley, Mercedes or

Maserati. Just an ordinary taxi. Courtney's jaw dropped. She chuffed, unable to find words.

"I don't believe this," Courtney finally managed.

Benoît looked up and straightened his posture when he realized that his passenger had arrived. Courtney's makeup had mostly worn off but her sea blue eyes made Benoît forget to breathe for a moment. Her messy ponytail gave her kind of a windblown look and a stray lock of wavy blond hair wandered over her forehead. Benoît suddenly couldn't move. He felt a buzzing sensation in his chest. He parted his lips and stood stupidly for a nanosecond, blinking.

"Stent?" Benoît finally said after swallowing hard.

Courtney nodded, staring at Benoît in disbelief.

Benoît felt like he was glowing inside as his mouth melted into a warm smile. *"Bonjour!"*

"Why isn't this a limo?" Courtney snapped.

Benoît gaped blankly at Courtney.

"I was supposed to be provided with a driver."

"That is me!" Benoît said jovially. "For the summer, I am yours."

"I was definitely not expecting this. *You.*"

"And I was not expecting *you*," Benoît said, tilting his hat in a reverent salute. "I imagined Stent to be the name of a humorless banker. You can imagine my delight when a beautiful..."

"Why are you dressed that way?" Courtney asked nervously, backing slowly away. "Are you a mime? I was told French mimes are pervs."

"No, I am just a driver."

"Really? Because I have a rape whistle."

Benoît cocked his head. "You have my word," he said chivalrously. "I would make a terrible mime. I am much too fond of talking."

Benoît cheerfully took Courtney's luggage and opened the taxi's trunk.

"Hey!" Courtney yelled as she grabbed her luggage from Benoît's clutches.

"I meant no offense."

"Bad!" Courtney scolded. "Bad driver!"

Benoît's eyes widened in confusion.

***

The silence in the taxi was deafening. Benoît had been driving for fifteen minutes and Courtney had not made a peep. He was distracted by a fruity aroma wafting around the cab. What kind of shampoo did she use? She smelled like a guava. Benoît heard a little sigh in the backseat. It was an exasperated sigh but it was still cute. He could not resist the urge to steal a glimpse of her through the rearview mirror. Her little pink lips were pursed tightly. She was so petite, like a little bird. And she was reading a book. How literary. Benoît craned his neck to get a better view of the title: ***"An American's Guide to Surviving Paris."***

Benoît burst into a snort of laughter.

Courtney looked up from her book and gave Benoît a suspicious squint.

Benoît sucked the laughter back in and held his breath for a moment. Who in the world would write a book with a title like that? Who in the world would *read* it?

Courtney was not really reading the book. She had already read it three times on the plane. She was merely hiding her face behind the book to disguise her nerves. Everything around her was unfamiliar. She couldn't read the street signs as they whizzed by. The guy on the radio was speaking in a foreign tongue. And she was feeling ill at ease being at the mercy of a strange man in a strange car, driving into a strange city. She watched the back of Benoît's head from behind her book, waiting for him to do something sinister. Her eyes meandered to the rearview mirror where she studied Benoît's chocolatey eyes with their long lashes. She noticed his eyes caught hers and they twinkled kindly at her. What was up with that?

"You there!" Courtney whistled to get Benoît's attention. "TAKE... ME... TO... AV...EN...UE...VIC...TOR...HU...GO!"

Benoît smirked at the unnecessary volume and tempo of Courtney's command. "I am French. I am not deaf."

Courtney felt her face flush. "Oh. My bad. I'm never quite sure how much you people understand."

"Taxi drivers?"

"French people. Your accents are so strong is a wonder you can understand *each other.*"

Benoît raised an animated eyebrow.

"Crap," Courtney was getting flustered. "Was that culturally insensitive? There's so many rules here."

"I am Benoît, by the way."

There was an awkward silence as Courtney rummaged in her purse for gum.

"Do Americans have first names?"

"How do you know I'm American?"

Benoît covered his mouth to stifle laughter.

"Why are you doing that? I'm unfamiliar with your customs."

Unable to contain it any longer, Benoît sprayed laughter all over his dashboard.

Courtney puffed herself up, consumed with insecurity. "In my country, laughing at people is considered rude."

"Americans are so cute. The way they want everyone else to be American."

"Wow. Gramma was right. French people are pompous."

"Is that what it says in your book?" Benoît stopped at a red light and playfully reached for the survival guide. "What else does it say? Let me see."

"I need that!"

Amused, Benoît read from the book. "*Expect poor service. The French are considered entitled, aloof, they have way too many poodles and wear necklaces made of garlic. The city is infested with bohemians and rakish fops. Even their cheese has a false sense of superiority..."*

"Sure, it sounds racist and absurd when you read it out loud like that."

"Like what?"

"You know, with all the twirly sounds. The moist consonants. The what-do-you-call-it. *Frenchness.*"

"I assure you, it is not my accent that makes this sound absurd," Benoît said before reading from the book again. *'Take extra caution when riding a taxi as the drivers are particularly surly.'* Ouch. *'When speaking English, a Parisian will squint and pretend not to understand you?"*

 "I suppose they also consider themselves more highly evolved love makers."

"That part is true," Benoît smirked.

Before Courtney could finish pretending to be morally outraged by the comment, Benoît rolled down the window and tossed the book out.

"You did that for no reason!" she protested.

"I did you a favor. Who writes a book about *surviving* Paris?"

"Arthur H. Flummery. Renowned American author of helpful travel guides."

"You don't *survive* Paris," Benoît said with verve. "You *absorb* Paris. I have lived here all my life and I never tire of the beautiful energy here."

"Are you going to tell me that Paris is the most magical place on earth? A place that's too beautiful to be real?"

"I was going to comment on our very efficient metro system. But okay."

"Are you making fun of me?"

"Yes," Benoît nodded emphatically.

"Are you this forthcoming with everyone or am I just special?"

"Yes."

"I don't follow."

"Have you never been flattered before?"

Courtney looked everywhere except at Benoît.

"Where is Mr. Stent?" Benoît asked after an awkward beat.

"Excuse me?" Courtney's heart throbbed at the question.

"People usually come to Paris with the one they love."

"I'm alone," Courtney said, holding her posture erect.

"Ah! Then you *are* here with the one you love!"

Courtney's mouth widened into an indignant letter O. "Love is counterproductive. I'm here on business."

"Really! What is it that you do exactly? Do you hate the French professionally?"

"I'm a fashion designer."

"From New York?"

Courtney let out a croak. She couldn't tell him she was from Colby Haven. That would be embarrassing. Courtney's mind swam around, thinking of all the closest cities and which one sounded the most impressive. Finally, she blurted out, "Milwaukee."

"*Milwaukee,*" Benoît said, savoring the way the word felt on his tongue. He had never heard of Milwaukee before. It was sort of a fun word to say.

"It's in Wisconsin. With the cheese?"

"Will you tell me your name? Are you a celebrity? Have I heard of you?"

Courtney hesitated. "Courtney."

"Courtney Stent? I have not heard of you."

"I prefer to keep a low profile," Courtney said softly as she thumbed through her sketchbook.

"What is that?" Benoît asked, gesturing with his head towards the sketchbook.

"It's my whole life."

"Better not lose it."

"They're my ideas. It's personal."

"You should talk to my cousin Étienne. You could say he dabbles in fashion like you."

"I don't dabble. I've been working towards this my entire life."

"How old are you?" Benoît asked, triangulating his left eyebrow.

"Twenty-three."

"Twenty-three? You have not yet *had* an entire life!"

"Why aren't you in a bad mood like normal taxi drivers?"

"Meeting new people is the best part of my job. Talking with people from all over the world."

"Doesn't that get on your nerves?"

"What do you mean?"

"Don't you think all other cultures are inferior to yours?"

"Was that in your book too?"

"Chapter eleven."

Benoit smirked.

Courtney squirmed, wishing she had her survival manual so she could decode the smirk.

"There is beauty in every culture, Courtney."

"Whatever."

CHAPTER SEVEN

Benoît drove up to a disappointingly average hotel and parked at the curb. Courtney looked up from her sketchbook as she heard Benoît turn off the ignition. Her face melted like a slushy pile of disappointed snow.

"Voilà!" Benoît chimed.

"Where are we?" Courtney asked in a lower octave than normal. "This isn't the hotel."

"This is it," Benoît said, rechecking the address. "Is something wrong?"

"I was expecting something snazzier."

"Do you require recommendations for dinner? A show maybe? I can drive you anywhere. You are my only responsibility for the next couple of months."

"That won't be necessary," Courtney tried to sound aloof.

"It must be 3:00 a.m. in MIlwaukee." Benoît really liked saying that word. "You must be starving. I know what you would like! There is a quaint place around the corner where you can enjoy a coffee and *pain au chocolat*."

"Ate on the plane," Courtney lied as she gathered her things. She eyeballed the sky where an ominous cloud was spewing rain. "Rain. Perfect."

"Just a flash storm. We have been getting quite a few of them this week. It will pass, I promise."

"I think you're supposed to have something for me?"

"Your itinerary! Here you go."

Courtney's hand accidentally brushed Benoît's fingers as she took the itinerary from him. She pulled away, not really sure why her hand suddenly felt dirty. She changed the subject by pretending to be surveying the weather. "The rain's not letting up," Courtney stated the obvious.

"You can stay here until it passes," Benoît offered. "There's no point in…"

"No I'm good," Courtney quipped as she bolted out of the taxi and ran for the hotel entrance.

Benoît deflated as he watched her sprint away. He then spotted Courtney's sketchbook which she had forgotten in her haste. He looked towards the hotel entrance and back at the sketchbook multiple times. What was Courtney hiding in those pages?

***

"*Attend!*" Benoît called as he burst through the hotel entrance, drenched from the rain and completely out of breath.

Courtney spun and found Benoît, panting and dripping. A stray curl of wet, black hair, stuck to his forehead like a shimmering letter C. His rich brown eyes danced with admiration. There were even raindrops lingering on his long eyelashes. Courtney gawked at Benoît with an indistinguishable expression when he offered her the sketchbook which he had kept dry under his jacket.

"They are very beautiful," Benoît said, looking down.

Courtney cocked her head, unsure of how to feel about Benoît's gesture.

"I looked at them. Your ideas. The designs." Benoît admitted. "It was not my place, I know."

Courtney glared at Benoît.

"I have made you uncomfortable."

Courtney swiped the sketchbook from Benoît. "Thanks. For keeping it dry."

"You are very talented," Benoît added quickly as Courtney turned to walk away.

"Is this your way of angling for a tip?"

Benoît looked stung. "Do you not have compliments in America?"

"Let's keep this professional," Courtney said, collecting herself.

"Of course. Your luggage is still in the trunk of my taxi. I shall get it for you."

"I can get it myself," Courtney sounded more defensive than she intended.

"You are most capable, I agree. But the rain is pelting out there. If for some reason you have an aversion to me handling your luggage, I will summon a bellhop to retrieve your things and bring them to your room."

"Bellhop. Sure."

Benoît handed Courtney his business card.

"I thought we were keeping this professional," Courtney said, seeming hesitant to take the card as though it might be a trick like one of those annoying hand buzzers.

"We are," Benoît explained. "You are my responsibility for the summer. If you need me for whatever reason, I can be reached at that number. Day or night."

"I'll need a ride tomorrow at seven."

"Of course," Benoît said, saluting Courtney with a tilt of his beret.

"Oh, and uh Bentley?"

"It is Benoît, actually."

"Can you wear something else from now on? That get-up is giving me the creeps."

"It will be my pleasure."

***

Courtney dinged a little bell at the front desk, causing an elusive expression to form on the face of a clerk who was literally standing right in front of Courtney. His face said something bitingly sarcastic, regardless of his poised silence. The clerk had a conscientiously trimmed mustache of the chestnut brown variety. His green eyes were slits of scrutiny but his mouth sported a customer service grin. His name tag which was pinned to his crisp shirt in geometrical perfection boasted the name *Jacques.*

"Courtney Stent." Courtney was startled by the unintentional abrasiveness in her voice while trying to sound important. "I'm supposed to be here?"

Jacques looked somewhat ill as Courtney looked around at her surroundings, scrunching her nose in revulsion.

"From the contest," Jacques said cordially. "We have been expecting you."

"Are the rooms less underwhelming than this lobby?"

"Pardon, Madame?"

"Seriously? It's too late at night for French," Courtney said stiffly, squinting at the clerk's name tag, "Jack Queasy."

"It is morning," Jacques said through rabidly polite, clenched teeth.

"Maybe here it's morning. But it's the like three a.m. normal time."

"Normal time, *Madame*?"

"Like in America."

"I see," the clerk sighed. "In that case I will forego the pleasantries so you can get to your room without any French interference. Your room card, Courtney Stent. Breakfast is served starting at seven. That would be *French* time, I'm afraid. Not *normal* time. Sorry for any inconvenience. Oh, and Ms. Fontrose left this for you."

Jacques handed Courtney a handwritten note.

"Dearest Courtney Stent: Wish I could be there to dote on you. Up to my spaghetti straps with industry related happenings. How daunting! I have left Tuesday wide open for you, my darling as I am sure you have read in the itinerary. Catch up with you later... Forever yours, Alexandria Fontrose. "

Courtney was so excited she nearly coughed up a fur ball. "Alexandria Fontrose? Wrote this? For me? Like with her hand?"

Jacques formed a smile that was a pin straight line with teeth. "It would seem that is the case, yes."

***

The *Right Said Fred* ringtone informed Benoît that Étienne was calling his cell phone. Benoît put his cousin on speaker phone as he drove his taxi through the bustling streets of Paris.

"*Étienne?*"

"*Was it an international spy?*"

"*No,*" Benoît answered, "*she wasn't.*"

Benoît heard Étienne's shriek of joy coming from the phone.

"*Have you made love to her yet?*" Étienne begged.

"*I literally just drove her from the airport.*"

"*What is wrong with her?*"

"*There is nothing wrong with her, Étienne. Not per se.*"

"*Per se? What do you mean per se?*"

"*She is not my type,*" Benoît lied, biting his lip.

"*You are much too persnickety, dear cousin. What are you saying? You cannot live with her eye color? Her derrière is not the shape of a ripe peach? What?*"

"*She is crass. She is opinionated. She has a deep rooted distrust for all things French.*"

"*Tourists are not so bad, Benoît. I deal with tourists every day. They are not nearly as annoying once you've unlatched their brassieres.*"

"*Étienne, please. I am not interested in her. At all.*"

"*You are such a bad liar.*"

"*Am not,*" Benoît squeaked.

"*Admit it. She has awakened your inner poet. Take her, Benoît. Take her like you are starving and she is the last croissant in the pâtisserie.*"

"*Étienne, no. She despises me. Besides she is almost ten years younger than I.*"

Étienne made a cat noise.

"I could not, Étienne. She is so small and young and naïve and helpless. I could not take advantage."

"Do not overthink things," Étienne said in his wise voice. *"That will only hinder your manly escapades."*

Benoît could never be annoyed by Étienne no matter how hard he tried. He shook his head affectionately and produced an amused dimple. *"I have the rest of the day off. Do you want to meet me at Le Marais?"*

***

The hotel room was shabby. There was a strong disinfectant smell and the bed with the floral comforter had a sag in the middle. The carpet was red, or at least it used to be before it was worn down from years of foot friction. A framed picture of an expressionistic croissant hung defiantly above the headboard of the sorry bed. The mattress sagged nearly to the floor when Courtney plunked her suitcase on it to unpack. She gave her lucky duck a squeeze before pulling the curtain to bring some sunlight into the gloomy room. Courtney gasped a little when she discovered a magnificent view of the city.

"Like my poster!" Courtney marveled to herself.

Courtney curled up on the window seat that was adorned with a nest of cushions. She studied her itinerary, trying to shake the jet lag from her foggy head. She blinked to stay awake as she read. She would not be meeting with Alexandria Fontrose until Tuesday but that would give her five days to mentally prepare. Key dates were printed in bold throughout the itinerary, including her big show in August. Sure, the accommodations were a bit of a letdown. And the luxury vehicle situation was a joke. But seeing her schedule in print made this whole thing overwhelmingly real. In five days she would meet her idol. Courtney felt invincible.

Her stomach snarled hungrily at her.

She needed to find some food but she had to be careful about spending money. Courtney had some savings from the shoe store but it needed to tide her over for the whole summer. Maybe there was a vending machine somewhere in the building.

CHAPTER EIGHT
(DAY 2 IN PARIS)

Benoît was twenty minutes early the following morning. The sun had decided to make an appearance after the previous day's stint of rain. Benoît leaned against his taxi, eagerly watching the front entrance of the hotel. Courtney was forty-five minutes late and walked out drowsily, her ankles wobbling on her yellow stilettos. She had dark circles under her eyes and she was wearing conspicuously more mascara on her left eye than her right. Her hair was tossed into a hasty French roll and she yawned as wide as a lion lazily roaring.

"Bonjour!" Benoît chimed cheerily.

"It's too early for that level of enthusiasm," Courtney grumbled.

"Is everything okay?"

"Rowdy neighbors," yawned Courtney. "They went at it pretty much the entire night. I pulled myself together though."

"I can see that," Benoît nodded uncertainly.

"Hey, you're dressed like a normal person," Courtney observed.

"I am a normal person."

"I'm not complaining," Courtney said, stretching. "You look way less freaky without that corny French garb."

"Thank you. I will dress this way from now on. Will that make you feel better?"

"Much," Courtney said, falling into the backseat.

"Where would you like to go this morning?" Benoît asked, sliding into the driver's seat.

"I have a date with Louis Vuitton."

Benoît's jaw dropped.

"Well," Courtney backpedaled, "not literally. I just need to go to the store on the *Champ Sally Say.*"

"Champs Élysées," Benoît swallowed a giggle, *"Tout suite."*

Courtney's eyes fluttered as she tried to stay awake while Benoît drove.

"You can sleep if you want," Benoît offered. "I can wake you when we get there."

"Nope, I'm good." Courtney was uneasy about sleeping in front of a stranger. What if she snored or drooled or passed gas? Or worse, what if she made herself vulnerable and her driver took advantage of her?

"What brings you to the Louis Vuitton store today?" Benoît asked jovially.

Courtney hesitated. "Business," she said stiffly.

"Obviously. But are you meeting with someone special? Is there an event?"

"A new product is launching."

"A product that you designed?"

"That's... confidential."

"Forgive me. I do not know the ins and outs of the fashion industry. I am just genuinely curious. I hope I did not sound ignorant."

"I think it would be a good idea to keep the conversation basic and minimal. For professional reasons."

"Oh," Benoît felt flushed. "I did not mean to cross any boundaries. I just thought that since we will be in a taxi together for two months..."

"I understand yours is a verbose culture. But you need to understand that I am not here to make friends. I am here to get discov... erm... promote my new fashion line. Let's not get too familiar."

Benoît did not have a chance to reply before Courtney answered her cell phone.

"Courtney Stent," Courtney had been practicing her grandiloquent phone answering skills.

"Since when do you answer the phone like that?" Chastity asked.

"Is this urgent? I'm on my way to a dire engagement."

"I see you're taking my advice and pretending to be important."

"Make it brief."

"So you're in the luxury vehicle right now?"

"Affirmative."

"What's the driver like?"

"Why?"

"Mom, Gramma and I are placing bets."

"On what?"

"Is he a greasy weasel?"

"I beg your pardon?"

"Did he try anything?"

"Such as?"

"Didn't you read Gramma's book?"

"I'll have to call you back. I'm entering the catacombs and I'm losing reception."

Benoît covered his mouth to stifle laughter as Courtney made static noises by crumpling some balled up paper.

"What does he look like?" Chastity asked gravely.

"I don't see the relevance…"

"If you disappear we'll need a description."

"I don't know. I…" Courtney tried to sneak a look at Benoît, hoping he would not notice. "Lean, smiley, medium tallness," Courtney whispered. "Black hair. Curly. No, wavy. But curly, you know?"

Benoît cocked his ear.

"Eyes, Courtney."

"Uh," Courtney stammered. "They're kind of..." Courtney craned her neck to get a better view. "Brown. But really dark. Deep, rich. Like chocolate cake."

Benoît smirked proudly and winked at Courtney through the rearview mirror. Courtney gasped audibly and diverted her eyes out the window. "That is all." And she quickly shut off her phone.

"That sounded important," Benoît said with staged seriousness.

"Caterer," Courtney lied. "Big event coming up. She wasn't sure what dessert to serve. It's hard, you know because in this industry everyone is on a starvation diet. I told her to screw it and just splurge for the..."

"Chocolate cake?" Benoît beamed.

Courtney felt her face redden. "Were you eavesdropping?" she asked, faking indignation.

"Louis Vuitton," Benoît changed the subject by stopping the taxi.

A ridiculously long lineup of people sprawled outside the Louis Vuitton store. A brand new style of handbag was on display in the window, like a revered monarch on a cushioned throne.

"All this fuss for a hideous, overpriced bag," Benoit gaped.

Courtney scrunched her face into an angry pout.

"Wait," Benoît asked. "Is that why you are here? I did not mean..."

"Wait for me here," Courtney said, offended. "I might be a while."

"You know my cousin Étienne sells similar bags at his shop for a fraction of the price. With the word Paris embroidered all over them. Perhaps you would prefer..."

"Are you implying that I can't afford a Louis Vuitton bag?" Because if he was implying this he would be correct.

"I was out of line," Benoît said humbly as Courtney trotted away on her yellow stilettos. "Courtney!" Benoît called after her. "You cannot do Paris in those shoes! All the walking on the cobblestones! The many stairs to climb! You will disfigure your little feet! At my cousin's shop you will find..."

"The shoes are fine," Courtney called, not looking back. "Later, Benoît. It's been real."

"But those shoes are ridiculous!"

Courtney stopped abruptly in her tracks. She spun around, squinting at Benoît in disbelief. "I designed these shoes."

Benoît felt suddenly queasy. He brewed a toothy smile and chimed back, "Then they are perfect!"

Courtney shook her head and gave him a disapproving glare as she walked away. Benoît banged his head against his steering wheel and groaned.

CHAPTER NINE:
(DAY 5 IN PARIS)

The saggy bed in Courtney's hotel room gave her even worse lower back spasms than her bed at home. She thrashed around in bed, putting the pillow over her face. The sadistic mattress was only part of the problem. Loud, drunken cackling, boisterous thumping and the occasional sound of shattering glass were throbbing through the walls and vibrating the whole room. The brouhaha was coming from the room across the hall. Courtney had not slept properly since she arrived in Paris. And she decided it was time to do something about it.

In her striped, faux satin pajamas, Courtney shuffled across the hall in an exhausted fury. She rapped on the rowdy neighbor's door with a purposeful fist. A drunk woman answered the door, askew but with an air of artificial dignity.

"Do you have any idea what time it is?" the woman asked in a breezily superior voice.

Courtney, with her hands forming into tight fists could not believe the nerve of this harpy denouncing the timing of her noise complaint. "Yes, I know what time it is. Do *you?*"

"Of course not, my darling. That's why I asked."

A man casually left the room, zipping his trousers.

"Well done," the drunk woman said to the man. "See you whenever."

"Do you have any idea how alert I need to be tomorrow?" Courtney exploded while holding the sides of her throbbing head. "Not that you'd care, but I'm meeting with arguably the most respected designer in the..."

The rage slowly drained from Courtney's face and was replaced with a look of epiphany.

"Oh my god," Courtney said hoarsely. "Alexandria Fontrose."

"Of course I am, Muffin. Who else would I be?"

"I've been following you since I was seven," Courtney was almost crying. "Your career. Your designs. The blanched almond maxi frock with the empire waist? The one that was featured on the cover of **God I'm Hot Magazine?** It gave me an asthma attack. In a good way, I mean."

Alexandria's Botoxed face was incapable of expressing emotion. Her voice presented a similar challenge. "How adorable are you? A fan of fashion, are we?"

"Uh, actually I'm Courtney Stent."

"I'm sorry, Baby Carrot. I have no idea what that means."

"It's... Me. You're supposed to be my mentor? I sort of won you. What about the note you left at the front desk?"

It is difficult to say whether Alexandria was really taken aback by the unexpected encounter with Courtney as her face was surgically altered to a permanent surprised expression. "Well color me fuchsia! You are Courtney Stent! You!"

"From Milwaukee."

"What a coincidence! I'm from Manhattan! We're cut from the same fabric. So refreshing to meet someone in Paris with whom I can communicate without using hand gestures."

"I know it's late. But would you like to scooch over to my room and see my summer line? I have sketches and the garments are in my closet."

"I'll bring the Vermouth."

***

"Your first time in Paris?" Alexandria said dotingly. "You're so adorable I could just put you in my pocket."

"I just can't believe this," Courtney quivered. "In a couple months my designs will be on a real Paris runway." Courtney winced at how much cooler that sounded in her head before she said it.

"I can't stop running my fingers over this chiffon," Alexandria marveled. "And this innovative use of yellow almost makes me want to believe in God. Is it lemon zest or canary? Either way, it's an eyeball orgy. Well done."

"Mentors have to say stuff like that," Courtney said in a daze, only half believing that her childhood hero was literally in her hotel room.

"Perhaps you are unaware that the contest people asked me to adjudicate the submissions."

"You?" Courtney's eyes glossed with wonder. "Picked me?"

"Why do you look so flabbergasted? Your sketches stood out. So much so, I wish I had come up with these ideas. I believe in you."

"Nobody has ever..." Courtney choked. "Oh, Ms. Fontrose."

"Call me Dree."

"Wow." Courtney was literally trembling.

"You need a little something for those nerves," Alexandria said, pouring Courtney some Vermouth into a little glass from the bathroom.

"Oh," Courtney said hesitantly as she eyeballed the boozy liquid. "I'm not much of a drinker."

"Nonsense. If you want to make it in the biz, you'll need to loosen up."

"I don't want any..."

"You're not Amish or something, are you? Because that would be gauche."

"No! It's nothing like that. Alcohol just isn't my favorite. The smell reminds me of... See, I grew up around a lot of... Besides, I'm small so it doesn't take a lot..."

"Come on Little Bird. Live."

Courtney winced as she took a quick swig. "Mmm," Courtney lied.

"You know I was thinking," Alexandria said while looking down her nose at Courtney's sketchbook, "there are some people you should meet. I think they would be very interested in seeing some of your innovations."

Courtney nearly choked on her Vermouth. "Seriously?"

"Oh yes, I am quite serious. We need to make you more visible. I have some colleagues from Soho NYC who have open minds about newcomers. They frequent a wine bar in the Latin Quarter most nights at around this time. It's a great little bar that American designers simply flock to. We should go. Promptly."

The Vermouth was churning in Courtney's esophagus and her head was slowly filling with swirling fog. "I should sleep. I'm still jet lagged and I feel kind of iffy. I should make sure I'm in top form since..."

"Get your schmooze on. You don't want to be invisible forever, do you?"

"But it's so late. Tomorrow I'm supposed to..."

"You were going to meet me," Alexandria laughed with a smoky rasp. "That's already happened. Come on, Turtle. Paris is just now waking up!"

***

Sleeping was futile. Benoît lay twisted in his sheets, staring blankly at the ceiling. His mind was racing like a greyhound whirring in circles around a track and his heart was thumping madly like a helicopter propeller. The darkness in the room seemed thicker than usual and the tick of his alarm clock was making him twitch.

His cell phone startled him. He answered, *"Étienne, what is it? I am in bed."*

"Am I interrupting anything?" Étienne asked coyly on the phone.

"Stop."

"Why then are you up?"

"I am feeling a bit sick."

"With love, no?"

"No."

"You expect me to believe you have been alone in a taxi with a beautiful woman, driving her around for five days and you have not…"

"Never once have I told you what she looks like."

"You are lying awake in bed at 3:00 in the morning. She is beautiful."

"Étienne, she is not for me."

"How do you know that for sure?"

"She grimaces at me like a gargoyle atop the Cathedral Notre Dame."

"That could mean anything."

"She is exhausting me with her opinions and her insults and her shoes."

"If you find her so tiresome, why are you not asleep?"

"She is crass, ignorant, prejudiced. I can barely squeeze her enormous ego into my tiny taxi."

"You are so hot for her."

"What?" Benoît squeaked.

"This is going to eat away at you, Benoît."

"You have an insane mind."

"What are you afraid of, Benoît? She is not Monique."

Benoît gagged on his own silence.

"Benoît?"

"Do not say that name."

"But that is YOUR name."

"Not mine. Hers."

"Monique?"

"Stop it."

"Is that why you refuse to..."

"This is personal, Étienne."

"But I care about you. We are family."

"Please leave me alone and let me... not sleep."

Benoît ended the call and smushed his face into a pillow.

CHAPTER TEN

Courtney really wished she had eaten more than a meager bag of chips from the hotel vending machine for dinner. Her hollow stomach was paying for it now, gurgling with resentment from that third glass of acrid wine. It burned like vinegar. Courtney was not accustomed to excesses such as these and was focusing hard on not throwing up. Her head pounded and her eyes squinted against the vengeful blue laser lights that pierced through the dark room. Why on earth would anyone design such a sadistic lighting system in a room full of drunk people who were addled with wine migraines? Courtney was no connoisseur, having been raised by a frugal brewmaster of cringe-worthy craft beer, but she was pretty sure wine was supposed to taste better than this.

Gripping the high glass table in case the spinning room whipped her right off of her wrought iron barstool, Courtney envied the way that alcohol emboldened Alexandria. Her mentor became more confident, outspoken and colorful with each glass she guzzled, while Courtney just prayed she wouldn't blurt something incriminating or barf on someone important.

"Courtney dear," Alexandria said, leaning towards Courtney confidentially, pointing at a gaggle of ostentatious men. "See those? Men of influence. Pants."

"What's that now?" Courtney slurred.

"Each of them contributed enormously to the design of high end leg wear," Alexandria said in a stage whisper.

"Oh."

"If you want to scale the wall of success," Alexandria said provocatively, "you must first scale..."

"I should go," Courtney said, nervously fumbling from her stool.

"How do you think I got my start?" Alexandria said reassuringly. "Don't look like such a scared labradoodle. It's only weird the first time."

Courtney mused on every level of wrong that applied to this situation. This was not what she signed up for. Besides, she was not all that attractive at the moment with her red eyes, profuse sweating, foul breath and lack of coordination. Even her hair looked drunk. "I don't know," Courtney stammered. "I don't feel all that comfortable around... you know... men. I've got these trust issues? There was this guy once. Paul..."

"I believe in you," Alexandria said soothingly.

"I don't think you get it," Courtney slurred. "I get taken advantage of a lot. Take Paul for example..."

"It's a rite of passage, Ladybird," Alexandria continued. "Mind over matter. It's normal to feel vulnerable..."

"We dated for a while, Paul and me," Courtney interrupted, being just barely self-aware.

"Oh we're doing this?" Alexandria said, looking at her watch. "Okay, dear. I'm all ears."

"I loved him, Dree. He had a decent job, unbelievable shirts and perfectly symmetrical earlobes. He was nothing like the other guys in my town. He was special. But then he went on a business trip to Canada and met... Paulette. She was French, Dree. How can I compete with that? It's not even fair."

"I hate them," Alexandria said with dignified contempt. "I hate them for what they did to you."

"She was skinny," Courtney recalled, swirling the wine around in her glass, "like a pencil. Kittenishly cute. With her stupid dimple and her flaxen curls and her freakishly small feet. Did I mention that she was demure?"

"She sickens me," Alexandria said, eyeballing some men across the room and straightening her up-do.

"Why did she have to be French? Men can't resist that trilly thing they do with the letter R."

"She cast a subtitled, French spell on him," Alexandria hissed. "The tart."

"I asked him why," Courtney recalled. "I mean I get that I don't have the allure of an ethnic chick. And that the names Paul and Paulette sound sickeningly cute together. But I thought we were soul mates. My family told me he was too good for me. Maybe they were right."

"No, darling girl. You must reject such toxicity. It will only hinder your success."

"I trusted him."

"Trust no one, Lamb Chop. Trust sets you up for disappointment and pain. You're so cute and unassuming. Like I was."

"Things are going to be different in Paris," Courtney said.

"No they're not," Alexandria said, shaking her head. "This is a tough city. Pretty but tough. You can't trust any of these quiche eaters."

"I uh..." Courtney said while holding her swimmy head. "I met a guy who was sort of nice. For a French guy."

"No you didn't," Alexandria cut her off. "It was a ruse."

"Huh?"

"You need to claim dominance. Empower yourself. Pee on your territory. Go outside your comfort zone and you will shatter ceilings. Show Paris who's the alpha female." Alexandria pointed at the acclaimed pants designers, "Now. It's time you learned what it's like to be on top."

"Wouldn't that be morally wrong?"

"Go ahead, Courtney. Pick any one you want."

Courtney's conscience sounded like a faraway scream, like a wispy fairy uttering a death cry on a fast moving train. It was desperate but convoluted. Courtney's knees unexpectedly buckled when she got up from her stool. She awkwardly stumbled towards a particularly flamboyant man.

"Not that one," Alexandria advised quickly.

Courtney teetered towards a different man dressed in a garish suit that most likely cost more than her parents' house. "Erm..."

"No," the man said bluntly.

"You're the least unattractive guy in this joint. Wanna' get out of here?"

"I would rather shop retail."

"I'm more important than I look."

"I have no idea who you are," the man said, aloof.

"Of course you don't, because I haven't told you who I am yet."

"Be brief."

"Courtney Stent."

"I still have no idea who you are."

"And you are…?"

"Wondering why you are still here."

"Name please."

"Garth Ambrosia."

"That's your name? Are you a leprechaun?"

"Be elsewhere."

Drunk she may have been, but Courtney knew when she was being rudely blown off. "Creep," Courtney said just a little too loudly. "You know something, *Garth Ambrosia?* Without pants, you are nothing!"

Courtney suddenly felt the penetrating glares of industry professionals all around her. "Dree?" she gulped.

Alexandria Fontrose was gone.

CHAPTER ELEVEN

A puddle of sleep drool was forming on Benoît's pillow. He was finally in a deep sleep, twisted in his sheets from hours of thrashing insomnia. Suddenly, he awoke with a jolt to the sound of his cell phone. He answered with his eyes droopy with sleep, his curls mussed and a voice deepened by semi-consciousness.

"Allo?" Benoît droned dozily.

"Benoît?" Courtney's voice was shaky and slurred on the phone.

Benoît sat up straighter in bed, instinctively covering his boxer shorts and feeling strangely self-conscious about being shirtless. "Courtney?" he asked worriedly, looking at the clock. "Are you okay?"

"I'm sorry to wake you," Courtney quavered. "Can you come get me? I'm... I'm alone."

"Where are you?" Benoît asked, already pulling on some pants.

"I... I don't know. Someone brought me here and I can't find them now. I don't know this place."

"It is okay. I am coming. Just describe your surroundings. I will figure it out."

"I'm sorry, Benoît. You gave me your card so..."

"It is not a problem, Courtney," Benoît said as he scrambled for his keys.

"I didn't know who else to call."

"I will be right there. Please stay where you are."

"I'm so drunk," Courtney sobbed.

"You will be fine. I am coming for you."

***

Blinding lights of purple, red and green lit up the Latin Quarter like an explosion of firecrackers. The buzzing neighborhood had no idea how late it was. Benoît drove around slowly, squinting at every passerby. His chest tightened when he spotted Courtney standing alone, looking so small and vulnerable. He patted the car horn gently three times to get Courtney's attention.

Courtney looked pale and sick but her eyes softened with relief when she spotted Benoît. She visibly exhaled. As she staggered towards the car, Benoît leaped out of the taxi to assist her.

"It's late, I know," Courtney slurred. "But you gave me your card..."

"Do not worry about it. It is my job," Benoît said politely.

Courtney's eyes widened as she suddenly heaved.

"Are you okay, Courtney?" Benoît asked, poised to assist.

Before Benoît had time to think, Courtney was retching with her face in a garbage can.

"Mon dieu," Benoît gasped as he instinctively held Courtney's head over the waste can, gently holding her hair out of her face. *"Ça va?"* Benoît said soothingly. *"Ça va aller. Je suis ici, mon amie."*

Courtney groaned as she lifted her head and used her sleeve to shelter her eyes from the beams of light coming from the vibrant marquis overhead. "You didn't have to do that," she said to Benoît, who was offering her a handkerchief to wipe her face.

"It is in my job description," Benoît shrugged affably.

"I don't usually do this," Courtney said, unable to look directly at Benoît.

"None of that is my business. My job is to get you back safely."

Courtney winced from her pounding headache.

Benoît winced too.

"How did you get here?" Benoît asked.

"Dree," Courtney moaned.

"I am unfamiliar with that word."

"My mentor," Courtney explained with effort. "She took me to this bar to schmooze with some industry bigwigs. She started flirting with this really old guy who apparently invented corduroy pants. Or had them banned, I don't remember which. She must have left with him because I can't find her anywhere."

Benoît cocked his head as Courtney rummaged through her purse.

"My head feels swimmy," Courtney moaned. "I have some aspirin in here somewhere."

"Excuse me please. Is that a duck in your purse?"

"I don't know," Courtney said quickly, trying to hide the duck.

"Is it an American custom?"

"It's for luck."

"Does it work?"

"Ducks are lucky. Ask around."

Benoît smiled when he opened the taxi door for Courtney.

"Courtney Stent!" A smoky voice came from across the street.

Benoît furrowed his brow. Where had he heard that voice before?

"Dree?" Courtney asked, dazed.

"Over here, Bella!" Alexandria called again. "The orange juice shooters are on me!"

"It's her!" Courtney said, trying to pull herself together. "Do I look okay?"

Benoît looked Courtney up and down. She was pasty. Her makeup was smeared. Her hair was sticky with sweat and possibly vomit. Benoît's lips parted for a moment before he replied softly, "You look extremely okay."

"I'm going to join her for a drink," Courtney said, gathering her things.

"Are... are you sure..."

"Every minute I spend with Alexandria Fontrose is a notch in my professional belt."

"Alexandria Fontrose?" Benoît asked.

"Come on, Poochie!" Alexandria called again, beckoning Courtney from across the street. "This tequila isn't going to drink itself!"

"Coming Dree!" Courtney called back, looking at Benoît defiantly.

Courtney ventured across the street. Her foot wobbled on her ridiculously tall stiletto heel, she lost her footing and fell headlong into the street. Benoît gasped when he saw a car dart from around a corner and head straight for Courtney.

"Courtney!" Benoît screamed as he leaped frantically towards Courtney, pushing her out of the way of the honking vehicle. Courtney toppled unceremoniously onto the sidewalk and Benoît found himself lying protectively on top of her. They both gasped for breath.

"Well," Alexandria said, standing over top of them, "that was a lucky break. You could have wrecked your shoes."

"Are you okay?" Benoît asked, ignoring Alexandria and still trying to find his breath.

Shocked, Courtney nodded.

"Please," Benoît said, trying to help Courtney to her feet, "let me..."

"You," Alexandria hissed when she recognized Benoît.

"Does anything hurt, Courtney?" Benoît asked with quavering concern in his voice.

"I'm okay," Courtney said, uncertainly.

Benoît found Courtney's duck, fallen in the gutter. With a playful smile, he offered it back to her. "Good thing you had this."

"Thank you," Courtney said quietly, accepting the duck from Benoît.

"Let me help you to the car," Benoît insisted.

"That won't be necessary, Raoul," Alexandria snarled with artificial charm.

Benoît froze when he recalled the last person who called him by that name. He spun around, slitting his eyes at the garish woman who had previously worn the toothpaste tube dress, who had hurled herself in front of his taxi with her mouth full of threats. "I am responsible for her," he said as though he was disciplining a dog.

"You are dismissed, Raoul," Alexandria said condescendingly. "Make haste."

Courtney blinked to keep herself from passing out. She was looking pastier and was hunched over as though she might throw up again. Benoît propped her up and escorted her to her seat.

"I'm sure if given the choice," Alexandria said, "our little artist would prefer to talk fashion with the genius who popularized faux fur than to sit in a stuffy taxi with... well, you."

"Forgive my insolence," said Benoît cordially. "I did not realize I was in the presence of greatness. I mistook you for a common lush."

"If that's some kind of French humor, it doesn't translate well," Alexandria said to Benoît. Then she turned to a very sickly looking Courtney and said, "Courtney, what would you like to do? Because

I'm fine if you want to toss me aside like a pair of discontinued culottes. I'm not petty."

Courtney's eyes looked like glass as she passed out. Benoît quickly caught her before she could thwack her head on the car door. Alexandria took this opportunity to switch off her false charm.

"You little worm," she stage whispered at Benoît. "Why are you still here? Why are you still driving? I lodged a formal complaint about you."

"I have a perfect driving record," Benoît said evenly.

"You assaulted me with your car, you murdered my sweet Louis, now you're undermining me in front of my protégé? I can see by your face that you are not picking up on my innuendo here. See, I loved my Louis Vuitton clutch. Like my own child."

Benoît muttered something in French.

"It was a limited edition bag!"

"Some mentor," Benoît muttered as he nested unconscious Courtney carefully into the backseat of the taxi.

"Don't get in my way, Raoul," Alexandria threatened. "You've been warned.

Alexandria huffed indignantly as Benoît drove away.

***

Courtney moaned in her sleep. Benoît glanced in the rearview mirror at the pile of Courtney in the backseat.

"That was a most unusual evening," Benoît tried.

No answer.

"Courtney?" Benoît tried again.

No answer.

After driving slowly and avoiding unnecessary bumps in the road, Benoît finally pulled up in front of Courtney's hotel. He gently tried to wake her but she was out cold. Now what? He couldn't just leave her in the taxi all night. And taking her home with him would be a serious faux pas. He discreetly unzipped her purse – gum, lucky duck, lipstick, wallet and some lady things that he pretended not to see – and found her hotel room card.

Her body was heavier than it looked. Courtney was tiny but she was limp and lifeless in Benoît's arms. His heart sagged with pity for her. He carried her to the lift, pressed the button with his elbow and felt his stomach dip as the elevator went up to the seventh floor.

When he got to Courtney's room, he put the room card in his mouth and opened the door, careful not to drop her. He carried her to the bed and laid her down daintily. He stood for a moment, wondering what to do with her putrid, soiled clothes. Biting his lip, he carefully stripped off Courtney's outer layer of clothing, peeled down the floral comforter and discreetly nested Courtney's limp body under the blankets. Careful not to wake her, he gingerly wiped her face with a warm, wet washcloth and rubbed some of the pungent stickiness from her hair.

Benoît left briefly, returning with three cans of ginger ale he purchased from the vending machine down the hall as well as a cellophane wrapped mini brioche. Next to the beverages, he strategically positioned a bottle of aspirin. Then putting the room card back in the sleeve, he left it in plain view on the vacant pillow next to her head.

He watched her sleep for a moment, musing on how her little body rose and fell with each breath under the comforter. Her nose, which was peppered with tiny freckles made a delicate whistle each time she inhaled. Her blond hair cascaded over the white pillow. Then he snapped out of his daze, realizing how creepy it was to watch his client sleep. He gently placed a wayward strand of hair behind her ear and padded softly towards the door.

CHAPTER TWELVE:
(DAY 6 IN PARIS)

Sunshine was aggressively forcing its way through the slits between the curtains. Courtney lay limp on her bed with her left arm dangling off the side of the mattress. The horrible phone rang on the bedside table. Each ring felt like screwdrivers in Courtney's eye sockets. Who on earth would have the nerve to call her hotel room at... noon?

Barely awake, Courtney answered the phone, croaking a feeble, "Hello?"

"Courtney Stent!" the voice on the phone seemed alarmingly chipper.

"Dree?" Courtney moaned as she sat up in bed, her eyelids still fluttering with sleep.

"Are you finally up? I've been banging on your door for the past hour."

"Up?" Courtney said dopily with a huge stretch. "I..."

Courtney looked around. She was in her underclothes from the previous night. Courtney's insides wobbled.

"How did I get here?" Courtney asked nobody in particular.

"Excuse me, what?"

"Nothing Dree."

"I'm coming over."

"Oh uh..." Courtney stammered. "I don't think..."

It was too late. Alexandria had hung up and moments later she was knocking on Courtney's door.

"Open up, Cupcake!" Alexandria said between assertive knocks. "I've got much to do today."

Courtney was overcome by her own stench. There was no time to change. Her stomach was gurgling acidly. She quickly opened the crinkly wrapper and took a liberal bite out of the brioche before attempting to get out of bed. The room was spinning and the floors felt unusually slanted like walking in a funhouse. Courtney stumbled across the room and answered the door.

"Headache?" Alexandria guessed. "Here. I brought you my favorite hangover remedy."

"Rum?" Courtney winced when handed a bottle.

"Snap out of it, Daisy Chain. We have a lot of work to do. Unless I've completely wasted my time compiling helpful feedback on your designs."

"Uh..." Courtney stammered, trying to make sense of this whole situation.

"Are those your undergarments from last night?" Alexandria asked accusingly, eyeballing Courtney up and down.

"I... I'm kind of confused. I don't really know what... how..."

"What did he do to you?"

"Who?" Courtney was caught off guard.

"You know who I'm talking about."

"I have no idea what you are implying. You are making no sense right now. My head..."

"Someone must have come back to the hotel with you. Else how could you have returned on your own? I saw the state you let yourself get into last night. You were puking all over yourself and barely self-aware."

"I passed out. I honestly don't know what happened after that."

Alexandria collected herself, exhaling a theatrical, cleansing breath. She closed her eyes momentarily and pinched her fingers together in a meditative way. "Courtney, you know you can be honest with me. If you have committed an indiscretion, you do not need to hide it from me. I am your mentor. And your friend. You can trust me."

"I seriously have no idea what's going on," Courtney whimpered.

"It was that beast from the taxi."

"You mean Benoît?"

"What is a Benoît?"

"My driver. That's his name."

"You gave him a name?"

"He came with a name."

"So you talk. To each other."

"Sometimes."

"Why."

"I don't know. He's sort of nice or whatever."

"Nobody in Paris is nice," Alexandria snarled. "Sure, they seem charming with their provocative accents and their strangely titillating accordion music. But under all those berets..."

"He's just my driver."

"I worry about you, Courtney Stent. So fragile, like a dewy hydrangea. You can't even tell when someone is trying to take advantage of you."

"Take advantage?" Courtney said, popping two aspirin and washing them down with a swig of ginger ale. "Benoît? You really think he..."

"Did you not see the way he looked at me? He knows I'm your mother chicken. And that I would do anything to protect you. That's why he wants to fill your head with poisonous little thoughtlets about me."

"I don't understand. He's never even mentioned you."

"Men like that prey on innocence. And once he's sucked the last of your innocence through a bendy straw, he'll kick you to the curb like an empty can of beans."

"But..."

"Like Paul."

Courtney gaped. "Paul? How do you know about Paul?"

"You told me all about him, my little gosling. Last night."

"I did?" Courtney felt sick. Well, sicker.

"You were a little tipsy so you may not remember the details of that conversation."

"How much did I say?" Courtney asked hoarsely.

"Oh Courtney, my sweet little tuft of dandelion fuzz. I didn't mean to startle you with my sudden outburst. It's just that I never had a daughter of my own. I get a little protective when it comes to you. I believe in you, my sweet. Like a mother."

"A mother?" Courtney swallowed.

"My passions get the better of me, don't they," Alexandria said. "It happens with artists such as we."

Courtney nodded.

"Listen," Alexandria soothed, "why don't you get yourself showered and cleaned up. I freed my schedule for the entire day for you which is rather impossible considering how sought after I am. Don't look at me like that, my darling, I did it because I love you. Now clearly you're going to need some time to defog your brain and make yourself presentable but don't take too long because we have a meeting scheduled at Nespresso and I just can't change it to another day. You know how thinly I spread myself. The time is in your itinerary."

"Yes Dree," Courtney said submissively.

"And I don't mean to scare you, but you really should call the police and have your hotel room investigated for French DNA."

"Uh..."

Alexandria spun around with a dramatic exeunt.

CHAPTER THIRTEEN

The taxi was eerily quiet.

Benoît did not want to mention what had happened the previous night and he was extremely nervous about the inevitable moment when Courtney would say something about it. The silence was unbearable. Benoît glanced in the rearview mirror at Courtney who was glaring out the window with her lips pursed tightly. Benoît drove with a purpose, trying hard to focus on the road and not on his rapidly thumping heart.

"How did I get into my bed last night?" Courtney finally blurted out.

Benoît swallowed hard.

"I want to know," Courtney said, crossing her arms.

"I uh…" Benoît cleared his throat to bide a nanosecond of time. "I did not want to wake you."

"Did… did you do anything?"

"What do you mean?"

"You know what I mean, Benoît."

"I do not."

Courtney took a deep breath and then blurted, "Did you do weird things to me while I slept?"

Benoît's heart felt like it had been stung by an unprovoked wasp. "Are you joking? Do you wish for me to laugh now?"

"You came into my room," Courtney said in a panic, "while I was passed out. What am I supposed to think?"

"How else could I..."

"I've been advised to call the police."

Benoît muttered something in French that Courtney could not understand.

"Don't do that. No fair saying French things."

"I did nothing wrong," Benoît said defensively.

"So you're saying you didn't take the opportunity to have your way with me?"

"You have my word."

"How am I supposed to know for sure what happened?"

"Do you think I am that kind of person?"

"I have no idea what kind of person you are. We met six days ago."

"Do you honestly think I would hurt you after... after what happened in the street last night?"

"I don't remember anything that happened last night."

"You remember nothing?"

Courtney shook her head.

"Oh mon dieu."

"All I know is that I was out with Dree, getting some trippy industry advice and the next thing I know I'm in my bed. Partially clothed."

"I would never..."

"Prove it."

"How?"

"This is very scary for me, okay? I was in a very vulnerable situation last night and anything could have happened. I barely know you. Oh my god. What if I'm pregnant? My career, my reputation, my hips... And if my baby is French how will he understand me?"

Benoît laughed explosively.

"What?" Courtney asked, horrified at the mockery of her emotions.

Benoît squeezed his eyes shut, trying to suppress the laughter which sprayed out of him again.

"What?" Courtney's voice quivered from the contagiousness of Benoît's laugh.

"Forgive me, Courtney," Benoît said, trying to catch his breath. "My response was inappropriate, given the grave circumstances." The word "circumstances" squeaked with cachinnation.

Courtney's insides quivered between rage and beguilement. She really wanted to be mad at Benoît. Why did he keep making that so hard?

"*Nespresso*," Benoît said with attempted professionalism as he pulled up in front of Courtney's stop.

"Wait for me here," Courtney instructed. "My meeting should be finished in a few hours."

"I will be here."

***

The clack of Courtney's stilettos echoed throughout the café. Alexandria looked up from her table and spotted Courtney from across the room. Alexandria made sure that every patron was aware of her presence.

"Well hello my darling raisin scone!" Alexandria projected theatrically. "Come. Sit. Let us discuss things of great importance!"

"Hi Dree."

"I've been thinking about your summer line," Alexandria said with her eyes popping with enthusiasm.

"I brought swatches."

"Good girl. What do we have here? I've never seen so many shades of..."

"I kind of have a thing for yellow."

"I can see that, Angel Doll. Tell me, why yellow?"

"Is there something wrong with yellow?"

"Not at all, dear. I am just curious about what inspires you. Let me inside your head, Courtney Stent. Tell me about your muse."

Courtney blinked. "I don't know if I have a specific muse. I just really like yellow."

"You really like yellow," Alexandria repeated with verve.

"It's happy."

"Yellow is happy?" Alexandria wrote that down.

"See, to me every color has a specific emotion. Blue is sad. Green is jealous. Pink is giddy. Orange is angry. Red is lovesick. Purple is proud."

"And your obsession with yellow means… you're happy?"

"Not exactly."

"So you're unhappy?"

"Yellow is sort of my utopia, you know? It's not necessarily reality based but more what I think the world should be like."

"I don't follow."

"I live in a basement so…"

"Maybe we should discuss textiles," Alexandria said, crossing something out in a notebook. "I see you are obsessed with chiffon. Along with other flowy materials."

"I like fabric with movement," Courtney explained eagerly. "It seems more natural to me. Stiff fabrics make people look like they are stuffed in envelopes."

"Very insightful. You are very cerebral in your process. I like that."

"Thank you, Dree."

Alexandria examined Courtney through her horn rimmed glasses, which she really did not need but rather wore for style. "So you're telling me you have no muse."

"Well, you are my muse in a way."

"Of course I am, darling. I inspire the world daily. But that's not what I mean. Every great artist has a muse. Someone in their life from whom they draw their passion. On an intimate level."

Courtney exhaled, embarrassed. "I'm pretty much alone, Dree. I don't really get my inspiration from a singular person. Nobody special anyway."

Courtney felt the intensity of the horn rimmed glasses scrutinizing her again.

"You are quite an innocent little thing, aren't you."

"I wouldn't say..."

"I'm not criticizing," Alexandria assured Courtney. "It's actually quite adorable. Makes me want to sit on you like an egg."

Courtney cocked her head at the unusual simile.

"Did you call the police?" Alexandria was no longer looking at Courtney but rather writing something down again. What did she keep writing down?

"I..." Courtney hesitated. "...No."

"Why not?"

"I don't know for sure that Benoît did anything wrong."

"Do you have proof?"

"No, but I have no proof against him either."

Still writing something down, Alexandria muttered and Courtney was pretty sure she heard the word *naïve*.

"Dree, I don't know what to think. He tucked me in. Do sex offenders tuck in their victims? Because I'm pretty sure they don't."

"It's a ruse," Alexandria muttered.

"He left me ginger ale and a little bread thingie."

"He's playing with your mind," Alexandria said in a sing-song voice.

"What if he's not all that bad? What if he's just a plain old driver? With no motives?"

"If you don't want to press charges that's your choice," Alexandria said firmly.

Courtney zipped her lip like an obedient pupil.

***

Benoît was slouched in the driver's seat with his head lolled against the window, fast asleep. He was suddenly awakened by a rapping on his window. He jolted awake, only to find Étienne, smiling animatedly and waving from outside. Benoît stretched and rolled down the window.

"Cousin!" Étienne cheered enthusiastically. *"How coincidental to find you here!"*

"Why are you not at the shop?" Benoît yawned.

"Why are YOU sleeping on the job?"

"It was an eventful night."

"I am so happy for you, Benoît!"

"Étienne, not everything I do involves convincing women to share my bed."

"My sincere condolences, Cousin."

"I was roused in the wee hours of the morning to retrieve my passenger. She was very drunk and confused."

"Aaah!" Étienne beamed. *"That is how I met Nanette! And now we have a beautiful exclusive relationship on alternate Thursdays!"*

"She was left all alone in the street."

"Who did that to her?"

"Her mentor. The most horribly plastic woman I have ever seen. Remember that garish woman I told you about a few days ago? With

the brimmed hat and the sociopath eyes? She crossed the street illegally and mindlessly walked into my taxi? THAT is Courtney's mentor."

"Awkward."

"I can handle her insults and threats because they are baseless. But the way she treats Courtney..."

"I thought you did not like Courtney."

"It is basic, human decency."

"Why would you care?" Étienne teased.

"Because I am nice. Besides, it is my job to look out for her."

"Is it?"

"I brought her safely back to her hotel room. I did what I could to make her comfortable and ensure her safety. But today she accused me of abusing the situation."

"She clearly does not know you."

"Right?"

"If she knew you, she would know of your paralyzing fear of intimacy."

"Exactly... she..." Benoît squinted disapprovingly at Étienne. "That is not true."

CHAPTER FOURTEEN:
(DAY 14 IN PARIS)

Alexandria Fontrose's availability had been sporadic for the past couple of days. However, she was gracious enough to rent Courtney a little studio complete with sewing equipment where she could develop her designs and prepare her garments for Fashion Week. Courtney's studio had a winsome view of a little cobbled courtyard with an artistic fountain composed of a lion's head spitting water into a clear blue pool. A roving croissant vendor frequented the courtyard every day. The smell of freshly baked goodness often wafted up to Courtney's window, making her salivate.

Courtney loved everything about her little studio. It was a sanctuary from the chaos outside and the blistering politics of the fashion industry. Here she could steep herself in a deep focus, giving birth to some of her most innovative creations yet. Her garments were developing more and more character with each passing day. She became so well acquainted with them that she would occasionally talk to the garments which was a bit psychotic but supposedly one of the perks of working in solitude.

"I am so proud of you," Courtney said delusionally to a yellow lace panel sleeved dress with an A-line princess scoop neck. I just know you are going to wow them at the venue during Fashion Week."

As Courtney looked out the window her glimpse of the fountain gave her a sudden idea. She scribbled several different elements into her sketchbook, including a magnificent dress with the flowing elegance of a spraying fountain. She imagined a dress that flowed like water, with a texture that resembled a rippling effect. The bodice mimicked the ferocity of a lion, spitting out a spaghetti strap. The perfect combination of womanish flirt and female power.

Glancing quickly at her watch, Courtney uttered a little gasp and scrambled to gather her things. Alexandria had squeezed Courtney in for a dinner meeting at a charming pizzeria on the *Champs Élysées*. Courtney had so much progress with which to update Alexandria. She had taken her mentor's advice on several things, including the incorporation of lace into her designs. And Courtney could not wait to make Alexandria Fontrose proud of her.

***

Outside the studio building, Benoît was waiting for Courtney as per her instructions earlier that day. Benoît looked up from his magazine when he heard the telltale clack of Courtney's stilettos. She hopped into the backseat without saying a word.

"Pizzeria?" Benoît asked. "Dinner meeting at 8:00?" Benoît had pretty much memorized Courtney's itinerary. What else did he have to do, after all?

Courtney nodded professionally.

"You have chosen your dinner venue wisely," Benoît said with his bright smile. "The place you are going serves some of the best pizza in the city."

"I didn't pick it," Courtney said, aloof. "Dree set it up."

Benoît cringed at Alexandria's ridiculous nickname. How could Courtney be so blind to her slime of arrogance? "I see," Benoît said.

Courtney looked out the window but watched Benoît from her peripheral vision. He had kind eyes. The kind that danced each time he smiled. Not that this was relevant because Courtney intended to keep all of her interactions professional on this trip. She was just making an observation.

"What vibrant creations have you been inventing in your studio?" Benoît asked cheerily, shrugging his shoulders with excitement.

"Why?"

"I am curious," Benoît said, bouncing in his seat to emphasize his eagerness. "What else do I have to wonder about while waiting for you each day outside your studio?"

Why did Benoît have to look so cute when he bounced like that? Courtney was bursting to tell someone about her progress but this was not the time or the place. What would Dree say if she found out Courtney had spilled her ideas to her manservant before conferencing with her? Did she just *think* the word *manservant*? Courtney shook that image out of her mind immediately.

"I can't say," Courtney lied. "It's too soon."

Benoît nodded with animated seriousness.

"I've been meaning to ask you," Benoît said quizzically, "I have not yet seen you with your beauteous new Louis Vuitton handbag." Benoît tried very hard not to make the word *beauteous* sound like a lip fart of laughter. He failed. "You waited all day in line to buy it. I thought you would be flaunting it at every opportunity."

Courtney's face turned into a pickled beet. She had saved her money for months to buy that handbag, only to have her credit card declined. It was humiliating.

"They ran out of inventory by the time it was my turn in line," Courtney lied.

"You know, at my cousin Étienne's shop…"

"No thank you," Courtney interrupted.

Benoît spotted the pizzeria up ahead. "Here is your stop," he said, looking over his shoulder to parallel park.

"I should be finished in a few hours."

"Have a beautiful time," Benoît nodded in a friendly salute.

***

Courtney clacked into the bustling pizzeria with her arms filled with sketches which she hugged close to her body. She scanned the room, tilting her head upward to find Dree's elaborate up-do over the sea of heads. She deflated when she could not find her mentor anywhere in the restaurant. She looked nervously at her watch, wondering if she was early.

"Dining alone, *Madame*?" a polite water asked.

"No," Courtney said uncertainly. "I'm meeting someone."

The waiter smiled, beckoning Courtney to follow him.

There was one empty table left and Courtney took the seat on the booth side, leaving the corresponding chair vacant. That would leave Dree enough room in case she wore one of her ostentatious, crinoline dresses. The seat was near the window which Courtney liked. She would be able to gaze at the view of the *Champs Élysées* illuminated for the night.

The waiter offered her a basket of fresh, sliced baguette but Courtney waved him away. She checked her watch again.

***

From the taxi, Benoît's eyeballs lolled up from his magazine periodically, each time he saw someone with big hair walk by. Of late, he had been oddly angered by big hair. More specifically, he found a particular, garish woman attached to said big hair vexing. Not a lot of people disliked Benoît. He had one of those bubbly personalities that people warm up to quickly. The fact that Alexandria Fontrose despised him spoke volumes of the tarry fathoms of her dark soul. The fact that Alexandria was sniffing around Courtney made Benoît shiver with antipathy.

Strangely, Alexandria Fontrose had not arrived at the pizzeria during the ninety minutes Benoît had been parked there. He tried not to gawk at Courtney sitting alone at her seat by the window, but her dejected face was impossible to ignore. She drew circles with her finger on the red checkered table cloth. She looked up with sad eyes at the sympathetic waiter, shaking her head every time he came to check up on her. The little tea candle reflected off of Courtney's forlorn face, illuminating a tear on her cheek.

CHAPTER FIFTEEN

"Madame," the waiter said, putting a sympathetic hand on Courtney's back, "perhaps this person you are meeting…"

"They'll be here," Courtney insisted in her most curt of voices.

The waiter nodded compassionately. "I see," he said softly. "May I at least offer you…"

"Two glasses of Bordeaux please, Jean-Louis," Benoît said blithely, putting a hand of familiarity on the waiter's shoulder.

"Benoît!" the waiter's eyes sparkled with recognition. "Yes, of course."

Courtney gawked at Benoît in disbelief. "What are you doing here?"

"Sorry I am late, *Chérie,"* Benoît said, pulling a chair out for himself.

"Oh my god, this is beyond unprofessional," Courtney said, hiding her face with her hand.

"I disagree," Benoît said, accepting a basket of sliced baguette from the waiter. "You see, my job is to make sure that your experience in Paris is *formidable.* You must never dine alone in this city. That is unacceptable. So here I am. Hi!" Benoît waved cutely for effect.

"This is silly," Courtney said awkwardly. "We should just leave."

Courtney's stupid stomach blustered with an incriminating snarl, not unlike a rapacious Bengal tiger.

"Hungry?" Benoît simpered.

"I'll get something out of the vending machine from the hotel," Courtney said, scrambling for her things. "Bugles. I like Bugles."

"But you are starving," Benoît argued.

"It's fine," Courtney mumbled. "I've been eating out of the vending machine ever since I got here."

Benoît's eyes widened into ping pong balls. That's *all* Courtney had been eating for the past two weeks? No wonder she was so sick that night in the Latin Quarter.

"You know," Benoît said while helping himself to a slice of crispy baguette, "part of the Parisian experience is to embrace the food. It would be a shame to leave without indulging a little bit. How often do you find yourself in Paris?"

"This is an Italian place though."

"They have French options to appease the curiosity of tourists."

"I…"

That baguette really smelled delicious. The freshly baked aroma was making Courtney's nostrils flare. But she could not admit to her driver that she could not afford to eat out. Not without Dree splurging for her.

"My treat," Benoît smiled, raising one of his signature eyebrows.

How did Benoît read her mind? Why was he trying so hard to be nice to her? Why was she not utterly revolted by his chivalry? Why was this whole thing so terribly wrong?

"I can't," Courtney said bluntly. "It would be inappropriate."

"How so?" Benoît asked, resting his chin on his hands in expectation.

"You forget that I have a reputation to uphold," Courtney answered primly. "What if an industry professional showed up? What would they think if they saw me eating with my manservant?"

Good God. Did she just say that out loud?

"Excuse me, what?" Benoît giggled.

"My driver!" Courtney nearly shrieked. "I can't be seen with my driver!"

Smirking, Benoît held a piece of baguette under Courtney's nose. She may or may not have moaned a little bit.

"Try," Benoît coaxed.

Courtney hastily grabbed the baguette from Benoît and snarfed it down. There was a delicate crunch. Fluffy, chewy heaven squished around her mouth with each bite. "Holy hell," Courtney said blissfully. "This is incredible! What do you people call this?"

"Bread," Benoît blinked.

Courtney realized how indelicate she must look, making out with the bread. (As they call it in France) She swallowed quickly and squinted at the menu, hoping to change the subject.

"I can translate if you'd like," Benoît offered.

"Do they have any squeaky cheese?"

Benoît sprayed water in mid-sip. "Excuse me, what?"

"Squeaky cheese. It's a thing. We have it in Wisconsin. It's like little curd balls. They make the coolest noise when you chew them. It's awesome."

"Cheese that squeaks," Benoît said, covering a snigger with his hand.

"Are you making fun of me?"

"Have you ever tried *escargot?*"

"Ew. No Eating snails is unsanitary."

Benoit blinked.

"Madame, Monsieur," the waiter said, "Two glasses of our finest Bordeaux."

"Oh," Courtney said with her mouth full of bread. "I don't really drink."

Benoît raised an eyebrow.

"Well," Courtney said sheepishly, "that time you found me on the... that was a special circumst... see, I prefer not to..."

"Do you mind if I try it?"

"Sure, if that's your thing."

Benoît nodded at Courtney as he swirled the wine around in the glass for a moment and inhaled. He closed his eyes and made a kind of sigh. He licked his lips, seeming to be in a faraway place. "Scintillating."

"How do you even know that?" Courtney said, popping more bread in her mouth. "You haven't tasted it yet."

The glint in Benoît's eyes – possibly from the tea candle – startled Courtney. "Wine is a work of art," Benoît said dreamily. "You can anticipate its flavor based on the blend of fragrances."

"You don't say," Courtney said, suddenly realizing her mouth was full of baguette. She swallowed conspicuously. "You never struck me as a wine guy."

"There is a lot you do not know about me."

***

Courtney goggled at the pizza that was placed on the table between she and Benoît. "Is that an egg?" she gaped.

"It is," Benoît said, sticking a napkin in the neck of his shirt.

"On the pizza?" Courtney was stunned.

"Why don't you try?"

"Because I don't eat things that are disgusting."

Ignoring Courtney, Benoît slid a slice on the plate in front of her. "How do you know it is revolting unless you try, *non*?"

Courtney examined the slice of pizza critically. The yoke was slithering down the side into a thick, yellow pool on her plate. She closed her eyes before taking a bite, hoping she could forget about the fact someone cracked breakfast on top of her dinner. Benoît leaned in expectantly, waiting for her to swallow. "Are you kidding me right now?" Courtney said emphatically. "That is literally the best thing I've ever..."

Courtney jerked a little bit when her cell phone rang. Again with the horrible timing. Courtney scanned the call display. It was Chastity.

No, Chass. Not now. This is the worst possible moment.

Benoît noticed Courtney staring at the call display and not answering. "Should you get that?" he suggested.

"It's not important."

The phone just kept ringing.

Awkward.

"Maybe I should just..." Courtney knew her sister would call relentlessly until she answered. "Yes, what?" Courtney lowered her voice as she answered the phone.

"Courtney, it's your sister Chastity."

Courtney rolled her eyes. She only had one sister. "I'm kind of busy here."

Benoît shifted proudly in his seat.

"Doing what?" Chastity said cynically.

"I'm in the middle of dinner," Courtney said, looking around nervously, convinced that everyone in the room was listening to her phone call, "and all the French people are judging me."

Benoît hid an amused smile under his hand.

"Whatever. Dad wants to know when you're coming home."

"I'm here until late August. Dad knows that." Courtney kicked herself. Now her driver would know how embarrassingly often her family calls to check up on her.

Benoît tried not to listen but the staccato of Chastity's voice was easily audible from Courtney's phone.

"Right," Chasity sighed. "But realistically, when will you be coming home?"

"What does that even mean?"

"Courtney, you know as well as anyone else that this whole Paris thing is going to crash and burn. You're not ready for this. Please come home before you embarrass yourself."

Benoît looked down with his tongue circling the inside of his cheek, trying to stop himself from speaking his mind.

"Can't talk, Chass. I'm in an important meeting."

Benoît perked up.

"Courtney," her sister lectured, "please don't make an ass of..."

End of call.

Courtney's face felt hot. She could feel Benoît's eyes on her. She dared not look back at him. She became jittery, feeling like she needed to leave immediately before she was further humiliated. "Where is the waiter?" she blurted nervously. "He hasn't checked up on us at all since he served the pizza." Flustered, Courtney muttered, "It's true what they say about the horrible service in Paris."

"Are you okay?" Benoît asked.

"I need to get out of here. Why hasn't the waiter come with the bill?"

"He does not want to disturb us."

"An American waiter would have swooped in seven or eight times by now asking if we need anything."

"That sounds annoying. It is rude to interrupt someone's meal. Restaurants are gathering places. People come together for celebrations, meetings, conversations, romance…"

"How the heck is the waiter supposed to know what I want?"

"You… ask him?"

"Yo!" Courtney said, snapping her fingers. "Gar-SON!"

Benoît reddened and sheltered an abashed expression with his hand.

The waiter looked sideways at Courtney, giving her a look of disapproval.

"Did you see that rude look he gave me?" Courtney stage whispered.

"Jean-Louis is a very attentive waiter. There is no reason to talk down to him, *Chérie.*"

"What the…"

"Try a little eye contact and a smile," Benoît explained, smiling at the waiter.

"For you, Monsieur Benoît," the waiter said with a nod as he placed the bill in front of Benoît.

Benoît said something to the waiter in French that made him smile and chuckle.

Courtney withered in embarrassment. She had no idea how to behave in this city. Why did Parisians have so many rules of etiquette? It was impossible to keep up with them.

Benoît reached for the wallet in his back pocket.

"You don't have to…" Courtney said, blushing.

"Please," Benoît said. "It is my treat, remember?"

"But that wouldn't be right."

"You are a guest in my city. I will pay."

Courtney fidgeted with the lucky duck in her purse. She really could not afford this dinner. But letting him pay would be like admitting…

"Benoît," Courtney began.

Benoît looked up.

Courtney bit the inside of her cheek. "You should know," she said quickly, "that this isn't a date or anything."

Benoît's face dropped. "I know," he said quietly.

"I don't want to hurt your feelings. I just don't want there to be any misunderstandings."

Benoît nodded. "No misunderstandings to be had. I am just the manservant." He could not help but smirk.

CHAPTER SIXTEEN
(DAY 21 IN PARIS)

Tall, skinny salted caramel macchiato with no whip and an extra shot of espresso. Benoît now knew Courtney's favorite coffee order by heart and had it ready for her each morning when he picked her up. Coffee in hand, Benoît stood straight when he saw Courtney approach. Like clockwork, she accepted the coffee from Benoît and systematically found her usual spot in the backseat. They had become like a well-oiled machine.

"What adventures do you have in store today?" Benoît asked.

"I have an event at the Palace Garn-ee-air."

Benoît had become an expert American interpreter. *"Palais Garnier?"* He could not hide the excitement in his voice.

"Is that someplace special?" Courtney asked, oblivious.

Benoît was bursting with glee. "This is my favorite place in the whole city. I cannot wait to see your face when you see this building. Your heart will explode!"

"Mmmhmmm," Courtney said distractedly, sipping her coffee.

"Ask me why *Le Palais Garnier* is my favorite."

Courtney was extremely focused on something in her sketchbook, with her brow intensely furrowed.

Benoît bounced eagerly in his seat, unable to contain himself. "Not only is it the most divinely ornate building in all of Paris, but... are you sitting down?"

Of course she was sitting down. They were in a taxi.

"My four times great grandfather's second cousin was," Benoît said, building suspense which was literally lost on Courtney, "Charles Garnier!"

Crickets.

Courtney looked blankly at Benoît. Clearly that name meant nothing to her.

"You know?" Benoît squealed. "THE Charles Garnier? The architect who designed the opera house."

"Okay," Courtney said, looking back at her sketches.

"I don't think you understand. You see, my name is Benoît Garnier."

Courtney wondered why Benoît was stating the obvious but then realized that all this time she had not known Benoît's last name. *Benoît Garnier.* Who knew?

"So as you can imagine," Benoît said with verve, "being a Garnier myself, this building holds a very special meaning to me. I have an extremely strong, spiritual connection with that place. I sometimes envy the pigeons who sit atop the statues outside the opera house. What an exquisite view they must have."

"Pigeons," Courtney said absently. "Huh."

"So what kind of event is being held at *Le Palais Garnier?*" Benoît was giddy when he said his own name.

"I'm meeting with Dree," Courtney finally looked up from her sketches.

Benoît's face melted into an expression of concern. Alexandria Fontrose had stood Courtney up for twelve scheduled meetings in the past three weeks. He could not bear that punctured look of rejection on Courtney's face one more time. Stewing, Benoît bit his lower lip.

"Why are you biting your lower lip?" Courtney asked.

"No reason," Benoît lied.

"People don't bite their lower lip for no reason."

"It is not my place," Benoît said humbly.

"Benoît, if there is something on your mind just say it. Don't go around biting your lower lip."

Benoît blew out some stress-infused air. Courtney was not going to want to hear this. "I do not trust her," he said almost inaudibly.

Courtney narrowed her eyes. "You're right. It's not your place."

"I am sorry, Courtney. But the way she treats you."

"She treats me really well!"

"She stood you up twelve times."

"She didn't stand me up. She is just really busy. Maybe you don't realize how important and famous and influential she is. *Alexandria Fontrose...*"

"Is that even her real name? It sounds like... what is that English word that sounds like a sneeze? *Pretentious.*"

"That is not true!" Courtney protested. "Don't you understand? It was very cool of her to fit me into her crazy schedule and it's not her fault when things come up unexpectedly! ... You're biting your lower lip again."

"You do not want to hear what I have to say so..."

"I don't."

"There is something wrong with her eyes," Benoît said anyway.

"Benoît..."

"I once knew someone with those same eyes. They see and then they take. You cannot trust such eyes."

"I have no idea what you just said but you are wrong."

"I don't want her to hurt you, Courtney."

"This is none of your business."

"Can you at least be careful?"

"Stay out of this, okay? You're just the driver!" Courtney instantly regretted this outburst. Her throat was strangled with remorse when she saw Benoît's eyes redden. She hated herself when he looked down at his steering wheel. She silently swore at herself.

"*Palais Garnier,*" Benoît croaked almost silently as he stopped the taxi in front of the lavish opera house.

"It looks cool," Courtney offered pathetically.

Benoît nodded. "Have a magical time," he nearly whispered.

Courtney gaped at Benoît stupidly for a moment before she left the taxi and headed for the front entrance of the *Palais Garnier*.

Benoît craned his neck to make sure she made it into the building safely. His concern was pointless. But he could not help himself.

CHAPTER SEVENTEEN

The inside of the *Palais Garnier* was like something from a dream. Lavish elegance enveloped Courtney from every angle. The sweeping, theatrical staircase seemed to welcome her as she walked obliviously through the front entrance into the grand foyer. Marble kissed her feet with each step she took on the magnificent floor. The ornate baroque art on the ceiling seemed to look down at Courtney curiously, protectively. But Courtney did not notice. She was utterly mesmerized by Alexandria Fontrose, following her around like a doting puppy.

"I reserved one the most extravagant salons for our meeting," Alexandria said with a dramatic flourish, almost as though she was trying to compete with the theatricality of the building itself. "I felt the ostentatious ambiance would grant you inspiration. And the acoustics in these rooms are fabulous so you will benefit from the commanding amplification of my voice."

"Awesome," said Courtney, who was still unsure as to why they needed so much empty space to have a meeting.

"I must offer a trillion apologies about my lack of availability of late. I feel abysmally for disappointing you. These little urgencies just keep popping up. I had to mediate another spat between Dolce and Gabbana. Vera Wang had no idea how to design a trumpet skirt for her new line of wedding dresses. Calvin Klein had an underwear emergency that only I could help with. Karl Lagerfeld couldn't find his keys..."

"Wait, didn't he..."

"You'll find out just exactly how daunting this life can be when you become a famous, adored and sought after designer."

Courtney felt her face literally glowing.

"We have a lot to catch up on, Lollipop," Alexandria said, pointing a manicured finger at Courtney. "I trust you have been taking advantage of the studio I rented for you."

"I am!" Courtney said eagerly. "Thank you so much for that! It was so nice of you."

"Yes it was," Alexandria agreed rather pompously. "But you are worth it, Pussy Willow. Consider it an investment. If you succeed, we both succeed. Now then, have you given any thought to the feedback I gave you about that splendid sun dress you've been working on?"

"Yes," Courtney said, opening her sketchbook. "I've been adding layers of texture. I've also been trying to elevate my designs."

"Smashing!" Alexandria said, eyeballing the designs in the sketchbook. "But I need to see more than just the sketches. I want to see these alterations in three dimensions. Did you bring any of the garments with you?"

"Oh," Courtney said quietly, "no, I hadn't considered bringing them with me."

Alexandria's eyes bulged dramatically.

"I'm sorry?"

"I forgive you," Alexandria said, aloof. "You are special, Courtney Stent. Regardless of your inexperience, it is an honor to be a part of your journey."

Courtney welled with emotion. "Can I hug you right now?"

"I'm wearing Chinese silk so no."

"That's cool," Courtney nodded.

"But I'm hugging you right now in my soul, my sweet tadpole," Alexandria said maternally.

"Dree, I was thinking maybe we could..."

Courtney suddenly noticed that Alexandria, now with a stiff, painted-on smile, was no longer looking at Courtney but looking at something just past Courtney in the distance.

"Dree?"

"Yes, dear," Alexandria said absently. "You know, why don't we wrap things up for the day and meet whenever. There's a good tot."

Courtney was stumped when Alexandria flippantly patted her on the head, walking slowly away.

"What's going on?" Courtney asked. "I thought we had access to this salon for the afternoon."

"Something's suddenly come up, Muffin. Be elsewhere."

"But I thought..."

"It's nothing personal. Just... make haste."

Courtney would have complied had she not been frozen to the spot in shock.

Alexandria clenched her teeth when she was recognized and approached by an utterly vainglorious designer who was wearing the most highfaluting scarf Courtney had ever seen. He trotted imperiously over to Alexandria, whose face was draining of color.

"Courtney," Alexandria hissed, "it's Gerald Featherstone. Why are you here still? Suck in your cheeks and pretend to be important."

Courtney urgently obeyed.

"Alexandria!" Gerald said with a dramatic flourish of his hand.

"Gerald!" Alexandria gasped, blowing imaginary kisses to him in the air. "Duckling," Alexandria said to Courtney whose cheeks were sucked in ridiculously, "would you mind giving Gerald and I a bit of privacy? It's critical that I talk to him about scarves."

"But I don't really have anywhere to..."

"Gerald, Darling," Alexandria said while discreetly pushing Courtney aside, "we absolutely must talk about your new line of neckwear. Oh, how your colors pop!"

"Over a latte of course," Gerald said smoothly.

"Is there any other way to discuss scarves?"

Looking around awkwardly, Courtney timidly cleared her throat.

Alexandria lolled her eyeballs towards Courtney, annoyed. "Yes, yes. Gerald, I found the most charming little novice. She calls herself Courtney. Isn't she a cracker?"

"A novice? How charitable of you."

"Isn't it though? Her sketches are absolutely adorable. Like a basket of kittens."

Kittens? Was she freaking kidding?

"Why is she here?" Gerald asked, looking down his nose. "If the question is not too forthcoming."

Courtney squirmed.

"I let her tag along. Thought it would boost her self-esteem a little. Give her some important hands to shake. Let her show off her quirky shoes. You don't think it's gauche that I brought her here?"

"Gauche? Bosh! Thinking it gauche would be impolite, wouldn't it."

"I have a show so..." Courtney felt the need to defend herself.

"A show?" Gerald said, with his eyes widening condescendingly. Courtney wondered why his mouth remained glued into the shape of the letter O long after he finished saying the word *show*. "You? Mind boggling!"

"Not really. I'm a designer. I'm here for Fashion Week."

After an awkward pause, Gerald burst into a spit-spraying fit of laughter that boomed through the room with a reverberating echo. Much to Courtney's anguish and humiliation, Alexandria followed suit and laughed along condescendingly. Courtney could feel tears stinging her eyes. Her heart thumped so loudly she was certain everyone in the building could hear it. Her face became so hot you could fry an egg on her cheek.

"Excuse me," Courtney squeaked as she sheltered her face with her hand and made a beeline out of the room. She found a crevice at the bottom of the opulent staircase and curled up in a ball underneath with her face in her arms. She wept. She could hear the voices of Alexandria and Gerald echoing from the other room. Their scoffing voices bounced off of every surface in the building – one of the many disadvantages of outstanding acoustics.

"I worry sometimes that she won't be able to keep up with the current," she heard Alexandria say.

"D'ya think?" Gerald said mockingly.

Courtney wanted to shrink into the floor and disappear. She curled more tightly into a ball.

A man with his hands in his pockets, admiring the lavish art on the ceiling, heard the arrogant cackles of Alexandria and Gerald. The man turned his head in the direction of the salon – it was Benoît. He recognized the raspy cackle and his eyes narrowed. He sauntered discreetly towards the sound and leaning against a pillar, he sneezed the word *"Putain!"*

As though answering to her own name, Alexandria spun around and found Benoît, staring challengingly at her.

"Hold my drink, Gerald," Alexandria seethed. "I have a foe to smite."

Alexandria left a very confused Gerald and walked with a purpose towards a police officer who was minding the building.

"You there!" Alexandria said, pointing intensely at the officer. "That wretched man over there? Leaning against that pillar? Have him removed."

"Madame?" the perplexed officer said.

"You should know," she whispered venomously, "he got me alone in the powder room and…"

"That man?"

"He is an animal."

The officer cocked a perplexed eyebrow.

"Go on now," Alexandria prompted. "Apprehend him. Be sure to make as big a spectacle as you can. I want him humiliated. Take him down. Like a hyena. Ravenously hunting an unassuming gnu."

"But I know him. He comes here all the time."

"He…"

"I am afraid you are drunk and confused. *Monsieur* Garnier is literally my favorite person. If his effervescence causes you discomfort then perhaps YOU should leave, *Madame*."

"Damn," Alexandria sneered. "Even the fuzz thinks he's charming."

CHAPTER EIGHTEEN

Courtney was indelicately slurping snot back into her nostrils as she squeezed tightly into a ball of disgrace on the floor of the opera house. She realized she had nothing to wipe her nose with, not even a sleeve. Why did she have to wear micro-suede? She hid her face in her folded arms, finding the sound of the footsteps all around her to be unbearable. Everybody was looking at her. She could feel their stares boring through her head. Everyone knew what a complete joke she was. Why did she even come to Paris? Her family was right. She was a failure.

One set of footsteps stopped in front of Courtney. She did not look up. She could not look anyone in the face right now. She would just stay in this ball on the floor forever. Maybe nobody would care. She was invisible, after all.

"Courtney?" a familiar voice said.

Courtney looked up and saw Benoît looking down at her. She became self-conscious of the streaks of mascara that were smeared down her cheeks. And the snot. So much snot.

Benoît kneeled down next to her. "Hey," he smiled. "No crying in Paris. We have a rule."

"What are you doing here?" Courtney snuffed.

"Did I not tell you I have a spiritual connection with this building?"

"I don't want to talk right now."

"Okay," Benoît said buoyantly as he nestled his butt on the floor next to her. "You do not have to say anything."

"You are really annoying sometimes, you know that."

"It is all part of my charm," Benoît shrugged.

"Nothing has gone right since I got here," Courtney blurted out before she had a chance to change her mind.

"Is something wrong with the duck?"

"This is nothing like the Paris I taped to the wall."

"I do not understand," he said, offering Courtney a tissue.

"I thought I'd be making a bigger splash," Courtney explained."

"I thought..."

"I can't go home without getting my break in Paris. I can't face them. I can't..."

"I thought you were a..."

"Nope. I lied. I am not a big shot designer. I'm not even from Milwaukee. I'm from a stupid little rural village called Colby Haven where literally nothing ever happens. I'm here because I won a stupid contest. It's not an esteemed contest and it's not for professional designers. It's for beginners. An artichoke could enter if it wanted to. I paid a whopping twenty-five dollar entry fee."

Benoît pursed his lips and nodded.

"I'm not as talented as I thought I was."

"That is not true."

"You heard what Alexandria said. Everyone in here heard what she said."

Benoît looked down, getting only a peripheral glimpse of Courtney. Every breathy snuff she inhaled felt like someone was punching him in the solar plexus. He exhaled loudly then stood to his feet.

"What are you doing?" Courtney asked, startled.

"Turn around," Benoît beamed.

Benoît turned Courtney to face the grand staircase. Courtney's eyes sparkled, partly from tears, partly from wonder. She had not really paid attention to the details of the opulent foyer when she arrived as she was focused on other matters.

"*C'est magnifique, non?*" Benoît said, showing her around. "Even the staircases are theatrical. Like Charles Garnier wanted the spectators to be part of the show. To be watched, just like an opera."

Courtney followed Benoît up to the staircase. She ran her hand over the sleek, marble banister.

"Papa used to bring me here all the time when I was a little boy," Benoît continued. "This room would bewitch my boyish imagination."

"So you have a crush on this building."

"Look at the detail," Benoît said in amazement, showing Courtney an intricate lizard detailed into the staircase. "It is a salamander. It is used to hide a gas line. So clever."

Courtney watched Benoît's face light up each time he explained a detail of the building. His eyes glimmered with enthusiasm. There was a bounce in his step. His energy was alluring.

"How can you be sad in here?" Benoît asked. "Won't you let me show you?"

Benoit bounded up the stairs and Courtney followed cautiously behind.

***

"Do you know the legend of *le fantôme de l'Opéra?*" Benoît asked Courtney as they explored the upper levels of the *Palais Garnier*.

"Everybody knows about the phantom," Courtney shrugged.

"Some people claim," Benoît said with eyes widening with mystery, "that the legend was based on Charles Garnier. He was obsessed with this building."

"Must run in the family."

"When he was finished, he did not want to leave. Because he knew every passage and corridor, some believe he would hide around the opera house and play pranks."

Courtney followed Benoît around a bend and towards a dark corner. Benoît stopped in front of a door that was nearly hidden in the shadows.

"This is the famous Box Five," Benoît said with playful secrecy. "It must be kept empty for the phantom."

"Then what are we doing here?" Courtney meant that on a number of different levels.

"Do you want to see?"

"I thought we weren't supposed to go in there?"

"I know a guy."

Courtney's eyeballs roved around, looking for a potential escape route.

"It is okay Courtney," Benoît teased. "I am not going to eat you. I just want to show you one of the greatest enigmas in the history of France."

Courtney inhaled and nodded.

The door to Box Five creaked when Benoît opened it. Courtney edged her way past Benoît to get a better look. It was very red and plush and velvety. Courtney walked up to the front and looked over the edge of the balcony, wincing. That was a long way down. She looked up and saw the biggest, most stunning chandelier she had ever seen.

"So what's the big deal about this box?" Courtney asked quickly to slice through the silence. "Why did the phantom like it so much?"

"Of all the boxes," Benoît said, turning to face Courtney, "this one is the most private." Benoît swallowed hard. "He liked to hide in the shadows so people would not know he was there. Only in secret would he startle patrons with his dark magic."

Courtney struggled to breathe for a moment.

"There is something otherworldly about this place," Benoît nearly quavered. "It is easy to lose yourself in this building's alluring fantasies."

They were suddenly interrupted by Benoît's phone buzzing with a text message.

"You're pants are vibrating," Courtney observed.

Benoît scrambled for his phone.

Have you made a move yet?

The text was from Étienne. Benoît fumbled to put his phone away.

"Who was it?" Courtney asked.

"Nobody," Benoît stammered. "It was nothing."

"Do you have to be somewhere or…"

"No," Benoît said with a breathy laugh. "I do not have to be anywhere. We have all the time in the…"

Courtney quickly changed the subject, turning to face the chandelier. "So that's the chandelier that caused all the brouhaha," she said.

"So beautiful," Benoît said almost whispering, moving a lock of Courtney's golden hair off her forehead, placing it carefully behind her ear. Crystals from the chandelier reflected in his chocolaty irises. He leaned in so close that Courtney could feel his breath on her neck. Everything seemed hazy when his lips nearly touched hers.

Courtney flinched.

Benoît pulled away.

"Courtney?"

"What almost happened?... Didn't happen."

"I am sorry to hear that because what did not happen was *incroyable*."

"Did you plan this?"

"No, I just..."

"Oh God," Courtney said, massaging her temples. "I can't do this."

"Why?"

"Please don't take this the wrong way, Benoît. You're just not my type. I can't be with you. Like ever."

All the animation drained from Benoît's face. "Why not?"

"Because you're Fr... frankly not my type."

Benoît ran his hands over his face as though trying to wash away the shame. He blinked hard, looking away. "If you would like to request a different driver..."

"No!" Courtney surprised herself with the urgency of her plea.

Benoît looked up, hopeful.

"I mean," Courtney stuttered, "why bother? A new driver would mean I would have to get used to a whole different French person."

Benoît raised an eyebrow.

"Can we just go?" Courtney spouted, scrambling for her things.

Benoît nodded, biting his cheek.

CHAPTER NINETEEN
(DAY 30 IN PARIS)

Courtney smelled funky. She lost track of when or how often she showered. Judging by the film that was forming on her hair, she estimated that her last shower was four or five days ago. She had no reason to leave her hotel room. The disgrace and humiliation was smothering her like the world's largest pillow. She had no motivation to work in her studio. What was the point? She thought Alexandria Fontrose was impressed by her talent but the truth was staring Courtney down like an outlaw in a spaghetti Western. Her own mentor was embarrassed to be seen with her.

Her precious garments she had meticulously and lovingly prepared for Fashion Week were carefully hung in the closet with the door open. They seemed to watch her, critically. *"Why did you create us, only to leave us on a hanger like a bunch of leisure suits at a rummage sale? We thought you loved us. We are your babies. Probably the only babies you'll ever make because you are a total spaz and screw up every relationship you've ever had. But that's none of our business."*

Who knew inanimate articles of clothing could be so judgmental?

And then there was the matter of Benoît... (shudder)

Unbeknownst to Courtney, Alexandria Fontrose had left a plethora of handwritten messages at the hotel front desk for her. Courtney had not left her room for the past nine days and had put the *do not disturb* sign on her door handle, so she had no idea these messages were waiting for her:

"Dearest, Dearest Courtney-Poo:

I must explain my behavior of late. It may have seemed on the surface that I was somehow trying to blow you off at the opera house. That was simply not the case, my love. The fashion industry is merely a series of mind games and that was precisely what I was doing with Gerald Featherstone. Gerald simply does not understand our unique bond and it would be pointless to explain to him. I was put on the spot, you understand. Let me explain further over some drinky-poos.

Fondly Forever,

Dree."

"Loveliest Courtney:

I am simply aching to meet with you. I had a dream last night about your luminous future as a fashion guru. I was so proud, my darling. I am quite wise and dare I say clairvoyant, lol. So I am confident my dream will come true, as will yours. Please forgive the sins of my past like a good girl and let us dine together Tuesday next.

Dree."

"To my shining star:

How I miss you, my darling. I trust you are making good use of your studio that I graciously provided. I am quite busy this week but I will be with you in spirit. I am aquiver with anticipation for this upcoming Fashion Week. The industry pros will be agog when they see your brilliant creations.

Your Humble Fan,

Dree."

"To my surrogate daughter (Courtney Stent):

I have spoken highly of you to my colleagues over at the Prada Convention and they are eager to meet you at your upcoming show. I told them that yours is a name they should watch for! I am so proud of you, my dear. I do hope I haven't done anything to offend you because you are truly the apple of my eye. A treasure, if you don't mind my saying so. I'm a little bit drunk right now but I'll be in touch within the next few days if you want to confide in me about anything deeply personal.

Maternally yours,

Dree."

"Dear Future Fashion Goddess:

Since your disappearance, I have not had the opportunity to give you one of my inspiring pep talks. I shall therefore do so in written form. You are glorious, Courtney Stent. You are a visionary. You give me hope for the future of fashion. In other news, I bought a fabulous hat. – AF"

"Yoo Hoo!

I may be a little sensitive given the current phase of the moon but I do get the impression that you are blowing me off. I am not used to this sort of treatment, you understand because I am astonishing. I should remind you that I handpicked you out of thousands of applications and have sacrificed my time, energy, money and dare I say reputation for you, love. Don't misunderstand. I do love you with all my being. If you are in a snit over something or other, I suggest you grow a thicker skin. This industry is not for the fainthearted.

Kisses!

Dree."

"Me Again!

Oh Courtney, if something is troubling you remember I am here to help. I am a devoted mentor and you are my darling sprig of parsley. I forgot to remind you in my previous letter that I am frequently quoted in the media. Those I hold dear get a respectable plug during interviews. I thought I should bring that to your attention. Because reasons.

Your Dreamweaver,

Dree."

"Hallooo my precious chrysanthemum:

This is Alexandria Fontrose. Or as I have lovingly allowed you to call me, Dree. I felt a moral obligation to inform you that I have explained everything to Gerald Featherstone and he now thinks you are a peach. You're welcome, dear. We both had a good laugh over the situation as I know you are doing right now as you read this. And please, next time try to not be quite so oversensitive. That will never do in this industry.

Love and Light,

Dree."

"To My Heart, Courtney:

I was just saying to Ralph Lauren the other day, that your designs could very well top the fashion charts in the coming year. Ralphie is intrigued. He may have implied that he wants to collaborate with you in the future. (wink, wink) I also wanted to see how things were going with your driver. If I can be candid with you, he was not a driver of my choosing, nor do I approve of him. Remember that conversation we had about French vices. You would be wise to heed my warnings. That man is odious. Don't ask me how I know that.

Love and Cuddles,

Dree."

CHAPTER TWENTY

"Why did you put so much pressure on me to make a move?" Benoît asked Étienne who was restocking his Eiffel Tower keychain inventory. "I have completely traumatized Courtney. She has not called for a ride in nine days."

"You mean to say nothing at all has happened between the two of you since her arrival?

"Of course not."

"Are you saying you have not tasted her sweet neck? Caressed her ivory cheek? Enjoyed her delicate sighs? You have not yet ravished that picturesque body that was created by the hand of our God? The same hand that sculpted the mountains and the sea?"

"I cannot just ravish her, Étienne. That would be indecent."

"What do you mean you cannot ravish her? You have the hot blood of a poet rushing through your veins, Benoît. Like me, you are devilishly handsome. Go to her, Benoît. Make wild passionate love under the moon! Or by the Seine. Or both. I am not particular about these things."

"I cannot. She is from a completely different world."

"You have lost sleep over this girl. She is all you talk about. She makes your soul climax. Deny it. I dare you."

"She despises the French. She basically said that to my face before she stopped herself for the sake of decorum."

"Decorum? That's an improvement! See, Benoît? She cares about your feelings! She is becoming a better person because of you! And do you know what this means, Benoît? She is imagining what you look like shirtless!"

Benoît shook his head in amusement with an unavoidable smirk. "You are a force of nature, Étienne. But no."

"Okay," Étienne said, patting a stool for Benoît to sit next to him. "Let us discuss. What exactly went wrong that day at the opera house?"

"I miscalculated things."

"What was she doing at that exact moment?"

"Looking at me."

"Looking at you how?"

"She looked at me in a way that made me think..."

"So you were acting on an instinct based on her body language?"

"It seemed like the moment was perfect."

"Were her eyes steamy? Were her eyelids drooping with lust?"

"I don't know."

"What was the energy like in the room?"

"It is hard to describe."

"Was there an animalistic force pulling you together like a giant fridge magnet?"

"I... what?"

"Did she close her eyes when you leaned in?"

"I think so."

"Did your lips actually touch?"

"Almost. They grazed a little bit."

"What did it taste like?"

"You are getting a little too into this."

"I am only trying to help, Cousin."

"It seems wrong to be talking about this."

"Do you love her?"

"It does not matter how I feel. I have made things awkward for her. I encroached when she did not want me. My culture repels her. I have no chance. I..." Benoît jolted when his cell phone rang. He fumbled around until he found his phone with Courtney's number on the screen. *"Mon dieu!"* Benoît said, gawking at the number. *"It is her."*

CHAPTER TWENTY-ONE

"Benoît?" Courtney choked on the phone.

"Courtney?" Benoît's voice made Courtney jittery. "Are you oka... Do you require a driver today?"

Courtney looked at herself in the mirror. She was still wearing her pajamas – the same pajamas she had been wearing for the past nine days. There were dark circles under her eyes. She was pale and her eyes were red from sleeplessness and tears. She was pretty sure she would never be able to put a comb through her hair ever again. Her shoulders looked bonier than usual and her collar bone was protruding. The last decent meal she had was that freaky egg pizza she ate with Benoît.

"Are you there, Courtney?" Benoît asked, trying to mask his concern.

Courtney opened her mouth to reply but the words hung silent in the air. She had no idea what to say to Benoît. She had no idea if she ever wanted to talk to him again. But she was feeling herself disconnecting from reality and she did not know who else to latch on to.

"I..." Courtney stammered right before she was rescued by call waiting. "I have to put you on hold," she said as she switched calls. "Hello?"

"It's Mom."

Courtney deflated. Why did she not check the call display?

"Hey."

"Something's wrong. What's wrong?"

"Nothing's wrong, Mom."

"Don't lie to me, Courtney Agatha Stent."

"Never say my middle name ever again."

"What are you hiding from me?"

"I'm on another call. I have to go."

"Who is it?"

"That's none of your business."

"I'm going to keep pestering until I get some answers."

"Okay fine," Courtney sighed. "I've had a crummy couple of weeks."

"I knew it."

"I've taken a little break. To regroup."

"Typical. You can't handle this. Dad and I will be on the next flight to bring you home."

"I'm not going home."

"Why are you taking a break? What does that even mean? What happened?"

"There was just a little hiccup…"

"How long have you been on this little break? Did you humiliate yourself? Did Fashion Week fall through?"

"I've been working hard. I just needed…"

"What have you been working on? I want pictures."

"You have no interest in my work."

"Work. Pish. You're just coloring and playing dress-up with your friends."

"What *are* you?"

"A concerned mother, that's what. Cut your losses and come home. I don't know what you're trying to prove but we've played along long enough."

"I don't want to come home."

"Bruce has been asking about you."

"Bruce is morally repugnant."

"He's a good match for you, Courtney. He's tall. He's local. He doesn't have any major substance abuse problems. And he is open-minded about your shortcomings."

"I don't want to go back to Colby Haven. Not now."

"You admitted that it's not working out in Paris."

"I didn't say that."

"Be honest, Courtney. You don't belong there. You belong in Colby Haven. You have a life waiting here for you. A supportive family. Fulfilling career. Bruce."

"I've got to take this call mom," Courtney said as she flipped the phone back to Benoît. "I'm back."

"I am here," Benoît replied on the phone. "Do you require my services?"

Courtney's mind wafted to something inappropriate. But her brain zipped back to reality like a record player needle. "Uh... yeah. I need to go to my studio. Right away." She winced when she saw her reflection again. "I mean, give me an hour."

CHAPTER TWENTY-TWO

Benoît was suffering from a sudden bout of restless leg syndrome while waiting for Courtney in the taxi. He turned his head rapidly every time he saw someone walk out of the front entrance of the hotel. Would Courtney ever arrive? And what would he say when she did? Would things be weird? Of course things would be weird. Benoît crossed a serious, professional boundary.

Startled, Benoît bounced an inch off of his seat when Courtney suddenly closed the taxi door and was seated in the backseat. He secretly bubbled.

"Studio please," she said blandly.

Benoît nodded and started driving.

"You disappeared," Benoît said, concocting a bright smile despite his nerves.

"I was on hiatus," Courtney explained.

"Very understandable."

"What is that supposed to mean?" Courtney asked defensively.

"I only mean to say that it must be common among creative geniuses to need time to refuel. It must be exhausting with all those brilliant ideas swirling around your brain all the time."

"That's not what you meant."

"Then… what did I mean?"

"You think I was hiding in my hotel room for nine days because I was afraid to face you. Oh my God, Benoît! That's so smug, even for a French dude."

"I did not say…"

"Nothing happened. We agreed on it."

"You brought it up so…"

"Speaking of nothing happening, we should agree on some ground rules."

"Okay."

"I realize that this thing that happened, which didn't happen, was partially my fault. Not that I've been lying around thinking about this for the past week because that would be pathetic."

Benoît perked up.

"It should have occurred to me," Courtney continued, "that I should have established boundaries earlier on. Seeing as how we are spending so much time alone together. An attractive young girl and an okay-ish looking guy."

Benoît covered his mouth to shelter a giggle.

"All kinds of indecent things could happen if we don't have some kind of agreement ahead of time. I've heard that impulse control is hard for you people."

"Where did you hear that?"

"Television. There is a lot of educational programming on the subject."

"Such as?"

"For starters…"

"Other than that skunk from Loonie Toons."

"Whatever, never mind."

"Okay," Benoît's said with his voice breaking in an attempt to stifle laughter. "Name the boundaries."

"I mentioned before that we should keep things professional. Maybe the word professional means something different in your language. Or maybe culturally, it's normal to kiss random people on the mouth. I don't know how things work here but in America we don't neck with our co-workers. We have a thing called HR that prevents that kind of behavior."

Trying not to laugh was causing Benoît physical pain.

"A good rule of thumb is that if you think I'm giving you a signal of some kind, I'm not. For example, if I'm gazing at you like a screech owl it doesn't mean I'm into you. You might have gunk in your teeth. Or I'm baffled by your strange culture."

Benoît nodded.

"Second point. If I seem clingy it is only because I am far from home and under a ridiculous amount of stress as Fashion Week approaches. It does not mean that I want to form a romantic relationship with you, nor do I want you to grab my knockers."

Benoît snorted loudly.

"Is something funny?"

"Yes!" Benoît squeaked between laughs. "I mean no!"

"Benoît if you can't take this seriously... Oh skip it. Gramma was right. Boundaries don't exist in this city. If you cross the line again I'll just have to slap you. Deal?"

Benoît nodded, gasping for breath.

"Forgive me, Courtney. Your American whims are most entertaining. I will be on my best behavior from now on. We will only speak of pick-up times and destinations in a curt manner."

Courtney gaped for a moment. "Let's not take this too far. If you feel the need to launch into some of your effervescent, French banter, I have an open mind."

"What do you mean?"

"You know how you get. When you talk with all that gusto? You get all cartoonishly animated. I don't hate that."

Benoît smirked.

***

Courtney gaped blankly at a naked seamstress dummy in her studio. She narrowed her eyes into slits of concentration, trying desperately to drum up some new ideas. But the words of Alexandria

Fontrose that once echoed off the walls of the *Palais Garnier* were now echoing throughout the caverns of her brain.

"I worry sometimes that she won't be able to keep up with the current."

No amount of squinting was helping Courtney to conjure inspiration, even after three hours. She was distracted by the humidity in the room and the aroma of fresh croissants wafting through her open window. She skipped breakfast and those obnoxious croissants would taunt her until she sunk her teeth into one.

Courtney abandoned the studio and scuttled down the narrow stairway to the door that led to the courtyard. Sure enough she spotted the croissant guy, flaunting his wares in a way that she interpreted as smug.

"I need one of those!" Courtney yelled to him, not even caring how crass she sounded. "Did you hear me? I said I want a croissant. Like today."

The croissant guy gave Courtney a disapproving glare and turned away from her. Courtney walked with a purpose towards him.

"Yo! French Guy!" Courtney said a little too hungrily. "I'm entitled to some service here!"

The croissant guy replied in French.

"Look Buddy," Courtney said grumpily, "I really need a croissant. I won't go into the details of my day except to say that I'm starting to question the reason for my existence and my eyes ache from too much squinting." She put her hand out conspicuously and sighed, "Croissant."

The merchant threw a croissant at Courtney and said something unintelligible in French. The croissant bounced stupidly off of her head and fell to the ground.

Courtney griped, picking the croissant up quickly and cramming some in her mouth. As she walked away she distinctly heard the croissant merchant speak cordially to another passerby in English.

"Oh my god!" Courtney said with her mouth full of croissant.

***

Courtney was in a funk as she slammed the door of the taxi. Benoît's eyes widened when she started muttering psychotically to herself.

"Of all the rude..." Courtney muttered.

"Excuse me?"

"Not you, Benoît. It was that douche canoe that sells croissants outside my studio. He pretended not to speak English. Can you believe that? All I wanted was a croissant."

Benoît raised an eyebrow.

"Dude. What's with the eyebrow?"

"Were you being your usual delightful self when you approached the merchant?"

"Of course!"

Benoît grinned ironically and nodded even more ironically.

"Stop being elusive. It bugs me when you do that."

"Courtney, did you have a bad day?"

"That's personal."

"I cannot advise you unless you tell me."

"Okay fine. Yes, I had a bad day. The worst."

"Is there any chance that perhaps you took it out on the merchant?"

"That's irrelevant."

"How so? Parisians are people too."

"Elusive people who do things that make no sense."

"Courtney, I know nothing about the code of etiquette in your country..."

"Obviously."

"...but around here..."

"...you hold people to unrealistic standards. And you seem pretty proud of yourselves for it."

"I am proud of my city and am excited to share it with visitors. But there are certain things we simply cannot..."

"Are you implying..."

"How do you expect a person to behave if someone is being rude, disrespectful or abusive? You are a guest in our home. Do you behave disrespectfully when you are in someone else's home? What reason would we have to tolerate that?"

Courtney gaped stupidly, her face reddening.

Benoît noticed Courtney's face sagging into a confused stupor. He decided to snap her out of it. "No need to thank me for the advice," he bubbled, "it is all part of my service."

"I… ugh… I get a little moody when I'm feeling uninspired."

"But you are in the most inspirational city in the world!" Benoît said with fervor.

"I'm busy with work. There's no time for sightseeing."

"But if you are feeling uninspired…"

"No."

"… maybe you should take some time to…"

"Not interested."

"… clear your head and get inspired…"

"Do you even have ears? I said I don't want to…"

"… by all the things that made you want to come here in the first place."

Courtney blinked. "I…" she hesitated, "I don't know my way around."

"I can give you a metro map. Pick any attraction. I will drop you off."

"I…" Courtney was nearly hoarse from straining a humiliated whisper, "I've never really had to find my way… I'm alone so…I don't usually do big cities." Courtney winced at the stupidity of her statement.

Benoît's face melted into an expression of empathy. "I see."

"I'm not a loser or anything! I just…"

"You require a guide!"

"Yes!" Courtney exhaled in relief.

"You want to experience the allure of Paris through the lens of someone who knows the city intimately."

"Do you know anyone?"

Benoît blinked.

CHAPTER TWENTY-THREE

"There it is!" Benoît said, spinning around to see Courtney's expression. "Is it not the most exquisite thing you have ever seen?"

Courtney followed Benoît's face as it turned upwards to admire the impressive height of the Eiffel tower. "Gosh," Courtney said sardonically. "You're acting like it's the first time you've ever seen this thing. You'd think it's become such a stereotypical landmark, the French would be bored of it by now."

Benoît's eyes glowed with wonder. "Maybe to some. But not me. I look at it and it reminds me of everything that is beautiful about my city. It is distinct. It is artful. It brings people together. It inspires culture, light, love..."

Courtney cleared her throat. That tower watched over her from the poster she taped on her bedroom wall at home. She would lie in bed, staring at it for years. It had been the one thing she had focused on throughout her journey. The one thing she clung to whenever she felt like giving up. And now there it was, casting an intimidating shadow over her. This was like a religious experience.

"It's pretty," Courtney said casually.

"Are we going up?"

"Up the tower?"

"You did not come all the way here to stand in its shadow?" Benoît laughed. "Come. I will take you."

"Sure," Courtney said, clacking her stiletto heels to keep up with Benoît's pace.

"Wait," Benoît said, noticing her stilettos. "You are not wearing those shoes?"

"There is nothing wrong with my shoes," Courtney said defiantly.

"They are lovely. But Courtney, the stairs."

Courtney goggled at the many stairs winding up to the top of the tower. "I don't see the problem," she lied.

Benoît looked at Courtney as though she was green. "You are saying you have no issues scaling the steps..."

"They are very versatile shoes, Benoît."

"Okay!" Benoît shrugged. "In that case, follow me!"

Benoît walked with a purposeful briskness towards the tower entrance and Courtney could barely keep up, already regretting her decision not to take Benoît's advice.

* * *

Benoît bounded effortlessly up the stairs in his Nike trainers. Courtney panted and massaged her feet at every landing, praying they would reach the top soon.

"Courtney?" Benoît called eagerly when he noticed they had become separated.

"Coming!" Courtney huffed desperately.

"We are nearly there!" Benoît called from deep within a dense crowd. "Follow my voice!"

Courtney's foot buckled and she heard a horrible crack. "Oh God, no!" She salvaged what was left of her beautiful shoe. The heel had cracked right off. Courtney literally whimpered as she cradled the shoe mournfully in her hands.

"Courtney! You are missing everything!"

"Benoît?" Courtney squeaked, surveying the crowd.

Courtney spotted Benoît's hand reaching through the crowd towards her. She grabbed his hand and felt herself being pulled through the throng until sunlight found her face.

"Lots of stairs, *oui?*" Benoît grinned sunnily.

"I..."

Benoît gaped at the broken shoe in Courtney's hand.

"I can fix it," Courtney insisted.

"Did I not tell you that you cannot do Paris in those shoes?"

"I screwed up, okay?"

"That does not matter now, Courtney," Benoît said, turning her to behold the spectacular view. *"Voilà!"*

Courtney croaked with wonder.

"Look!" Benoît said, guiding her to a different angle. "You can see everything from up here."

Courtney could not find words. For that matter, she could not find breath either. She could possibly die up there from asphyxiation but she could not think of a better way to go. She turned to look at Benoît whose eyes sparkled magically like the sun reflecting off the Seine.

"Formidable, oui?"

"So um…" Courtney said, trying to remain cool. "How am I supposed to get back down with one stiletto shoe?"

"The elevator," Benoît smirked.

Courtney blinked.

***

"Surely you brought more than one pair of shoes?" Benoît said as he drove the taxi down a narrow, winding street.

Courtney blushed.

Benoît's eyes widened.

"Don't judge me," Courtney muttered.

"Not to worry!" Benoît chimed. "My cousin Étienne…"

"No."

"But he sells the most comfortable shoes in all of Paris!"

"I'm not wearing shoes from a souvenir store."

"Okay. In that case I will drop you off on *Rue de Passy*."

With all the internal controversy stirring inside Courtney's brain regarding whether or not she was a loser, she could not bring herself to admit that she could never afford to shop on *Rue de Passy*.

"Your cousin sells shoes?" she asked. "And you say they're comfortable?"

"I thought…"

"I wouldn't want to be rude to your cousin. You know. Since apparently being rude is morally wrong here."

"We are not far from the shop. That is my cousin up ahead!" Benoît said, parallel parking the taxi.

Courtney craned her head to get a better view of Benoît's legendary cousin. "Hot damn!" she thought to herself when she saw Étienne. At least she hoped she had not said that out loud.

"Benoît!" Étienne said as he spotted Benoît approaching with a very awkward Courtney. Étienne put his arm around a sultry woman with legs that went on forever. *"This is Suzette. We met twelve beautiful minutes ago. I have taken her as a lover."*

"Allo, Étienne. I am looking for shoes."

"For you or for the object of your desire?" Étienne asked, gesturing towards Courtney.

"Étienne, no…"

Ignoring Benoît, Étienne startled Courtney by kissing her hand. For Courtney's benefit, he spoke to her in English. "Dear, sweet, savory Courtney. Benoît has spoken relentlessly of you."

"He did what now?" Courtney's eyes popped in shock.

"Étienne, please," Benoît begged through clenched teeth.

"Pick any item in my store, Courtney. My cousin has told me many amorous tales about…"

"*Mon dieu,* Étienne!" Benoît withered in humiliation. "I have shared with you no such thing! Courtney and I are on professional terms."

"New love is so beautiful," Étienne said, wiping away a tear of joy as he looked at Courtney. "See? I have tears!"

"What is he talking about?" Courtney uttered a cumbersome stammer.

"Do not listen to him, Courtney. Étienne is a man of many passions. He has lost his mind."

"Benoît," Étienne said confidentially, "if you want to do it behind my display of Mona Lisa T-shirts, I will create a diversion to discourage onlookers."

Courtney paled with stupefaction.

"Shoes, Étienne. Courtney needs shoes, comfortable for walking."

"*Voilà!*" Étienne said theatrically, presenting Courtney with the corniest pair of shoes she had ever seen.

"I…" Courtney stuttered. "I can't wear those."

"I can give you one of my special discounts," Étienne winked.

"Do people actually wear these?" Courtney asked, scrutinizing the shoes. "I mean people with eyes?"

"Courtney," Benoît said in her ear, "you will hurt Étienne's feelings."

"I'm just saying your cousin isn't selling a quality product here. Étienne, people only buy this junk because you're a real live French guy. They want to see you up close. Like a car accident or an exotic mushroom."

"Thank you," Étienne said proudly.

"Courtney," Benoît whispered, "Can you perhaps be a little less... honest?"

"Shoes are kind of my thing," Courtney said, suddenly feeling in the zone. "Étienne, these shoes have excellent arch support and for that, you have my respect. The soles are squishy, which I'm sure is very foot-pleasing. But these colors are putrid. And what you've got here is a shoe that can't decide if it's a loafer or a clog."

"Perhaps," Étienne said coyly, "my business would flourish more with a woman's touch."

"Okay, we're done!" Benoît said pulling Courtney away as Étienne puckered his lips provocatively.

"What?" Étienne called as Benoît grabbed the hideous shoes and ushered Courtney to the car. "I figured if you are not enjoying her..."

"I'll pay you later for the shoes!" Benoît called out the window as his tires screeched and the car zipped down the narrow street.

***

Courtney wiggled her toes which were currently being held against their will inside the gruesome shoes from Étienne's shop. Benoît was correct in that the shoes were insanely comfy. Too bad they looked like a couple of graphic nightmares.

"I must apologize for my cousin," Benoît said as he drove. "I had no idea he would speak to you that way."

"Do you?" Courtney asked.

Benoît turned to look at her, not understanding Courtney's meaning.

"Do you talk about me relentlessly?" Courtney was focused on her wiggling toes and not returning Benoît's inquisitive look.

Benoît's mouth moved but he could not find words.

"Do you complain about all the crude crap I say to you?"

"I do no such thing," Benoît assured her.

"Did you make stuff up about me? About you and me? Us, I mean? Is that why he started talking like a smutty Harlequin romance novel?"

"No. That is how my cousin always talks."

Courtney nodded.

"We are almost at your hotel," Benoît remarked.

"Right," Courtney said, looking out the window. "Benoît... If you want to do something like this tomorrow... I mean... What's the point of Paris when you can't plunge right into... no that didn't come out right... there's a few more things I'd like to... since it's your job and all... and keeping things professional of course..."

"I will pick you up tomorrow morning at nine."

CHAPTER TWENTY-FOUR
(DAY 31 IN PARIS)

The ridiculous shoes made a squishy sound as Courtney walked through the hotel foyer. In her imagination she was wearing Jimmy Choo glitter sling-back pumps, but the shoes' telltale squish sucked her back into reality. Courtney checked the time on her phone and quickened her pace. She was late again.

Jacques was manning the front desk and he greeted Courtney with green slits of suspicion which he also used as eyes. A polite smile reluctantly crept out of its hiding place under his mustache.

"Bonjour, Madame," he said cordially.

"I'm in a hurry, Jack," Courtney said bemusedly.

Jacques tightened his smile, exposing more teeth. *"*You have several messages waiting for you, *Madame.* It seems you were unreachable for the past nine or ten days. An additional letter was left for you this morning which I have added to the pile. Would you care to retrieve them now or are you stockpiling in case of a famine?"

Aghast, Courtney stopped abruptly in her tracks.

"And it is pronounced, *Jacques."* Jacques articulated with extreme Frenchness for Courtney's benefit.

Courtney scrunched her face into a raisin of outrage as she grabbed the letters from Jacques, not giving him the satisfaction of a response. Her protruded lower lip said it all.

The green slits narrowed even more, daring Courtney to say something.

"Listen, Jack…"

"*Jacques.*"

"Don't think you can come at me with that snooty 'stache and those slivery, neon, alien eyes and…." Courtney stopped herself. She pressed the rewind button on her brain and recapped her various encounters with Jacques, who she had presumed to be an egomaniacal, French bastard. It was as though he physically strained to smile at Courtney. His eloquence was stilted. His manners were plastic and forced. Courtney pondered for a moment, wondering if it was really that much of a burden to serve her.

"Ah frig," Courtney accidentally said out loud.

Jacques looked physically nauseated by Courtney's choice of words.

"I uh…" Courtney stammered. "Thank you for the letters," she said humbly. She curtsied for effect, which was weird.

Jacques cocked his head, taken aback by Courtney's sudden splurge of manners.

"Say, Jack… Do you like ferns?"

Jacques cocked his head. "Ferns?"

"Yeah, ferns."

"They are passable."

Courtney nodded thoughtfully and walked away.

***

The stairs went on forever. Courtney's claustrophobic anxieties were causing her to perspire profusely as she carefully trudged up the steep, winding, narrow, cramped staircase. Her feet squished each time she put her foot down on one of the irregular, slippery steps. The walls squeezed in tightly around her with barely enough room to spread her arms. She braced herself by clutching a wall with each hand all the way up. Walking directly behind her nimble driver, Courtney had a direct view of Benoît's butt, which was the one aspect of this traumatic experience that she hated the least.

The sunlight nearly blinded Courtney when she approached the top as her eyes had grown accustomed to the gloom of the bell tower's interior. She could hear Benoît squealing something in French from outside. She followed his elated voice which led her to the top of the *Cathedral Notre Dame*.

"This is it!" Benoît was practically twirling as he presented the sublime rooftop. "If this does not grant you inspiration, I do not know what will!"

"Holy hell, that was a lot of stairs," Courtney panted.

"Good thing you are wearing practical shoes."

A gargoyle startled Courtney.

Benoît took a seat in between Courtney and a gruesome gargoyle that looked alarmingly similar to Alexandria Fontrose with its sneer and angry beak.

"Sorry I'm flaking out like this," Courtney apologized. "I really don't like the feeling of being boxed in. I go all squirrely."

"I appreciate the effort," Benoît said, offering his own water bottle.

Courtney instinctively took a swig from Benoît's bottle, realizing abruptly afterwards that she put her mouth on something which probably contained traces of Benoît's saliva. She wiped her mouth, hoping to hide the blush of her cheeks.

"When I was a boy," Benoît said dreamily as he gazed out at the view, "I used to think the *Cathedral Notre Dame* was looking at me. Did you see the windows when we were at street level? Do you not think those sad windows on the bell towers look like eyes? With emotion even?"

"I didn't really think of it like that," Courtney said, cocking her head. "Why did you think the cathedral was looking at you? Why would it be sad?"

"I do not know," Benoît shrugged. "This building contains many secrets which I am sure it will never tell. Perhaps the cathedral has memories of when it was once forgotten."

"Wait, what? Who would forget this place? There's like a trillion tourists here. Even I find them annoying and I'm not even a local."

"Did you know that Quasimodo saved the cathedral?"

"Like the fictitious character?"

"The cathedral was falling into disrepair, but when Victor Hugo wrote his hunchback story, *Notre Dame* became famous. They were prompted to restore it."

"You really are up to date on all your literary allusions."

"Our culture is marinated in creativity," said Benoît who was physically stirring with irrepressible energy. "Paris inspires artists and as a result the art becomes a part of us. Even the architecture awakens the creativity of our writers. The energy in these buildings makes our characters come alive, as though Paris itself created them."

"That's deep, Dude."

"Do you not celebrate writers in your country?"

"Most writers where I'm from are treated like cat turds."

Benoît's face morphed into an expression of shock and revulsion, as though he just witnessed someone kicking a puppy. "You are not serious."

"That's not a thing here?"

"We name streets after our writers."

"Well. That's... respectful."

"Have you ever read any French literature? I can lend you a few books. It could really give you some insight into our culture."

"Aren't French books kind of long?"

Benoît blinked.

Courtney felt a tide of stupidity crash over her. She rapidly changed the subject. "Jeez," she said, miming hunger. "Who do you have to sleep with to get a crêpe in this city?"

Benoît blinked.

Courtney winced in humiliation. "What I mean is..."

"Are you hungry, Courtney?"

"Do you know where I can find a crêpe-ist?"

Benoît blinked.

"Please never say that word ever again."

"But I feel like crêpes."

"I can never un-hear that word now."

"I thought there were crêpe-ists on every corner around here."

"And you said it again."

"What am I saying wrong?"

***

"Crêperie," Benoît enunciated clearly, ushering Courtney to a semi-casual restaurant that opened into a patio. "Here you will find the most delectable crêpes. You have my personal guarantee. Might I suggest the crêpe with apple compote and ham, listed under the savory options?"

"You mean it's not called a..."

Benoît put a finger up to Courtney's lips, shushing her. "Enjoy your crêpe, Courtney."

Courtney was perplexed as she watched Benoît amble down the street by himself. "Wait!" she called.

Benoît turned around.

"Where are you going?"

"To wait in the taxi."

Courtney gaped.

"Is there something wrong, Courtney?"

"Dude, I can't let people see me eating by myself. They'll think I'm a doofus."

"Sooo you want me to... find you a lunch companion?" Benoît was looking around animatedly as though trying to scope out an invisible date for Courtney.

"I just thought..." Courtney hesitated. "I mean you're already here and you haven't eaten..."

"Are you asking me to..."

"Think of it as business..."

"... join you?"

"... and it's meaningless, really."

Benoît looked down with a bashful smile.

"Look, Benoît. I can't eat by myself. That's just weird."

"You are the one who made the rules…"

"Which is why I am the one who's allowed to alter the rules when doing so can save me from humiliation."

"Would it be improper?"

"Oh probably."

"That response does not give me reassurance."

"Let's call it a business lunch. We can even write it off for when we do our taxes."

Benoît threw his head back and did one of those laughs where no sound comes out – only a kind of nasal snuff. "Business. Okay."

***

The plate was set in front of Courtney and her eyes turned into saucers. Having ignored Benoît's recommendation, she went ahead and ordered a crêpe with chestnut spread, dark chocolate shavings and a dollop of Chantilly. Benoît's savory crêpe was emitting an intoxicating odor that gave Courtney a mild case of plate envy. She forgot herself for a moment and realized all too late that her nose was hovering dangerously close to Benoît's plate.

"Do you want to try?" Benoît smirked.

"Who me?" Courtney asked much too quickly. "I wasn't…"

A morsel of savory crêpe appeared on the end of a fork just below Courtney's nostrils.

"You can have a taste if you want."

"I prefer sweet crêpes," Courtney said, trying to sound dignified. "I'm not so much into…"

Courtney was suddenly distracted when Benoît put the forkful of crêpe into his mouth, closed his eyes and savored.

"…savory…" Was Courtney fantasizing about ham with apple compote, nestled in a refined sheet of eggy wonderfulness? Oh probably.

Benoît gestured towards the stack of letters Courtney brought in her purse. "Are those business related?"

"These?" Courtney felt like she was caught with her hand in the cookie jar. "Yes. I guess."

"You seemed to come alive when you were reading them," Benoît said, choosing to look down at the knife and fork as he sliced another bite of crêpe.

"Yes well things are working out well again."

Benoît knifed through the crêpe a little more roughly. "With her?"

"Benoît…"

"I am only curious."

"Can we not get into this here?"

"I know it is none of my business…"

"Nope."

"And I do not mean to overstep…"

"Then don't."

"I only think that you should consider finding a new mentor."

"Where? I'm a nobody, remember? I blurted that out to you in a moment of weakness."

"You are talented, Courtney. I saw your sketches. They are beautiful."

"You think everything is beautiful."

"Why do you worship her? She is a monster!"

"Provide examples."

"That night in the Latin Quarter when you were passed out in my arms…"

"Wait, what? Your arms?"

"…she said the most disturbing things to me."

"It was the Schnapps talking."

"That Schnapps had a lot to say."

"She's a little eccentric, sure. But who cares?"

"She threatened me."

"You're making this about you?"

"I have a very bad feeling about her."

"Whoa. What are you accusing her of exactly?"

"I knew someone like her once…"

"Again, this is not about you."

"She has dangerous eyes."

"How dangerous can eyes be? Yeesh."

"Why do you try so hard to turn everything into an argument?"

"Why do you even care?"

Benoît dropped his fork and stared at his plate.

"Okay, fine. Yes, the letters are from Dree. Here's the 411. The whole thing at the opera house was a total misunderstanding. I overreacted, okay? It was my fault. Dree really thinks I'm special. She's going to make big things happen for me. Why can't you regard that as a positive thing?"

"I am happy things are working out so well for you," Benoît said despondently.

"You don't sound happy."

"I am happy," Benoît said glumly. "See? This is my happy face."

"That's your sad face, Benoît. Don't mess with me."

"In my heart, I am laughing right now."

"No you're not. That's dumb."

"Tra-la-la. See? Happy."

"Dude, I've never seen you like this. It's like all your verve drained out of you through a slow leak. Your sparkle sizzled out. You lack zeal. It's weird."

Benoît put his face in his hands.

"Oh my God," Courtney gasped in horror. "I broke Benoît."

A muffled, explosive laugh came out of Benoît from behind his hands. Courtney furrowed her brow.

"Courtney, why do you keep doing that?"

"What'd I do this time?"

"You make my head explode sometimes, you are so frustrating," Benoît smiled, "but you are just so…"

"Well color me fuchsia," came a serpentine voice, suddenly pulling Courtney and Benoît out of the zone.

A dark shadow loomed over Courtney and Benoît's table, causing them each to look up. Hovering above was Alexandria Fontrose, staring down at them disapprovingly like the vengeful God of the Old Testament. A few on-looking diners crossed themselves.

"Dree?" Courtney quavered.

"Courtney Stent," the serpent hissed. "I didn't expect to see you here. You vanished in a puff of elusive, purple smoke and now I find you here? With your *driver?*"

"It's a business lunch," Courtney said, looking down at her unfinished crêpe.

"Courtney," Alexandria said with a painted on smile, "can I speak with you privately for a moment?"

Benoît instinctively stood up, inadvertently pushing his chair back which caused several diners to turn their heads. He shifted his weight from side to side like a Rottweiler getting ready to protectively pounce.

"Sit down, Raoul," Alexandria barked.

"You don't have to talk to him like that," Courtney said sheepishly.

"Courtney, my sweet cherry," Alexandria said, spreading on the charm thickly, "I am only thinking about your reputation. What if an industry professional came in here and saw you eating with your *driver?*"

Benoît winced.

"I don't mean to embarrass you, Bunnyhop. But if I don't look out for my adorable little ingénue than you'll be casually tossed to the slobbering hounds like a raw pork chop. You know how those industry professionals are. Standing around like judgmental crayons in their vintage zoot suits and flattering mermaid gowns. They don't look at you though a maternal lens like yours truly... Jesus Versace, what are you wearing on your feet? Have you died from the clap and gone to shoe hell?"

"I didn't think..."

"No you didn't, Inchworm. You didn't think at all. About the shoes or about fraternizing with this sketchy bastard. I'm sure Raoul here *didn't* have intentions of *taking you* in a grungy alley behind an artisanal meringue shop. But it's best not to take any chances when it comes to the likes of him. Those snail suckers are the basest of all creatures."

"I'm standing right here," Benoît reminded Alexandria.

"Shush, Raoul. I'm not talking to you."

"We should go," Courtney said, wilting like a humiliated geranium.

"Yes, Pet. Let's be somewhere that lacks pestilence."

"Benoît is my ride so..."

"Uh. Well yes, I supposed he is. So inconvenient that we have to be served by the underclass. How daunting. Just watch where he puts his hands and if he does anything suspicious with his eyebrows, call the authorities."

"I'm still here," Benoît said raising his hand.

"I can't stay any longer. I'm being recognized by peeping diners and I can't muster the energy for autographs at present. Did you read the letters, Courtney?"

"Not entirely."

Alexandria blew the pretentious bangs out of her face in frustration. "Read them. Pronto. We will discuss further when I have time. Have a safe drive home. Hopefully this hopeless bug won't sell you to human traffickers on the way back to the hotel."

"I am literally right in front of you," Benoît sighed.

Courtney gaped at Alexandria Fontrose as she trotted out of sight.

CHAPTER TWENTY-FIVE

There was a funk in the hotel room. Courtney waved away some weird, weedy smelling haze that was wafting around in the air as she entered. The odor was asphyxiating. The hotel guests who just moved in next door must have been smoking something with the evidence creeping in through the vents. Courtney headed straight for the window to let in some fresh oxygen. She could tell this would be a long night.

Plopping herself on the saggy bed, Courtney perused the letters Alexandria had written her. Her eyes widened more and more with each line she read. Her eyeballs scanned the sentences faster and faster. Her heart fluttered with anticipation. Ralph Lauren? Prada? Endorsements? Pre-Fashion Week hype? Courtney could hardly believe what she was reading. It was too good to be true!

After leafing through all the gushy letters, she picked up the final message that Jacques had added to the pile at the last minute. Tears welled in her eyes as she read:

Darling Courtney Stent: I have the most splendid news! I have arranged the most spectacular event in Évian which will be taking place on the seventh of August. Naturally you will be invited, Doll. All the industry's finest will be in attendance and as I mentioned earlier, Ralphie is on pins and needles to meet you! Wear your most impressive gown, my lovely. I've arranged this event for your benefit and all eyes will be on you. This meet & greet will be more pleasure than business so leave all your work behind and just bring your gorgeous self. You will be back in Paris in plenty of time for Fashion Week preparations. This event will do wonders for your image, which is quite literally everything in this business. What an excellent networking boost as a prelude to your big show. Are you as excited as I am? Of course you are, dear. Of course you are. – AF

Courtney covered her mouth, partly from girlish excitement and partly to shield her respiratory system from second hand marijuana smoke. Was this even happening? Was it all real? If there had been any question about whether or not Alexandria's eccentricities were worth putting up with, these letters put Courtney's mind at ease. However, the buzz of Courtney's cell phone instantly stole her thunder.

"What," Courtney said bluntly, answering the phone.

"It's Chastity."

"I know."

"Dad wants to know what day is best for you."

"For what?"

"For meeting you at the Paris airport to bring you home."

"That's not happening."

"Mom said you're on a break. Translation – you screwed up need your family to bail you out."

"You can bite me because I'm going to meet Ralph Lauren in seven days."

"Don't lie."

"What's so unbelievable about that?"

"Why would he want to meet you?"

"There's going to be an event held for my benefit."

"That's daft."

"No it's not."

"Why you?"

"Because I'm making a splash here."

"Where is this... and I use air quotes... event?"

"Évian."

"Like the bottled water?"

"It's a real place. I googled it."

"Why isn't it in Paris?"

"The French Alps are gorgeous. You should look at pictures."

"I'm going to ask this again and this time I'll say it slower. Why isn't the event in Paris?"

"Why is that even relevant?"

"Because you keep droning on about how Paris is the center of the universe."

"People work in Paris and party in the Alps."

"You're making that up."

"Can you try a little harder to be excited for me?"

"What makes you think you deserve all this special treatment?"

"Because Alexandria Fontrose…"

"Who's that? Your imaginary friend?"

"Read a fashion mag once in a while. Dree is basically a queen."

"Dree?"

"We're on a first syllable basis. Didn't Mom and Dad tell you about Dree? I won her in the contest."

"By contest you mean scam."

"Your lack of support is getting a bit predictable at this point."

"You expect me to believe that you're successfully blending with all those fashion snobs?"

"I'm glorious. Dree said so herself."

"Are you high?"

"I might be a little bit. There's a lot of green fog in the room right now."

"Whatever. Look, that's not the reason I called."

"You mean you didn't call to slurp away the last of my self-esteem through a bendy straw? Are you okay? Do you have the bird flu?"

"It's about Paul."

"Paul?"

"He's been sniffing around, looking for you."

"Why?"

"I think he wants to see what his chances are."

"Be more specific."

"For reasons that are far beyond my grasp, he seems eager to reconnect with you."

"That makes no sense."

"Right?"

"What about Paulette?"

"He didn't mention her. Obviously things didn't work out between them."

"But their names match."

"I guess that didn't impress him as much as it did you."

"But she's French."

"Maybe that's why he can't stand her anymore."

"You are so ignorant."

"Me? You're the one with delusions of..."

"I don't want to talk about this anymore."

"What about Paul?"

"He left me."

"And it crushed you. What if he wants you back?"

"Mom and Dad said he's too good for me."

"And I agree. But if he wants this..."

"Nobody asked what I want."

"Because you want things that will never happen."

"Maybe Paul isn't my type."

"You said he was your soulmate."

"Maybe I changed my criteria."

"Excuse me, what?"

"Maybe I have my eye on someone already."

"What?"

"Shut up. I'm high."

"Clearly."

"Look, before you called I was reveling in my boundless success. Your psychological abuse is kind of dampening the mood."

"If you don't come home, you're crazy."

End of call.

Courtney rolled over on her bed, half moaning from the loopy feeling in her head, partly giggling from the loopy feeling in her head.

Courtney stopped giggling for a moment when the sound of Chastity's voice started ringing in her head, as though her brain had the acoustics of a Catholic church. The word *Paul* echoed to infinity inside her mind. Why was Paul looking for her? She was finally coming to terms with the fact that her life with Paul was something in her remote past. Images of his face, which was adorned with a hipster soul patch, once consumed every inch of her mind. There was a time when the memory of his sardonic laugh, sleepy eyelids, Rascal Flatts tattoo and amazing selection of shirts would haunt her. She spent many nights, lying awake, hungry for one of Paul's sloppy kisses or one of those inappropriate butt-slaps he was famous for. She and Paul had even named their future children. There would be five of them. Declan, Dash, Daria, Derby and Paul Junior. They would have been born in that order.

The breakup had been unexpected and heart-wrenching. It happened in February. A Monday. As if Mondays didn't suck enough as it was. Thankfully it happened on a leap year on the last day of the month which would spare Courtney years of traumatizing breakup anniversaries. Paul invited Courtney on a date to a fondue restaurant. Their table was next to a big, stone fireplace, boasting orange, crackling flames. Courtney wore a dress she had designed herself, thinking this was going to be a special occasion. There was only one semi-romantic restaurant in Colby Haven, and this was it.

All smiles throughout the evening, Courtney kept her eyes peeled for a ring box. She and Paul had been together for six years, after all. They were high school sweethearts since the day they shared a beaker in Chem. By the time dessert arrived, (a caramel parfait with two spoons) Paul admitted to Courtney that he had been secretly banging Paulette for almost a year.

The reasons were explained to Courtney as she stared in a stupor. Paul was a driven person and had ambitions of growing a lucrative camembert brand. Cheese was plentiful in Colby Haven but sorely lacking in variety. The locals were suspicious of ethnic cheeses. Colby

Haven was holding him back and he was itching to break free into a more urban scene where businesses flourish.

Paul met Paulette at a French cheese convention in Montreal and her ambitions aligned with Paul's. She also had an irresistible accent and according to Paul, she was a smoke show. Courtney seemed to be in a holding pattern, destined to be stapled to Colby Haven indefinitely. Paul got tired of Courtney's fashion whims and pretending that her quirkiness was a turn-on. It had been fun when they were kids but Paul felt that Courtney never really grew up. He thought she was holding him back and that their differing interests and motivations were causing him to be less attracted to her. He felt it was important to have a more poised and elegant woman on his arm when he networked during corporate cheese events. Courtney was a lot of things, but she was not refined. Or French.

All of that, Courtney had put behind her. But her stupid sister resurfaced all of those painful memories. She would be lying to herself if she did not admit she still hurt from Paul's abrupt exodus. She would be an even bigger liar if she denied her jealousy of Paulette. Why would Paul dump Paulette? They were clearly perfect for each other with their shared cheese fetish. If Paul was looking for her, would it even matter anymore? Should she open that door again? She had invested six years of her life with Paul. She grew up with him. Until he broke up with her the previous year, he was the only thing Courtney really knew. But could he make her happier than...

Whoa! Why did Benoît suddenly pop into Courtney's head? He was not even a viable option. Even if there was something brewing between Benoît and Courtney, and even if she put down her defenses and went along with it, the best she could hope for was a brief summer fling. Would that be worth forfeiting a life with Paul? If she could prove to Paul that she was not a loser and that she did have a bright future ahead, would he love her again?

Things were much less complicated before the hotel room filled up with green smoke.

CHAPTER TWENTY-SIX
(DAY 32 IN PARIS)

A potted fern suddenly plunked in front of Jacques on the front desk. Jacque's eyes popped open, looking like a pair of green cat's eye marbles.

"It's a fern," Courtney said.

Jacques slowly cocked his head.

"Fern," Courtney enunciated more clearly.

Jacques raised an eyebrow.

"For you," Courtney explained.

"A fern," Jacques repeated.

"Is there something wrong with it?"

"I..."

"I wasn't sure what the custom was..."

Jacques picked up the potted fern and analyzed it carefully.

"Because I've been a jerk."

Jacques narrowed his eyes in confusion.

"I have a meeting," Courtney said, inching away from the front desk. "I hope the fern... sparks joy."

Courtney fumbled away.

Jacques curled the corner of his mouth into the world's most subtle smile.

***

Courtney poured runny batter into the waffle iron in the hotel breakfast lounge. As she waited for the beep she scoured the room for Alexandria Fontrose, who had squeezed her in for a breakfast meeting before enduring a day of back-to-back photo shoots. Alexandria finally made her entrance, wearing dark sunglasses and a very wide brimmed hat – her usual attire after a full night of schmoozing. Courtney quickly scraped her waffle onto a plate, adorned it with slippery strawberries and teetered towards the table Alexandria had selected in the corner.

"Morning, Dree!" Courtney bubbled, taking her seat and liberating her cutlery from their napkin swaddle. "You are going to freak when you see my sketches from last night. I had a strangely rapid flow of ideas all of a sudden. Oh my god, I had the best ideas. Do you want to..."

"Love, what are you eating?" Alexandria said, lowering her sunglasses down her nose.

"Waffles."

"Carbs are satanic. They have been formally banned by the fashion industry. You must scrape that poison into the garbage post haste. Consider your thighs, dear. We want you slipping smoothly into your gown for your big debut. We don't want to look like a ghastly sea cow, now do we?"

"Sea cows are freakishly adorable, actually..."

"I would hate to see you make a bad impression in Évian."

Courtney looked dismally at her plate. "I was super hungry this morning."

"Here, swallow this breakfast pill with a mouthful of carbonated water. You will remain nourished for the next twelve to twenty-four hours. That is the secret to my enviable figure, which is not unlike Praxiteles' divine statue of the goddess Aphrodite."

Courtney pinched the breakfast pill between her thumb and index finger, studying it carefully.

"So tell me about last night's accomplishments," Alexandria said, pouring the contents of her flask into a glass of orange juice.

"I just discovered my new passion!" Courtney gushed. "Capes!"

"Fascinating!"

"Right?" Courtney beamed as she rapidly flipped through the pages of her sketchbook. "Capes are boss! You can put them on literally anything! I added capes to tent dresses, peasant dresses, pinafore dresses, bouffant dresses, yoke dresses, tunics, off-shoulder, halternecks. And wait until you see what I did with these skorts!"

"Dazzling! My mind is literally whirring, Poodle. Like a tropical cyclone. Do you mind if I borrow your sketchbook to review? I'd like to peruse them more thoroughly and tragically I'm only able to set aside fifteen minutes for our cherished breakfast meeting."

"I kind of need my sketchbook."

Alexandria let out an exasperated sigh "Are you saying this is posing some sort of inconvenience for you? Because I do have other things to do. I am merely offering to give your creations the attention they deserve, which I assure you is more than any of those other beady-eyed opossums in the industry would do for you."

"I appreciate it but…"

"UGH! Never mind, Bobolink. I revoke my offer. Far be it from me to offer my scarce time and expensive brain waves to perpetuate your cute little career."

"But…"

"We have some catching up to do, haven't we? What has been on Courtney Stent's agenda the past couple of weeks?"

Courtney gaped.

"Are you keeping some kind of a secret from me, dear? You know you can tell me anything. I am your spirit animal."

"Well, I went on hiatus."

"Is that wise? You're only in Paris for a brief time."

"I needed time. For my process."

"And eating crêpes yesterday? Was that part of your process also?"

"I..."

"You are certainly not obligated to follow my sage direction."

"Dree..."

"I can expedite your success with a flick of my twig-like wrist."

"I know. See, about yesterday..."

"But my mind has been known to change on occasion."

"Wait, what?"

Alexandria leaned across the table and locked eyes with Courtney.

"Drop the driver," said Alexandria, momentarily dropping her charm like a slippery mango.

"I don't understand."

"I don't feel comfortable with you driving around with that scandalous European imp."

"But what's wrong with him?"

"Grow ears. I have given you countless warnings..."

"What am I going to do without a driver?"

"Take the metro."

"But Benoît was part of my prize package."

"I'm telling you this because I love you, Courtney Stent."

"But I was promised a guide. A concierge. That's totally not fair. I'll be completely lost. I'll..."

"You will thank me when you don't get indecently assaulted and left for dead in the teeny tiny trunk of a Fiat."

"How will I get to Évian?"

"Take an Uber."

"I don't mean any disrespect, Dree. But I think you're wrong about this. I've gotten to know Benoît a little bit…"

"You did *what?*"

"I'm not saying that I want to shag the guy. I'm just saying that he basically shatters all the French stereotypes you keep flinging around."

"You are so naïve."

"What if I'm careful? Then can I keep Benoît?"

Alexandria took a brief moment to take a deep breath and melodramatically fan herself.

"Dree?"

"I can't tell you what to do. You're a grown woman with a free will."

"Thank you, Dree."

"But I also do not have to go along with your decisions if I feel they are toxic to your career and ultimately my reputation."

"What are you saying, Dree?"

"I'm saying that if you continue fraternizing with that shifty French bulldog, I will renounce my mentorship."

"But…"

"You are precious to me, River Pebble, but you've proven time and again that you cannot be trusted to use your own discretion about things. You are hypnotized by Raoul…"

"Benoît."

"… by his false charm. His superficial flattery. His mind games. Tell me, do you want to be a designer or not?"

"More than anything."

"The last thing you need is to enter the industry with a scandal clinging to your ass like a dryer sheet. And the last thing I want is to be the one who lead you into the spotlight when the whole world is judging you. Do you understand the stakes here, Courtney?"

"Yes, Ma'am."

"Then do the right thing," Alexandria said as she stood up, tugged at her mini skirt to prevent it from riding up, then started her pompous trot towards the door. "I may or may not see you Thursday, depending on your transportation arrangements."

Courtney stared down helplessly at her gummy waffle.

***

Courtney was not prepared for the sight she beheld when she walked like a zombie through the hotel entrance after breakfast. Benoît was sitting on a lounge couch, looking down with one restless leg, elbows resting on his thighs as though thinking about something important and holding a giftwrapped parcel in his hands. When he looked up and saw Courtney, he smiled one of his famous, ear-to-ear grins and waved at her enthusiastically. She stopped in her tracks. She had forgotten that she had arranged a ride with him the previous night. But with the unexpected breakfast ultimatum she was now faced with the awkward task of turfing Benoît in person. This was going to be a lot harder than she thought.

"Benoît?"

"*Félicitations!*" Benoît bubbled, waving the present sheepishly.

"What's going on?" Courtney asked hesitantly.

"I am violating protocol," he grinned as he handed Courtney the gift. "You have officially survived one month in Paris! I thought this was reason to celebrate!"

Courtney turned the present over and over in her hands, as though she was surveying a peculiar potato from an alien planet. She looked up at Benoît who watched her in anticipation and her heart stung.

"You didn't have to..."

"It is just a small gesture," Benoît shrugged. "But I think you will like it."

Courtney carefully undid the tape and neatly pulled off the wrapping paper as though trying not to rip it. Benoît was practically jumping up and down, waiting for her to finish opening it."

"It's..." Courtney said softly, "... it's a French/English dictionary."

"So you won't feel like a tourist anymore," Benoît explained. "I thought if you learned a bit of French you would not feel so far from home."

"Benoît..." Courtney's voice cracked.

"And now when I mutter things in French, you will understand me!"

A tear snuck out of out of Courtney's eye.

"What is wrong, Courtney? Do you not like your gift? I can exchange it for a snow globe containing the Eiffel Tower."

"You're making this really hard."

"I did not mean to upset you. I just thought..."

"Benoît, you can't be my driver anymore."

Benoît's jaw dropped. He looked down, as though trying to locate an unruly marble rolling around the floor. "I guess I should have gone with the snow globe," he mumbled.

"You didn't do anything wrong," Courtney said, dabbing her moist eyes. "It's stupid, really. Dree gave me this ultimatum."

Benoît looked up, unnerved.

"She said if I don't drop you as my driver she'll cut me off."

"She said *what*?"

"I'm not happy about it," Courtney whimpered.

Benoît's eyes softened.

"I mean you have decent driving skills. And if I dump you, I'll lose my guide and concierge. This is a big city, Benoît..."

"Courtney..."

"I told you before that I'm from a small town. As much as I hated it there, I've never really been anywhere else. I've never travelled, especially not alone. I'm nervous. I'll be lost. This whole thing is a rip-off because I won that prize fair and square. I won a full-service driver, not the right to purchase my own damn metro pass."

Benoît chewed the inside of his cheek in contemplation.

"I'm sorry, Benoît. I know you were expecting to show me around today. You woke up at ridiculous o'clock for nothing."

"Let's go," Benoît said quickly.

"What do you mean? Dree said..."

"You were promised a guide. You are getting a guide."

"But I can't ride in your taxi."

Benoît smirked mischievously. "We are taking the metro."

CHAPTER TWENTY-SEVEN

"We are SO going to get busted," Courtney said nervously while clinging with a death grip on a subway hand rail.

"I do not think you will be seen by your mentor. She somehow does not strike me as one who rides public transit with ruffians like *moi*," Benoît teased.

"I don't think you understand what's at stake here, Benoît. I don't have a chance at making it as a designer without Dree's help. If she finds me here with you..."

"May I please ask why she forbade you to be seen with me?"

Courtney hesitated, looking around for potential moles. "She said you are a sociopathic predator."

Benoît nodded.

"Why are you nodding? Never mind. She was worried for my safety because she questions my judgment. Not sure what that's all about. She also thinks you'll destroy my reputation. And also hers indirectly."

"What do you think about all that?" Benoît asked, looking down.

"I think it's a crock of shitake mushrooms. You're a little quirky but I'm pretty sure you're not a sociopath... You're not a sociopath, are you?"

"I would never admit it to you if I was."

"This is a very bad idea. I should just go back to the hotel."

"You have dreamed of exploring Paris for such a long time, Courtney. This is the chance of a lifetime! Hiding in your hotel room for the next month would become the greatest regret of your life."

Courtney huddled, looking around nervously.

"You have let that beast get inside your head."

"Dree is not a beast," Courtney snapped. "She's gone to a lot of trouble for me."

"And yet she makes you afraid."

"I'm not afraid of Dree specifically. I'm just afraid of her finding me here."

"My mistake," Benoît said ironically.

"I agree she's overreacting about the whole driver thing. But she's not a bad person. She promised to hook me up with all kinds of powerful industry people. I mean yes, this ultimatum seems frivolous, but on the other hand it's a small price to pay considering everything Dree is doing to launch my career."

Benoît pursed his lips.

"She planned an event in Évian just for me. I'm going to meet literally all of my fashion heroes. Nothing like this has ever happened to me before."

Benoît nodded silently.

"Benoît…"

"I can give you recommendations for transportation to Évian…"

"Stop looking so disappointed. You're making me feel bad."

"May I suggest the high-speed train…"

"It's not my fault, Benoît. I have to think about my career."

"Or you could rent a limousine…"

"I can't afford either of those options."

"Elle est la pute du diable."

"What are you saying?" Courtney asked nervously, scrambling for her French/English dictionary. After reading the translation she gasped melodramatically. "Dree is not the devil's whore! That's just rude!"

"I see my gift was an excellent investment."

"You can't go around saying stuff like that about my friend!" Courtney said in a huff. "And to think I defended you."

Benoît perked up. "You did what now?"

"Nothing," Courtney grumbled.

"When did you defend me?"

"Don't listen to me. When I'm mad I blurt things out that don't make sense."

Benoît beamed.

***

Sweat was beading conspicuously on Courtney's forehead as she waited with Benoît in an insane lineup outside *Le Louvre.* She really wished she had not used that wimpy deodorant made from snapdragon nectar. She was starting to smell herself and was praying nobody would identify the stench as hers. The sweltering heat was making her relate emotionally to barbecued meat.

"It feels like Paris is basically a series of endless lineups," Courtney complained.

"We are making progress!" Benoît cheered. "The surly man in the orange pants who stood thirty-eight persons ahead of us has now advanced to the front entrance!"

"Why does Paris have to be so damn crowded all the time?" Courtney grunted.

"It is crowded because everyone wants to be here!" Benoît bubbled with his arms spread in celebration.

"I don't think it's smart to stand right out here in the open like this."

"Don't let Alexandria ruin this experience for you."

"The humidity already ruined it for me."

"Courtney, how can you be morose when you are about to experience some of the most famed and cherished artwork in the world? I am excited and I've seen Mona Lisa's elusive smile seventeen times!"

"I don't know if I can do this. It feels wrong."

"Did you not say that your mentor will be in photo sessions all day today? There is literally no chance of her finding you here. Consider it an adventure!"

Courtney started breathing with fast, short breaths. The beaded sweat started to flow more profusely. Fear soaked her eyes.

"Courtney?" Benoît asked, concerned.

Courtney gasped for breath, holding an up and index finger as a signal that she would be fine in a minute. However, the passing moments only fed her anxiety, making her pant more desperately.

"You are having a panic attack," Benoît said urgently. He scrambled to find a person who might have a paper bag.

"No," Courtney gasped. "It's... heat."

Benoît instinctively put his arm around Courtney in an attempt to calm her. Courtney pushed Benoît away.

"Don't!" Courtney said loudly enough to make people turn their heads.

Benoît stood motionless, blinking.

"I told you," Courtney wheezed, catching her breath and clutching her chest, "boundaries."

"You need help," Benoît offered.

"You can't do things like that," Courtney scolded pathetically. "What if... I... I can take care of myself, you know."

"You need to hydrate. There is a Brioche Dorée down this way on the Champs Élysées."

"What about the Mona Lisa? You said..."

"She will wait for you. She is very understanding about these things."

Benoît guided Courtney down the street, being careful not let his body accidentally brush against hers in any way. The task was challenging given the crowd of people closing in around them. Still shaking, Courtney did not notice Benoît hold open the café door for her. She failed to notice him ordering two bottles of sparkling water and a baguette sandwich with chicken and sliced egg. He pulled out a chair for her and she obliviously sat at a small café table by the window. Benoît offered her a beverage and placed half of the sandwich in front of her.

"The sandwiches here are my favorite," Benoît chimed, rubbing his hands together in anticipation. He took a liberal bite and chewed enthusiastically.

"I'm on the pill," Courtney said absently.

Shocked, Benoît suddenly spewed sandwich into his napkin.

"I mean I'm feeling stuffed because I took the breakfast pill this morning."

"What is a breakfast pill?"

"It's a meal replacement capsule that stops you from craving food."

"But food is beautiful. Artful. Food brings people together. Craving it is part of the experience."

"You feel pretty strongly about that sandwich."

Benoît laughed in a way that made his eyes turn into sparkling, crescent moons. It made the side of Courtney's mouth curve upwards.

"Why in the world would you want to stop eating, Silly Woman?"

"Eating is considered obscene in my industry. I have to look good for my event in Évian. Everyone will be looking at me."

Benoît secretly envied the people Courtney referred to. He tried not to look too intently at Courtney. It was hard.

"You have nothing to worry about. You are resplendent," he muttered inaudibly.

Courtney squinted at Benoît. She was not sure what resplendent meant. Was he complimenting her or was that some kind of a fancy insult? Her contemplation was interrupted by the distinct Skype ring on her phone. Groaning, she pulled out her phone and her eyes widened. It was Paul. A picture had popped up on her screen – one that Courtney had not bothered to change – of Paul lustily nibbling Courtney's ear while she shrieked with giggles.

Courtney froze. She stared stupidly at the picture which was in full view of Benoît. When she realized how publicly she was displaying the picture, she fumbled to turn off the phone, quickly burying it in her purse. She prayed that by some miracle Benoît had not seen the picture.

Benoît bit his lip and looked down, dejected. He felt as though something was crushing his chest.

"Sorry about that," Courtney said, trying to sound blasé.

"Was it important?" Benoît asked quietly.

"Pffft! No!" Courtney fake laughed. "It was just someone from my family checking up on me again."

"You must have a close family," Benoît said ironically.

***

The metro station was bustling. Benoît had to speak at a slightly higher volume to be heard above the throng as he told Courtney he was going to obtain some tickets from the metro pass machine.

Courtney stood awkwardly waiting for him, hiding her feelings of displacement by people-watching. As Courtney scanned the metro station, being somewhat jostled, she became fixated on a bubbly metro employee who was graciously speaking perfect English to several tourists who needed assistance. She had the most poetic French accent which made it hard not to study her smiling mouth. Courtney tried to move her mouth into similar shapes, wondering what the trick was to speak with such phonetic flair. Courtney mused on the employee's willingness to help, no matter how insignificant the request. She would greet each tourist as though they were an old friend, and send them on their way with a warm comment and a friendly wave.

The penny dropped.

Maybe Benoît was not a Parisian anomaly. Maybe this level of enthusiasm, warmth, graciousness, energy and well-mannered hospitality was somewhat normal in Paris.

Suddenly a crass sound cut through the white noise of the metro station like a rusty round saw slicing through sheet metal.

"DO...YOU...SPEAK...ENG...LISH..."

Courtney spun around when she heard a British accent speaking much too loudly, slowly and condescendingly. Courtney spotted a British backpacker, hovering over the metro employee in a way that he probably thought was intimidating. Courtney smirked when she noticed the employee maintaining her impeccable charm.

"DO...YOU...UND...ER...STAND...ME!" the backpacker bellowed again. "DO...YOU...SPEAK...ENG...LISH...LIKE...A...NORM...AL...PER...SON?...OR...ARE...YOU...TOO...BLOODY...STU...PID?"

"Je suis désolé," the pleasant metro employee said with extreme sweetness, "si tu insistes d'être un bâtard d'être ignorant, je ne peux pas t'aider."

Intrigued, Courtney scrambled for her French/English dictionary and quickly leafed through the pages.

"LEARN...ENG...LISH...LIKE...A...CIV...IL...IZED...PER...SON!" The backpacker reminded Courtney of a foghorn.

"Écoute moi, putain d'imbécile," the metro employee said in a voice that was as sweet and bubbly as a glass of champagne, "pourqoi devrais-je faire des efforts pour communiquer avec toi alors que tu me traits comme une merde?"

Courtney snorted with laughter when she translated with her dictionary.

"YOU...ARE...COM...PLETE...LY...USE...LESS!" the backpacker thundered. "I...SHALL...GO...ELSE...WHERE!"

The cheery metro employee smiled like an angel and waved sweetly saying, *"Mange de la merde et meurs doucement et avec douleur!"*

Following along with her dictionary, Courtney buckled with wild laughter. "Oh my God!" she laughed to nobody in particular. "Parisians are awesome!"

Courtney did not see Benoît approach her from behind with a pair of metro tickets.

"Why thank you," Benoît could not help but produce a charming dimple.

"Benoît!" Courtney could barely catch her breath from laughing so hard. "You missed it! It was a hoot! That metro lady over there? She was being all nice and speaking English to all these tourists and stuff. Then along comes this abusive dickweed with some kind of a Norwegian accent or whatever. And he's all *"talk English like a normal person,"* and *"I'm all civilized and whatever. You're just a stupid French twit."* Then the lady... this is the good part.... the lady is all cute and sparkly like you, with this big smile and she goes, she goes, *"I'm not helping you 'cause you're an ignorant bastard. If you treat me like shit I'm going to pretend like I don't speak English."* And, and, and the kicker? She pisses the guy off, he storms away like, *"Look at me, I'm an asshole and I'm mad now."* And the lady waves all sweet like and tells him to eat shit and die! This is the best city in the world!" Courtney wailed with laugher.

Benoît could not resist the contagiousness of Courtney's hysterical howls. He crumpled with laughter and cackled along with her. "She got him good," Benoît snorted.

"Right?" Courtney said, gasping for breath. "People here really know how to stick it to a-holes, huh?"

"It is so true!" Benoît laughed, dabbing his eyes.

"Is everyone in Paris this badass?" Courtney wailed.

"Pretty much!" Benoît squeaked breathlessly.

"I could totally live h..."

Courtney stopped abruptly.

Benoît stopped abruptly.

They looked at each other silently for a moment.

"I mean..." Courtney stammered.

Benoît rescued her. "Nobody ever wants to leave, Courtney. It is Paris, for God's sake."

"Right. I mean I will have to leave at some point."

"Of course you will."

"It's not home."

Courtney watched Benoît's expression carefully.

Benoît paused briefly before shaking his head.

CHAPTER TWENTY-EIGHT
(DAY 33 IN PARIS)

"She has a WHAT?" Étienne said, agog and clutching his chest. He pulled a rack of souvenir T-shirts over to give Benoît and himself a hedge of privacy from Étienne's on-looking customers.

"Courtney has a man waiting for her in America," Benoît sighed. "There was a picture of them in a lustful embrace on her phone. He attempted to have a video conference with her while we were at the Brioche Dorée together."

"No! No, no, no, no, no, no, no..."

"Yes, Étienne."

"But she said nothing of him to you."

"What reason would she have to delve into matters so personal? With her driver?"

"But this cannot be so! She is so cute and flowerlike! And you are as virile as an intact bull mastiff! The universe will fall out of kilter if you do not make gallant love to her!"

"This would explain all the boundaries upon which she insisted."

"I will not accept this! I do not approve of this other man!"

"I have no right to her, Étienne. She does not belong to me."

"We can make this right!"

"We?"

"You have another month with her in your taxi. Think of the connections you could make during that time. Consider all of the erotic sparks that could fly like a dazzling display of firecrackers!"

"About that..."

"What now?"

"She cannot ride with me anymore. Her mentor threatened to abandon her if she is seen with me."

"What the..."

"It makes no sense."

"The very mentor who threatened you after lunging maniacally in front of your taxi?"

"The same."

"She must be deranged."

"She has some kind of delusional vendetta against me. And apparently she has sucked Courtney into her delusions."

"If you cannot drive Courtney, then how did you escort her yesterday?"

"Metro. But I do not know how long we can keep up that strategy. Her mentor has her on a very short leash."

"Ai, ai, ai, Cousin! How did you get entangled in such a melodrama?"

Benoît shook his head.

"In that case," Étienne shrugged, "you will just have to try harder."

"What do you mean? She has a boyfriend."

"Did you see a ring?"

"I am forbidden to be her driver."

"You cleverly meandered around THAT orange pylon by sneaking out with her on the metro. I am so proud of you, Benoît. I had no idea you were so crafty!"

"She had an anxiety attack for fear of being discovered with me."

"A trifle!"

"She does not want to be with me. At all! She is much too worried about losing everything she has worked for."

"And yet she agreed to risk her career to accompany you on your excursion to le Louvre yesterday. She could have said no."

Benoît pondered.

***

Huddled in a ball on her hotel balcony, Courtney stared blankly at the missed Skype call on her cell phone. She had not seen that ear-nibbling picture in over a year and it pinched her heart. All it would take would be a simple click of the callback button and she could see those sleepy eyelids again. She could hear his lulling voice again. Maybe all the agony of the past year would wash away like little seashells being swept away by the redemptive tide. She could feel secure again.

Paul could be handing her a tangible opportunity to build a legitimate, grownup life together. Courtney would not have to feel like a floundering loser anymore, alone and aimless. People would take her seriously if she was in a long-term relationship, on the fast track to marriage and five kids. She actually tried camembert the other day and it tasted pretty good. It was not as fun as squeaky cheese but it was okay. Courtney could easily acclimate to the cheese life. It could give her a financial buffer while she built her fashion career.

It would be so easy to click that button.

So why did it feel so hard?

Courtney swallowed hard and quickly dialed before she could change her mind.

"Hello?"

Staring at her phone for a moment, Courtney took a deep breath before replying. "Benoît. It's me, Courtney."

"Courtney..."

"Please try not to sound so sunshiny. It'll make this harder."

"What is wrong? Do you need me to..."

"That's the thing, Benoît. I won't be needing you."

The foreboding silence that followed punched Courtney in the conscience.

"Ever?" Benoît asked squeakily.

"It's nothing personal."

"Right."

"This is the opportunity of a lifetime. I can't just throw it away."

"Uh-huh."

"We can't be sneaking around all the time, hiding from Dree. I need a guide and all but I'll go barking mad if I have to worry about being spotted with you. It feels dirty and frankly terrifying. I could lose everything, Benoît. Dree is powerful. All my hard work could end up in the crapper."

"I see."

"I'm not just mindlessly turfing you, you know. I thought long and hard about this."

"Courtney..."

"I'm at this critical point in my career where I have to jump through hoops and prove myself..."

"Please do not explain."

"Will you still get paid in full for the whole summer? That wouldn't be fair if..."

"Do not worry about me, Courtney. You have enough on your plate."

"Will... will I ever see you again or whatever?"

"I... I suppose that would be your decision."

Courtney opened her mouth to reply but Benoît had already said *au revoir*.

***

"Cousin?" Étienne said cautiously as Benoît covered his eyes with his arm and clenched his teeth with emotion.

Benoît wordlessly shook his head.

"Who was that on the phone? Was it..."

"It is over."

"No."

"She made her choice. I am a liability to her career."

"No, you cannot accept this."

"She is free to choose her own path, Étienne. She is not my property."

"No, no, no, no, NO!" Étienne was practically twirling in frustration, knocking over a rack of Quasimodo hats. *"You must not let that Fontrose tart take away what is yours! She is a supercilious buzzard with styrofoam in her soul!"*

"Again, Courtney does not belong to me."

"*But she belongs WITH you, Benoît! Why are you just standing there like a droopy spear of damp asparagus? Who extinguished the fervid wildfire that once consumed your valiant spirit? Do you not have the red wine of desire coursing through your veins?*"

"*Étienne, this is her dream.*"

"*I see what you are doing, Benoît. You are projecting your own pain...*"

"*This is a different matter.*"

"*Pursuing Courtney is not the same as...*"

"*I know what it is like to lose... everything you hoped for.*"

"*This is not the same. Not nearly the same.*"

"*Monique was...*"

"*... a sociopath. She is dead to us. It is time for you to find your own happiness. A happiness to which Monique has no claim.*"

"*Courtney's happiness is important to me. Her dream...*"

"*What about YOUR dream, Benoît? What about YOUR happiness?*"

Benoît leaned back against the wall with a thud, squashing a tear with his palm.

CHAPTER TWENTY-NINE:
(DAY 36 IN PARIS)

"Courtney's phone," Courtney exhaled while brisk walking down *Avenue Victor Hugo*.

"Babe."

The monosyllable on the other end of the phone made Courtney's throat constrict. Only one person ever called her Babe. She could feel the color drain from her face.

"Paul?"

"I found you."

Courtney abruptly stopped walking. The steady current of people continued down the sidewalk like a school of fish. Realizing she might get stampeded by rush hour foot traffic, Courtney continued brisk walking. Her ridiculous shoes squished against the sidewalk with each step.

"You found me."

"Your folks tell me you're gallivanting across Europe."

"They would say that."

"Paris?"

"That has always been the goal."

"I have to admit, I had my doubts about you, Babe."

"Paul, it's really hard to talk right now. I'm on my way to the studio. I can't really hear you with all these weird, European sirens…"

"Are you blowing me off?"

"No! You just caught me at an awkward moment."

"I need to talk to you about something important."

"I know. I mean okay. I just… can I get back to you when I get to my studio? There's a lot of commotion right now."

"It can't wait."

"Not even seventeen minutes?"

"I want to ask you something, Babe."

Courtney's stomach flip flopped. "Oh my god. Um… Bye." Courtney hastily shut off her phone and winced at her own stupidity.

A text message beeped. ***"Skype me. Tonight. 7:30 Paris time. Bring wine… Pauly Wog."***

Wine?

Courtney's mind whirred with a trillion theories of why Paul would want her to bring wine to a Skype date. Paul was nothing if not elusive. Though Courtney knew virtually nothing about wine, she did know that wine was an accessory to wildly romantic situations. Her heart flapped around like a nervous trout.

Wine!

Scanning the tree-lined streets, Courtney spotted a wine shop and awkwardly stumbled inside, conspicuous to the poised cliental around her. Avoiding the curious stares in the room, Courtney ran her finger along the labels of wine bottles, pretending to read them. She had no clue what she was doing.

"Madame?" a mild clerk said curiously.

"I... have no idea what's going on," Courtney admitted.

The clerk smiled, amused. "Do you have a particular occasion?"

"Skype," Courtney nodded bluntly. "I mean... I need something romantic. Do you have any romantic wine?"

"I am afraid all of our wine is romantic."

"Well that bungs things up."

"Red? White?"

"Which color is good for romantic video conferences? I think I'm getting engaged tonight."

"Via Skype?" The clerk's eyes bulged.

"Maybe not engaged. Yet. He might want to take it slow. We haven't seen each other since he was banging Paulette over a year ago. He might want to woo me all over again, if you catch my drift."

The clerk's eyes bulged more.

"I can tell by your expression that there isn't a specific wine suited to my situation."

"Not uniquely, no."

"I see. Well maybe I'll just wing it then. I'll look for a cute label or something."

The clerk smiled tentatively as Courtney inspected a bottle of wine with a funky emu logo. Lost in a jungle of wine, Courtney examined dozens of bottles, scrunching her nose at the label descriptions, comparing the artistic merit of each logo graphic and squinting at the elusive liquid inside. She was becoming apathetic until a bottle caught her eye on an endcap display. A tiny gasp escaped her throat. She gawked at the label for a full thirty seconds before reality seeped into her brain. There was a picture of Benoît on the bottle. A postmodern, expressionistic version of Benoît, but still. The resemblance was uncanny.

An earsplitting smash instantly turned the heads of everyone in the room. Courtney stood frozen like a stunned moose unexpectedly challenged by an oncoming transport truck. Her hand which held the bottle was now empty and trembling. Tiny shards of glass formed a rug of menacing triangles all over the floor and velvety red liquid pooled and trickled around Courtney's feet.

"I..." Courtney stammered to a roomful of stunned onlookers, "I am so sorry about that."

The mild clerk was already on the scene, sweeping away the shards. "Are you okay, *Madame?*"

"Um... this stain is never going to come out of my skorts but otherwise..."

"What happened? Did you have some kind of episode? Should I call an ambulance?"

"No, I just… I saw someone I know." Courtney collected herself. "I'll pay for the wine and just get out of here before I…" Courtney grabbed a bottle of Benoît wine. "…and I'll take this one too."

***

"What is going on here?" Courtney thundered at her plush lucky duck that was staring back blankly at her from her studio desk. "It's only been five days since I've seen Benoît and now I'm having delusions of seeing him on wine bottles? How did he get inside my head? I put up all my defenses, I set boundaries, cut things off amicably. Have I lost my freaking mind? Is he messing with me? Is he using some kind of wonky French voodoo to manipulate my thoughts? Am I obsessed with him or something? What is going on here? *Why am I seeing him on wine bottles?*"

And still, the duck stared blankly.

"I thought I figured out how to do Paris without someone to show me around. I mean, I'm always lost, I'm late for everything, I'm oblivious to the culture, my feet are yelling at me for firing my driver and I'm finding it surprisingly difficult to order my own coffee. But I've survived for the past five days without being kidnapped, mortally injured or accidentally walking to Belgium. That means I'm competent, right? Independent. I don't necessarily need…"

Benoît's face seemed to gleam on the wine bottle that was peeking out of Courtney's bag. How did the artist capture his twinkly essence? The way his eyes curved with friendliness. Courtney shook it off. That was not Benoît on the label. It was merely a figment of Courtney's tortured imagination.

"I can't think about Benoît right now!" Courtney shrieked into her hands. "Something is brewing with Paul. I can just feel it. Paul is what I've always wanted. He's long term. He's stable. He's familiar. I need that in my life right now. I need something to ground me. Jaysus! This is driving me..."

"...a little batty, are we now dear?"

Courtney spun around and found Alexandria Fontrose, standing elegantly in the doorway.

"Dree," Courtney whispered hoarsely.

"I see you're talking amongst yourself," Alexandria said with an air of piety. "Is this a private conversation? Am I intruding?"

Courtney quickly stashed her lucky duck out of sight. "Of course not, Dree. I was just..."

"Nerves? Understandable. You are setting off on a life-altering adventure tomorrow. Are you ready? Are you packed? Have you made travel arrangements?"

"Almost?"

"Almost? In what sense? And why do you say *almost* interrogatively?"

"I'm mentally preparing. I've shortlisted my wardrobe and... I'll figure something out in regards to transportation."

"You're not thinking of..."

"No! I've been without a driver for five days."

"There's a good girl."

"I'm just working out the details…"

"You haven't hired a car? Booked high speed train tickets? Chartered a flight?"

"I sort of can't afford those things? See, I was counting on this prize package. When I was rationing my money – you know, for food and other things that are keeping me alive - I didn't count on having to pay my way to the Alps."

"Did I completely go out of my way to arrange this soirée for absolutely no reason?"

"No! I'm going, I just…"

"I didn't realize that having a significant event arranged for your benefit – and ONLY your benefit – would be such a burden, my love."

"I sort of figured that since you confiscated Benoît you would probably take responsibility to arrange…"

"They told me not to be charitable with my time but did I listen to the deafening voice of reason? I did not. You expect me to pay for everything for you? Is that what I am to you? A priceless, genuine silver, diamond-studded gravy train?"

"Dude, I have to eat."

"No you don't. And never call me Dude again. That is irreverent."

"I have to eat occasionally or I'll topple over."

"Priorities, Baby Gerbil. Figure it out."

"That's literally what I'm doing."

"Alright my little hazelnut, let me tell you what I will do because I am benevolent. I will hire a car for you. Will that relieve you of your worries?"

Courtney exhaled in relief.

"I will take care of everything, love. Just leave it all to me. A driver from *Tellement Débile Limousine Service* will retrieve you at 7:00 am on the dot. I find their drivers to be most punctual so I do hope you are an early riser. No need to thank me. It is my deepest pleasure to help."

Courtney nodded humbly.

"Details, my love," Alexandria said, snapping her fingers to seize Courtney's attention. "I wanted to iron out every detail with clarity so you will be prepared for your special moment. I will be wrapped up with PR madness for the next twenty-four hours, but I will be meeting you in Évian two days from now, August 7th, promptly at nine. I will be visible at the front entrance of the *Château Lemieux*. Only the most opulent venue for my precious chickpea. You will be following two steps behind me, punctually and dressed in your finest gown."

Courtney nodded. She did not own a *finest gown*.

"Refreshments will be served by gloved catering staff but you are to politely refuse, regardless of how tantalizing those cocktail shrimps and pigs-in-blankets look. You must look stylishly hungry and musn't smudge your lipstick with frivolous finger foods. Wear slimming pantyhose and walk with erect posture. All the biggest names in fashion will be there, after all and this is your only chance to make a first impression. Did I mention Ralphie's heart is palpitating with anticipation to meet you?"

Courtney nodded.

"Advice. If Tommy Hilfiger wants to talk denim, let him drone on for as long as he likes and nod emphatically. Restrict your fashion observations to those of a flattering nature. Rear ends were designed for kissing, my darling girl. And try not to talk too much about yourself. Let others compliment you first and then describe your work with feigned modesty. There is nothing more off-putting than a cocksure novice."

Courtney nodded.

"Never mention tweed to Giorgio. It's a sensitive issue. Don't ask. Avoid the color orange. And please have a makeover before the event. You're beautiful but... well. You will be seated at Table 9 for the dinner, and I use that word loosely as you will not be eating but merely moving food around with your fork. Please review proper fork usage before you arrive to avoid any embarrassment. There will be VIP accommodations onsite, one night prior to the event and one night after. So just bring your little ticket thing to Manfred and he will take care of you."

Courtney nodded.

"Remember to smile at all ti... Mother of Gabbana, are you still wearing those blasphemous things on your feet?"

"I didn't have a chance to..."

"Uh! Dispose of them. They are insulting my eyeballs."

Courtney looked down sheepishly at her feet. The shoes she got from Étienne molded so comfortably around her feet she had almost forgotten how ugly they were. Alexandria may have been repulsed but her arches were shouting *hallelujah.*

"I love you with all my heart, Courtney dear," Alexandria said, kissing the air next to each of Courtney's cheeks. "I trust I will see you in Évian. Alone, as God intended."

"What?"

"You know what I mean."

Courtney cocked her head.

"Big things are in store for you, Courtney Stent!" Alexandria said with dramatic flourish on her way out the door. "Enormous things!"

***

Her suitcase was only half-packed when the time rolled around for Paul's Skype date. Courtney set the bottle of wine beside her with a plastic cup, heaving a nervous breath. Paul was already ten minutes late. Paul was never late. Her left leg twitched and she was breathing short breaths. She could feel her face flushing.

When the Skype ring finally startled Courtney, her heart thumped loudly. A scrambled image of Paul appeared on the screen and his voice was garbled.

"Paul?" Courtney squinted at the screen. "Can you hear me? We have a bad connection here."

"&*#DT#YH Courtney? &IE^^%D*$%# hear me #%&^#&#$F^ now?"

"Paul?" Courtney said, adjusting her computer. "You sound like you're possessed with demons and you look like an ocular migraine."

"&(^*%&%$&* Crummy &&%($%#uf%& connection. %(*&%%#%&J dammit."

"Paul, what did you want to ask me?"

"#&^#%$*&*T^$^%$&%"

"Paul, what do you want to ask me?"

"^&$%&#$*&&T$*^%$ important. *^$%#(&*%%."

"For the luvva... Paul! I can't freaking understand you! Can you call me back?"

"$%&^%#$%#&^% You %^$&*^$*^$ me."

"Paul? Oh my god, Paul just call me back. Can you hear me? Just call me back!"

"&$%$%$&^$$ Screw this."

The screen went blank.

Courtney fell backwards onto her bed with an unopened bottle of wine in her hand. She stared at the ceiling, trying to catch her breath. She suddenly noticed that she had been sweating.

Would he call back?

He did not call back.

CHAPTER THIRTY:
(DAY 37 IN PARIS)

Courtney's eyes fluttered open at dawn. Once she blinked the sleep from her eyes, reality creeped around the crevices of her brain. Today she would embark on a life altering journey. One more sleep until the big fashion bash. Panic strangled her when she realized she had fallen asleep before finishing her packing. She was kind of dreading the idea of busting free from her cocoon of blankets. She was woefully unprepared for this trip.

When she rolled over she realized she had been holding the wine bottle in her arm while she slept. Her eyes bugged open when she saw an expressionistic interpretation of Benoît's face smiling at her from the pillow next to hers. She scrambled out of bed, as though embarrassed to be seen with drool cake on the side of her mouth. She stood by her bed, looking strangely at the bottle of wine.

Courtney frantically shoved some clothes into her suitcase which had been strewn around the hotel room. She had planned to carefully strategize her wardrobe for the trip but there was no time for that now. She did however, make sure that she remembered to bring her best dress – nothing suitable for a night at the Oscars, but it was one of her own designs and it was her favorite – and zipped it in a garment bag to hang up in the... car.

"Oh my god, the car!" Courtney said, nearly giving herself whiplash as she urgently swerved her head towards the clock. It was already 7:20. She looked out the window and could not see a marked limousine. The front desk had not buzzed her. She scrambled for the phone and pressed the front desk button.

"*Reception,*" Jacques said blandly.

"Stent. From room..." Courtney stopped herself abruptly when she heard Jacques exhale on the phone. "I mean, good morning Jack. I was hoping you could help me."

A long, confused pause followed.

"Jack? Are you still there?"

"It would be my pleasure to assist you, Courtney," Jacques said in a surprisingly affable voice.

"Whoa. Okay. So apparently somebody hired me a limousine? It was supposed to arrive at 7:00?"

"My apologies, but no limousine has arrived for you."

"Are you sure? *Tellement Débile Limousine Services* are supposed to be known for their punctuality."

"Oh dear."

"What?"

"You say somebody hired you a car from *Tellement Débile?*"

"Did I pronounce it wrong?"

"No, no. You said it perfectly it's just..."

"It's really important. I'm getting my big break tomorrow at this thing in Évian…"

"My dear, I do not mean to upset you, but I do not think anyone will be retrieving you today."

"I don't understand."

"*Tellement Débile* is… oh my. How to I say this?"

"Are you having trouble translating or…"

"They do not exist."

"… What?"

"I am not sure who it was who made these arrangements but…"

"No no, they're real. It's a thing. My mentor arranged…"

"I am so sorry, *Madame.*"

"So they like went out of business?"

"Okay. We can go with that."

"Oh my God. How am I going to get to Évian?"

"Perhaps our concierge can suggest…"

"I'm broke, Jack. I don't have many options."

"I see."

"Thanks though, Jack. For being nice and stuff."

"Please take care, Courtney."

End of call.

Feeling woozy with panic, Courtney flopped on the bed and searched for options on the internet.

Should she rent a car? – Ouch. Nothing available last minute.

Taxi? – Yikes! Taxi fees in Paris are startlingly higher than the American rates.

Uber? – Nope. Not after the freaky Uber incident she had back in Wisconsin.

Train? – (sigh) More expensive than a taxi.

Hitchhiking? – Tempting. But terrifying and possibly illegal.

Courtney was seized with anxiety. How could she possibly get to Évian without a vehicle? How could she face this incredibly stressful situation alone? Having no clue how to find her way around? Everything would be strange and intimidating and flustering and foreign and confusing and taxing and French and nerve racking and overwhelming and...

Courtney felt a wave of nausea rise up inside her like a tsunami. She dashed to the bathroom sink to throw up. She caught her breath, wiped her mouth and looked up at her apprehensive reflection in the mirror. Her fretful eyes looked back at her, pleading.

"Uh," Courtney choked. "Get over yourself, Stent. Just do it already."

***

Box Five was Benoît's bubble of comfort. Private, quiet, hidden from the throngs of Paris and elegantly cozy. This is where he would retreat whenever life threw him a bunch of stale beignets. It was the perfect place to think, tucked in the shadows of the elusive loge. He felt like the walls of his beloved *Palais Garnier* were hugging him, nurturing him, protecting him. There was no place on earth where he felt safer from the pressures of the outside world.

The past six days had been wrenching for Benoît. He knew he would miss Courtney but he had not anticipated the gigantic, gaping, Courtney-shaped hole that would be gauged out of him. She was obnoxious, he told himself. She had no filters. She hurt him more times than he could count and she was impossible at times. Regardless, his taxi felt morbidly empty without her. Benoît rubbed his palms into his stinging eyes as he sat despondently in a red, plush chair.

He let out a long, agonizing exhale when his cell phone rang.

"*Allo,*" Benoît groaned into the phone.

"Benoît?"

Benoît sprung back to life like a wilting impatien reconsidering things after a rain shower. "*Oui,* Courtney. It is me." Benoît had no idea why he felt the need to fix his hair at that moment.

"This is embarrassing."

"What happened?"

"I... I think I need a ride. To Évian. Like right now."

"Oh," Benoît hesitated. "I thought..."

"Look, I have no idea who else to call. I'm kind of desperate here."

"I... I don't know if I should..."

"I'm scared, Benoît. I don't know what to do. I don't know anyone else. I'm... I'm so scared."

Benoît swallowed hard.

"This is so important, Benoît. I know I turfed you before and I know it's risky but if you don't help me out..."

"What about Alexandria?"

"She has her own ride."

"You know what I mean, Courtney."

"She... she doesn't have to know."

"Pardon?"

"There's a back entrance to the hotel. Next to the dumpster in a back alley. Meet me there, okay? Is that okay?"

"Are you sure?"

"Pack a bag or something. It's a long trip. I'll meet you by the dumpster in about an hour. Does that leave you enough time?"

"You are serious."

"Deathly. I'm not missing my big moment, Benoît. I've worked my arse off for this."

"Mon dieu," Benoît said, running his hand through his hair.

"Drive right up to the back door and I'll hop right in. Don't get out of the car, do you hear? Remain inside the car. Dree would never use the back door. She'd rather retch on a turkey bone than be seen using the same entrance as the servants. Are you game?"

Benoît gaped.

***

Jacques deflated like a nettled balloon with a slow leak when Alexandria Fontrose trotted haughtily into the lobby. She stopped with a huff in front of Jacques, coughing a boozy smoker's hack into his face.

"Checking out so early, Ms. Fontrose?"

"Can't get one past you, can I, *Pâté-For-Brains.*"

"You will be missed," Jacques sarcastically hissed.

"Of course I will. The pleasure has been all yours."

"I thought you would be staying with us until Fashion Week."

"You expect me to stay in this seedy dive for another month? You have mistaken me for someone with low standards. I only agreed to imprison myself in this roach motel for the sake of charity and altruism."

"You must be exhausted from the effort."

"UH! You have no idea. The sooner I get out of this hellhole..."

"What about Courtney?"

"Heh?"

"Is she not the object of your selfless altruism? Are you not her mentor during her stay here in Paris?"

"That floundering little underdog?"

"She is a shockingly sweet girl."

"Barf."

"She gave me this fern."

"What the..."

"I like this fern."

"Whatever. Just take this room card before your vulgar shirt gives me a seizure."

"Courtney might surprise you..."

"Grunt."

"... if you give her a chance to prove herself..."

"I'm doing her a favor. If she can't take care of herself in this city then she'll never make it. From now on mind your own business."

Jacques' eyes turned into slits of disgust. A faint growl emerged from deep in his throat.

***

Yellow construction tape brought Benoît's taxi to a halt. Benoît leaned out his window and got a whiff of the strong, tarry odor of fresh asphalt. He cringed and banged his head in frustration on his steering wheel. They were repaving the road by the back alley. Benoît did not have access to the rear entrance where he was supposed to meet Courtney. He drove around, looking for an inconspicuous parking spot. Finding one in the shade of a large, unruly shrub, Benoît parked and dialed up Courtney to tell her about the change in plans.

Alexandria Fontrose floated outside like a self-absorbed ghost with feet. She grinded her teeth when her driver was not immediately at her disposal. As her eyeballs scoured the parking lot for the tardy knave, her eyes froze into laser beams of hate when she found Benoît seated in his taxi, preoccupied on his cell phone. Alexandria sinisterly hid her identity with her huge, brimmed hat, dark sunglasses and shaggy collar of her unseasonable faux fur coat. She watched Benoît discreetly from behind a potted pyramid cedar.

He did not see her as he darted through the front, revolving hotel doors.

***

"Chérie!" Benoît said bouncily as he spread his arms in a sunny declaration of his arrival when Courtney opened her hotel room door.

"Shush!" Courtney hissed as she pulled Benoît into the room. "What if Dree..."

"Jacques said she has left the building already. You can let those tendons in your neck unravel now. You are safe."

Courtney had to mentally tell her arms not to hug Benoît.

"The taxi is parked discreetly behind a large juniper."

"Not the juniper near the front entrance of the hotel? Right out where anyone can see?"

"Oh, the scandal!" Benoît said playfully with his eyes widening with animated intrigue.

"It's not funny, Benoît."

"It is a little bit."

"I feel like I'm going to throw up."

"Am I that repulsive?"

"Stop being adorable. This is not the time or the place."

"May I take your bags?"

"What if somebody catches you being chivalrous?"

"It would save us a second trip to the car. And it is my job so..."

"Alright, alright. But don't do anything sweet. I don't want rumors to circulate."

"On my honor," Benoît tilted his head in a reverent bow.

"Stop that!" Courtney spat.

Benoît cackled with laughter that echoed all the way down the hall.

CHAPTER THIRTY-ONE

"Floor it," Courtney muttered from the backseat of the taxi, slumping down and shielding her face with the peak of her pageboy hat.

Despite Courtney's wonky behavior, Benoît felt a fresh squirt of revitalization having her in the taxi with him again. Warmth consumed him like the long awaited thaw after a frigid, dreary winter. He was so giddy in fact that he pretended not to notice how determined Courtney was not to be seen with him.

"Are you sure you do not want to sit up front? It is a long drive to Évian."

"Nope, I'm good."

Benoît glanced at Courtney in the rearview mirror, shaking his head good humoredly. She was slinking so far down in her seat her pelvis was practically sliding onto the floor. Her hat was now hiding her entire face.

"Nice hat," Benoît said.

"This is going to be a long drive."

"In the literal sense, yes. But I am a fun guy with many intriguing antics. The time will just whiz by."

Courtney curled into a ball.

"Are you going to be this like this the whole way? Because that would be amusing."

"Look, I'm not sure about how I feel about this, okay?"

"But this is an adventure!"

"What if we get caught?"

"It is not an adventure if it is easy."

"It's scary, okay? I don't want to mess this up. I have everything to lose here. Not to mention I'm in a car for eight to ten hours with..."

"What?"

"Nothing."

"Wait, is this about..."

"No."

"This game you play, pretending like nothing happened in the loge..."

"Nothing happened. We agreed on it."

"You agreed with yourself. I was not involved in that agreement. Besides, if I made you that uncomfortable why did you agree to be with me in the days that followed? At the tower? The cathedral? *Le Louvre?* Now?"

"Don't make things weird, Benoît."

"You are cowering in the backseat like a traumatized hedgehog. I would say things are already weird."

"Only because you…"

"…followed your cues."

"What's that supposed to mean?"

"You were thinking of kissing me back."

"Was not."

"Your eyes were closed."

"I was drowsy."

"You were staring at my mouth."

"There was a hunk of duck meat stuck in your teeth."

"You had this hazy look…"

"Headache medication."

"You leaned in a little."

"I thought you were about to tell me a secret."

Benoît sprayed out a laugh.

"Why are you laughing at my embarrassment and shame?"

"Why are you so nervous?"

"I'm encased in a taxi for practically a day with some guy…"

"Some guy?"

"…who may or may not try to snog me. It's a delicate situation."

"Courtney, I am not going to snog you. I do not even know what that word means."

Courtney fearfully looked around at the surrounding cars on the bustling street.

"You must allow yourself to enjoy this experience. May I ask though, if you are so nervous about all this why did you call me for a ride?"

"I told you already. My ride fell through."

"How so?"

"Dree ordered me a car..."

Benoît rolled his eyes.

"Stop that, Benoît. You didn't even let me finish. Dree hired me a car from *Tellement Débile Limousine Services* and for some reason nobody showed up this morning."

"Oh dear."

"Why does everyone keep saying that today?"

"Courtney, I think you have been deceived."

"Oh here we go. Are you going to slam Dree again? Come on, Benoît. Stop being so judgmental."

"*Tellement Débile Limousine Services* is not real."

"They went out of business. They used to be real."

"*Tellement Débile* means *so stupid*. Or you know. *Gullible.*"

"Are you saying I'm gullible?"

"No. I am just the unassuming translator."

"That's not what it means."

"It does mean that though."

"No, *débile* is a kind of car..."

"I am pretty sure it is not."

"So *tellement débile* means..."

"*So much stupid.*"

"Oh stop. Nobody would name their company that."

"Exactly."

"Don't lie, Benoît."

"I am not lying."

"You're lying."

"I do not lie. To lie is a sin."

"I don't believe you."

"Look it up."

Courtney resentfully thumbed through her French/English dictionary and gulped loudly.

"So... it means... what you just said."

"I am sorry, Courtney. I do not mean to be hurtful."

"I don't understand."

"It is over. You are in the taxi. Move on."

"Why would Dree make up a fake limousine service? When she knew I needed a ride?"

Benoît bit his lip.

"Benoît, just stop."

"I said nothing."

"I know what you're thinking."

"What am I thinking?"

"You're thinking all kinds of nasty things about Dree that are not true."

"I just do not understand..."

"And I don't understand *you* half the time with an accent that's as thick as margarine. And yet here we are."

Benoît struggled to blink back laughter. Why was Courtney so adorably hilarious when she was mad? It was not fair at all.

"Look, Benoît. Dree is a complex person. She has many layers. Many facets. What you see on the surface is merely a persona. You have to stand out in my industry. You have to exude confidence. You can't reveal any weaknesses. Dree is just putting on a show. But she is a really swell person under all that faux fur."

"So what is she really like then? I think I am missing something."

"Well... she says things that make me believe in myself."

"Example?"

"She called me her sprig of parsley."

"What does that even mean?"

"I have no idea. But I'm ninety-seven percent sure it was a compliment."

"What she did to you at the opera house…"

"That was my fault. We've been over this."

"She lied to you about hiring a car."

"There must have been a mix-up."

"Do you not see what she is?"

"Why are we still talking about this?"

"Because I am afraid she is going to…"

"Benoît, can you just frigging not?"

"I am only trying to…"

"Just do your damn job and drive, will you?"

BOOM.

"*Merde!*" Benoît cussed as the taxi vibrated from a loud banging noise. The taxi swerved and the tires shrieked to a sudden halt. "Get out of the taxi, Courtney," Benoît said, instantly unfastening his seatbelt.

Thick, black smoke was swirling ominously from under the hood.

"What just…" Courtney gasped, gripping the armrests with a strangulating hold.

"Get out of the taxi now!" Benoît said at a volume that Courtney was not used to as he flew from the car.

"But we're in the middle of the street," Courtney quavered as she surveyed the taxi's diagonal position in the middle of the bustling road. Horns were honking furiously all around them as Benoît's hand yanked Courtney from the car.

Benoît lifted the hood and his expression made Courtney worry. She watched in horror as Benoît pulled out huge chunks of blackened fur that had been crammed into several automotive mechanisms. She became paler and paler as he pulled out more and more charred, stringy fibers.

"*Putain!*" Benoît swore.

***

Benoît was abnormally quiet which made Courtney immensely nervous. He was staring intensely at the road as he drove.

"Holy crap, that was scary," Courtney said in a quaky voice. "What was it, do you know?"

Benoît tossed a mound of oily fur into the backseat. Courtney whimpered and dropped the bristly grossness in revulsion.

"Faux fur," Benoît spat.

"What?"

"Crammed into the engine mechanisms. Curious."

"Don't *even*."

"Who else do you know who lacks a conscience and dresses like a Kodiak bear?"

"Oh come *on!* What logical reason would Dree have to sabotage your taxi?"

"Maybe she does not want us to arrive safely in Évian?"

"That doesn't make any sense."

"Courtney, both of us could have been seriously hurt. That woman is dangerous."

"How do you know?"

"I... I knew someone. She... she had no conscience. Do you know what a person is capable of when they lack a..."

"You are taking this way too far. I get that you don't like her but *come on*. Nobody is that psycho."

"What do you think happened, Courtney? Did a cult of squirrels make a covert suicide pact under my hood?"

"I know what this is about. You are in a snit because I rejected you."

"*Pardon?*"

"I read all about this in my Gramma's handbook. It's your vainglorious, French pride."

"What are you talking about?"

"Don't get so defensive. It's not like you can help it. You just assumed I would mindlessly swoon over you because..."

"Stop."

"... vanity. Which appears to be a sin in every culture except yours."

"Why are you..."

"No fair taking it out on me, just because your ego was shattered. I'm not obligated to kiss you just because you feel superior to me."

Benoît's mouth dropped open as a dozen silent, French swears manipulated his jaw up and down. "Just stop."

"What did I do this time?"

"Stop *French-splaining* my culture to me."

"I'm not doing that. That's not a thing."

"It is now because that it was you are doing. Again."

"Nobody is *French-splaining* anything. Take a valium."

"So you simply know more about me than *me?* You have been in France, what? Five minutes?"

"This is so typical."

"Why don't you just shut your *bouche?*"

"My *boosh* is none of your business!"

Benoît screeched the taxi to a sudden halt, making Courtney thrash backwards in her seat. Stunned, Courtney watched Benoît get out of the car and listened with a cocked head as he went on a French tirade, screaming to himself, uttering a string of French profanities and flailing his arms in the air.

The tirade lasted several minutes.

When Benoît was finished, he got back into the car, slamming the driver's door.

Courtney gaped at Benoît for a long moment.

Benoît revved the motor much too loudly.

"You have something to say?" Benoît asked Courtney through clenched teeth.

Stunned, Courtney shook her head.

"Good," Benoît said as he screeched down the street.

CHAPTER THIRTY-TWO

Courtney had been sleeping in the backseat for what seemed like several hours. Benoît's heart sank into a puddle of guilt as he watched her curled up innocently into a daintily snoring nugget in the backseat. He retraced the moments leading up to his outburst, rethinking every scenario, wondering if he could have concluded their disagreement more amicably.

Benoît was suddenly distracted by the beep of a text on Courtney's phone. He tried to ignore it by remaining focused on the horizon at the end of this seemingly endless country road. But the phone beeped again. And again. Curiosity squeezed Benoît's innards like a juicy, Florida orange. He consciously shook his head. Nope. Courtney's texts were none of his business. But the phone beeped repeatedly in a kind of antagonistic morse code.

Benoît pulled over to the side of the road, gravel crackling under the tires. He reached for the phone in the backseat and making sure Courtney was still dreamily murmuring in her sleep, he snuck a look at some of her incoming texts.

"Worried sick. Please tell me you didn't get into a car with a French maniac. Call me if you're alive"

He scanned a series of other messages.

"You're wasting your time in that European cesspool. Come home."

"Stop embarrassing the family."

"Gramma has filed a missing person's report."

"There is no morality code in Paris."

"Cut your losses and marry Bruce. So what if he groped you?"

"Did Paul get through to you? Use your brain and talk to him."

"Are you dead yet? Gramma and I are placing bets."

"Paris is sketchy. Watch your back."

"Avoid fricassée – contains date rape drug."

"Don't talk to anyone named Maurice."

"Just admit that you are a failure."

Benoît gawked at the phone in disbelief. These people were Courtney's *family?* The ones who nurtured Courtney during her formative years? No wonder Courtney was so cartoonishly insecure. No wonder she had a chip on her shoulder the size of *Mont Pelvoux.* No wonder she had an irrational fear of French hats. Courtney was literally the *least* unhinged member of her family. Pursing his lips guiltily, Benoît quickly deleted every text from Courtney's phone.

***

Groggily, Courtney opened her eyes, realizing the taxi was not moving. She shifted nervously, looking around like an anxious bee that realized all too late that it was trapped inside a soda can. Benoît was gone.

"Benoît?" Courtney screeched in a panic. Shaking, she scrambled out of the deserted taxi, finding herself on a dusty road in the Burgundy countryside, surrounded by endless vineyards.

"Oh my god!" Courtney wailed to herself. "He turfed me!"

Courtney staggered down the desolate street, looking around frantically. "Benoît? Benoît!"

Courtney approached a city limits sign, taunting her with the name *Dijon*.

"Dijon?" Courtney squeaked in despair. She called out in a feeble scream, "Benoît? Benoît, I'm sorry! I'll keep my gob shut for the rest of the drive! I promise! Please don't leave me alone in Mustard Town!"

"Over here," Benoît said, ambling down the street with a paper grocery bag and a rolled up newspaper.

Breathless, Courtney stumbled emotionally towards Benoît, throwing her arms around him as she sobbed unintelligibly. Benoît's body stiffened with surprise, but slowly relaxed when he felt Courtney melting vulnerably in his arms. He enveloped her. "Hungry?" he asked, playfully mussing her hair.

Suddenly realizing in whose arms she had impulsively clothed herself, Courtney sucked in her emotion as convincingly as she could and pulled away. "I thought..."

"You thought I just left you on the side of the road?"

"I.. wouldn't have blamed you. And it wouldn't have been the first time something like that..."

"I did not mean to scare you. We missed lunch so I thought I would let you sleep while I slipped up the street to the market."

"You don't have to be nice to me. We could have just as easily stopped at a petrol station and picked up a bag of Bugles."

"Of course I had to be nice. I am a nice guy. I cannot help myself. The impulse is uncontrollable at times," Benoît smirked, tossing Courtney a fresh baguette. It was still warm from the oven. "There you go. I got your favorite. Baguette. The bread that makes you moan."

"I don't moan."

Benoît giggled.

***

"You honestly thought I would abandon you in the middle of nowhere. In my own taxi."

"Can we let it go now?" Courtney mumbled, embarrassed. "I had just woken up and I was disoriented."

Benoît hesitated. "What did you mean when you said it would not have been the first time someone did that to you?"

"I was dopy with exhaustion. I was speaking gibberish."

"You were so shaken when you thought I was gone."

"I have weird attachment issues. But I'm not comfortable discussing those."

"Drivers make excellent therapists," Benoît offered.

"No they don't. End of story. Full stop."

"Who left you alone?"

Courtney shivered. "That's none of your business."

"I know. But you do not deserve to be hurt. And if nobody else is going to tell you that then I will make it my business to say something."

"You don't know me," Courtney said hoarsely.

"I am trying to know you," Benoît said under his breath.

"Well don't. You're just setting yourself up for disappointment."

"Courtney..."

Courtney's mind whirred in a panic, trying desperately to find a way to change the subject. Her attention zeroed in on Benoît's French speaking GPS device.

"Can you turn that thing off?" Courtney said hastily.

"I can if you want to end up in Kathmandu."

"I don't understand it."

"And I do not understand you. So we are even."

"Nobody understands me," Courtney thought to herself in a huff, curling into a pouty ball.

"Courtney? Do you have anyone else to talk to?"

"About what?"

"About... whatever it is that makes you feel so confrontational."

After a silent pause Courtney replied, "Sure. I have family back home. And..."

The hairs on the back of Benoît's neck bristled as he waited for Courtney to complete her sentence.

"Paul," Courtney said bashfully.

Benoît deflated. "I see."

"What, did you think I was some kind of a social recluse?"

"Of course not. I just..."

"Are you one of those guys who gets all obsessed with girls who they think need to be rescued? Because I don't need to be rescued."

"Courtney, no. I..."

"I have friends. I have a family. I have a... Paul."

"He sounds special," Benoît blinked.

"He is."

"You have known him long?"

"Forever. Well, not literally. Just since school."

"Lucky," Benoît swallowed.

"Yep. It was dumb luck, really. Colby Haven is ridiculously small. There weren't a lot of guys to choose from and they weren't the classiest fellas. Most of the guys didn't really know how to treat a girl, you know? But Paul was okay. He chose me despite everything."

"What do you mean?"

"You know."

"I do not understand," Benoît shook his head in puzzlement.

"Paul stuck with me for six years. That's gotta' count for something."

"And..." Benoît swallowed audibly, "... and he is good to you?"

"Of course he... why would you ask me something like that?"

"It... it would give me great pleasure to know you are happy, Courtney."

Courtney felt a strange, syrupy emotion pour over her, consuming her entire body. *What is up with this guy? Nobody is this nice.*

The next stretch of the drive was eerily silent. Courtney was fixated on her view out the side window, watching endless fields streak by. After an hour or so of dead silence, Courtney suddenly erupted with an explosive epiphany.

"Oh my God!" Courtney screamed. "Stop! STOP! It's an emergency!"

Benoît slammed on the breaks.

"What is happening?" Benoît panted urgently.

"Ideas! Look at them all!"

Courtney grabbed her sketchbook and darted out of the taxi before it came to a complete halt. Benoît craned his neck to see Courtney flailing towards a solitary fig tree in the middle of a vast field. It was swaying in the wind and the leaves were rustling.

Deathly focused, Courtney drew an innovative dress in her book, inspired by the tree. The color and fabric on the bodice swirled in spirals like the blowing leaves. She blended a plethora of greens, all swirling together. The sleeves were textured like the gnarly, sprawling branches. The dress flowed downward like the magnificent trunk, textured with the natural knots and grooves in the bark. She even imitated the pale, yellow sun, illuminating the dress from behind.

From the taxi Benoît watched Courtney thoughtfully.

Courtney's cell phone rang in the backseat, indicating that someone was calling her via Skype video. Benoît watched the phone resentfully. He squinted at the phone, as though trying to stop its ring with his mind. His eyeballs swerved back to Courtney who was obliviously soaked in inspiration outside. It would be a shame to pull her down from her blissful cloud of naturalistic rapture.

Benoît took a deep breath and quickly answered the phone, seeing the grimacing face of Courtney's Gramma on the screen.

"Who the hell are you?" Gramma sneered. "What have you done with Courtney?"

Benoît brewed the most fetching charm he could muster from deep in his soul. *"Bonjour!"* Benoît said in his most bubbly of voices. The bubbles of charisma were Benoît's secret weapon.

"Don't get fresh," Gramma hissed. "Your fancy French vulgarity has no effect on me."

"Excuse me please," said well-mannered Benoît. "Who are you?"

"If you have defiled my granddaughter…"

"What?"

"I know your kind," Gramma said, scrunching her face into a dried fig of revulsion. "The pants. The garlic. The hair product. Coffee in really small cups. You sicken me."

"Would you like me to leave a message or…"

"Put her on," Gramma barked.

"I cannot."

"Goddamit. Did she get herself into some kind of trouble? Honestly, I don't know how that girl dresses herself in the morning."

"Are we talking about the same Courtney?"

"The one with the boring hair, wasted potential and poor judgement? Yep. That's the one."

"I am afraid you have profoundly underestimated her."

"Heh?"

"Courtney has made quite an impression in Paris."

"Lies!"

Benoît's eyes bulged when he saw Courtney returning to the taxi. "I must go."

"Her parents are worried sick about her! Why hasn't she called? Are you holding her against her will?"

"You have no reason to worry. Courtney can take care of herself and French people are trustworthy and cute."

"That's just guff. We want her home where we can keep an eye on her and make sure she doesn't get any more of those nutty ideas about succeeding at things that are hard. We know what's best for her, Frenchie. She's not capable..."

"Do not call again. And please, no more texts. Courtney has no time for such *merde.*"

"Why I oughta'..."

Benoît quickly shut the phone off and tossed it into the backseat before Courtney got back into the taxi.

"Nice tree," Benoît said casually, lolling his eyes innocently.

"Yep," Courtney said, trying to sound cool.

"May I see..."

"Nah, it's dumb."

Benoît looked at Courtney's sketch anyway, despite her nervous wriggling.

"It's not finished," Courtney felt the need to explain. "It's disappointing, really. Not really what I had in my head. It's..."

"Very organic," Benoît said, tilting his head in an analytical way.

"What? No. My little nephew could have done the same thing with his crayons."

Benoît put the car into drive. "That is your opinion."

Courtney took another look at her sketch then squinted curiously at Benoît. "So you're saying…"

"I like it. Is that allowed?"

"But you're not a designer. You don't have the *eye*."

"I have two of them. And they both agree that you have cleverly reinvented the color green."

"But you're a taxi driver. You wouldn't know Italian twill from Italian salad dressing. I… Really? You dig the green, huh?"

Benoît smirked.

"You know, I realized my family hasn't tried to contact me in a while. That's weird."

Benoît hesitated. "Maybe… they do not want to bother you?"

"You don't know these people. They wouldn't stop bombarding me with opinions if they were all unconscious from carbon monoxide poisoning… I should text them."

"Do not do that," Benoît said quickly.

"Why not?"

"Roaming… fees."

"Why are you acting all squirrely?"

"I am not."

"What's going on, Benoît?"

"I just… I just think that perhaps your family has finally come to terms with you living a successful, fulfilling, adventurous life without them. Perhaps they now realize how valuable your time is and they are waiting eagerly for you to squeeze in a phone call updating them on all of your impressive accomplishments. They may be busy bragging to everyone they know about their pride for you."

"No, that's not it."

"But how do you know?"

"I should call…"

"Why?"

"Why should I call my family? Because they are my family. Because if I don't they'll freak out and think I fell in the Seine or was roped into a doomsday cult."

"You will not get good reception out here in the country."

"Benoît…"

"Consider the time difference. They may be asleep. Or doing American things. Or… being asleep."

Courtney scrunched her nose in perplexity then noticed her phone sitting incriminatingly on the seat next to hers. "You…"

"No."

Courtney's jaw dropped in revelation. "You totally deleted the texts from my phone!"

"Absolutely not!"

"Look me in the face and tell me you didn't tamper with my phone!"

"I cannot do that. You see, I am driving..."

"Did someone call? You didn't... did you answer my phone?"

"The things you accuse me of!"

"I thought it was unlike my family to vanish. Those messages were private. My personal phone calls. I can't believe you would do something like this!"

"I..."

"Thank you."

Benoît was agog. "I... what?"

"I didn't really feel like being verbally assaulted today."

"Oh Courtney..."

"It's fine, it's nothing. I'm used to it. They've tried really hard to keep me living in an insular capsule of averageness. Ever since I was three and rode my tricycle two blocks over to Brewster Avenue. I was confined to my nursery for two months, gorging myself with Arrowroot biscuits and binge watching *The Flintstones*."

"Do they not notice how passionate..."

"Fashion is frivolous to them. They don't get it."

"But it is the only thing that matters to you."

"They're just trying to be practical. They don't want to see me fail."

"Forgive me but are they not setting you up for failure?"

"You don't know them, Benoît."

"I do not think I want to know them if they have blinded you to your own worthiness."

"Are you insulting my family?"

"Yes."

"Oh yeah? Well…"

Courtney became distracted when the GPS instructed Benoît to make a turn towards some towering mountains in the distance.

"Whoa," Courtney said, "the sign says that Évian is in the other direction."

"The GPS found a shorter route," Benoît explained.

"But we're straying from the main road."

"The mountain route will save us twenty minutes."

"Are… you sure?"

Benoît smiled. "Trust me"

CHAPTER THIRTY-THREE

The narrow, treacherous, winding, single-lane mountain road was doing a number on Courtney's nervous system. Benoît navigated as best he could despite the taxi's lousy shock absorption and the road's conspicuous lack of guard rails. Every turn was a blind corner. Courtney was frozen in fear, clinging to her seat like a neurotic barnacle.

"We're going to die," Courtney whimpered.

"We are not going to die," Benoît assured her.

"I told you to stay on the main road."

"It is all part of the adventure," Benoît warbled happily, hoping he had adequately hidden the uncertainty in his voice.

Courtney ogled a sign with horror and confusion. "Whoa! What does that sign mean?"

"Falling rocks."

"*Falling rocks?* So this is how it ends."

"Courtney..."

"Keep your eyes on the road!"

Benoît swerved to avoid an oncoming Toyota Camry that was apparently possessed by a speed demon. Dangerously close to skidding off the side of the road, Benoît screeched the car back on course, inspiring a banshee death scream to fly out of Courtney.

"Really?" Courtney said, hugging the seat in front of her for protection and reassurance.

"I kept us alive, did I not?"

"Why are there no freaking guard rails?"

"Look on the bright side!" Benoît generated golden sunshine from his gleaming smile. "We are saving twenty minutes!"

The taxi wobbled ominously as a thundering rumble echoed from outside.

"Oh my god!" Courtney shrieked. "What was that?"

"Relax, Courtney. It is probably nothing."

***

Courtney shivered with consternation as she stood alongside Benoît outside the taxi, gawking at the enormous pile of fallen rocks in front of them.

"Falling rocks," Courtney stated the obvious.

"I am sure it is not as bad as it looks," Benoît said, putting his arm around Courtney's shoulder to calm her nervous shivers. She did not seem to notice or mind this gesture. Perhaps she was too traumatized.

"We're stranded, Benoît! Out in the middle of freaking nowhere!"

"We are not *nowhere,*" Benoît shrugged. "We are just... on a mountain."

"We're blocked in from all sides! Oh my god, what about my fashion event?"

"I will not let you miss it."

"What are you going to do, Benoît? Grow hooves and scale down the side of the mountain like a goat?"

Benoît dug his foot into a rocky crevice and began to climb the daunting rock pile.

"What are you doing?" asked Courtney.

"Finding help."

"You're just going to leave me here?"

"Get what you need from the taxi and come with me. I will help you."

Courtney shook her head in disbelief. "Would it have killed you to stay on the main road?"

***

Benoît was surprisingly agile, an observation that was not wasted on Courtney, who was huffing for breath and throbbing from a twisted ankle. Benoît steadied her by taking her hand as they scaled down the other side of the rockslide, revealing a remote, rural village. Goats and sheep wondered freely in the street. There was a quaint hotel up ahead.

"Well," Courtney said, shaking dust from her disheveled hair, "this is *rural*."

"I see a hotel," Benoît chimed.

"I think I stepped in something," Courtney announced in disgust.

They approached the hotel and watched agape at the scruffy looking people standing in line at the reception desk. It was strangely bustling for a remote town.

"Courtney, it is going to be okay. We will ask about the nearest road out of here."

"This place is so kitsch," Courtney said, looking around uncertainly. Was this entire building made of cork?

"It is not kitsch," Benoît sparkled, "it is quirky."

"That guy over there brought his goat."

"We will not be here long. It is only a slight glitch."

"*Madame, Monsieur?*" Amandine the hotel clerk said, luring the attention of Benoît and Courtney who did not realize they were now next in line. "Do you have a reservation?"

"No," Benoît replied, "we were on our way to Évian..."

"Using GPS?" Amandine winced.

"Told you," Courtney nudged Benoît.

"Our car has been blocked in by falling rocks," Benoît explained. "Can you tell me…"

"You will need a room," Amandine said bluntly. "The entire village has been encased by falling rocks. It will take at least twenty-four hours to dig out a passageway to the road."

"My event is tomorrow," Courtney quavered.

"Like I said," Amandine continued, "I can give you a room."

"Okay," Benoît sighed.

"Two rooms," Courtney said a little too quickly.

"We only have one room available," Amandine winced apologetically. "We are booked solid for the goatherd festival."

"One room?" Courtney turned pale.

"Only the luxury suite is vacant," Amandine shrugged. "I hope that is okay."

"*This* place has a luxury suite?" Courtney said, wrinkling he nose. "What does that even mean?"

"It is identical to all the other rooms," replied Amandine, "but it is more expensive and has imported bedsheets."

"Let's go to another hotel," Courtney said, tugging Benoît's sleeve.

"This is the only hotel," Amandine interjected. "People only come to this village during goatherd festivals and rock slides."

"I will take the room," Benoît said, pulling out his wallet.

"Then where will I stay?" Courtney protested.

"With me," Benoît replied.

Courtney gaped. "I'd rather sleep with the goat."

"You have a better idea?" Benoît asked.

***

With her face smushed into a pillow as she lay sprawled over the grandmotherish bedspread, Courtney let out a muffled moan of defeat. She felt the mattress bounce as Benoît sat down on the bed.

"It is not that bad," Benoît said.

"This bedspread smells like my Uncle Phil," Courtney muffled.

"The room is charming," Benoît said, looking around at the wallpaper adorned with some kind of mountain herb. The weathered, wooden floors were characterized by large knots and telltale scuffs from years of being tread upon. The bed was wedged tightly between a wall and the balcony door. Realistic looking goats goggled at them from several strategically placed, framed paintings around the room. Dim, beige light squeezing through an outdated lampshade made the room glow fuzzily with a kind of retro fug. For reasons unknown the room was making an ambiguous humming sound. "How often do you get to stay in a luxury suite?"

"This is beyond inappropriate. You. Me. In a hotel room."

"Things will remain professional, I promise. I will be nothing if not a gentleman."

"There's one freaking bed and barely enough floor space for a miniature poodle to sleep on. How is this going to work, Benoît? How are we going to keep this professional?"

"Relax, Courtney. We will figure something out."

"This is a nightmare. My event is tomorrow and I'm marooned in a remote village where goats outnumber bipeds. We're going to be stuck here forever," Courtney groaned.

"This could be fun!" Benoît chimed. "We could explore the goatherd festival."

"I'm afraid of goats."

"Goats are cute."

"Their eyes are demonic," Courtney said, unzipping her suitcase. "These paintings are going to give me graphic nightmares."

Benoît did a double take when he spotted a bottle of wine packed carefully between Courtney's faux satin pajamas and her hastily packed unmentionables. "Is that...?"

Courtney gasped a little and tried to hide the bottle under a flirty camisole. "I packed in a hurry. I probably threw in a few things..."

"You said you do not like wine."

"I don't. I just..."

Benoît put his hand out for Courtney to guiltily offer him the bottle.

"The resemblance is uncanny," Courtney explained pathetically. "I don't know why it made me think of you..."

"It *is* me."

"Huh?"

"That is my picture," Benoît said, musing on the bottle in his hands.

"Why is your picture on a bottle of wine?"

Benoît sighed. "It is my creation."

"You make wine? Then why is the brand called *Monique?* Who's Monique and why is her name on your wine? And not to sound repetitive but *you make wine?*"

"I used to," Benoît said nostalgically. "I had my own brand."

"Why are you speaking in the past tense? What happened?"

"Monique happened."

Courtney could not control the emotional bile that gurgled upwards through her esophagus. She was confused as to why the name of another woman instilled such crude jealousy. "Who the eff is Monique?"

"She was a mistake," Benoît said, tossing the bottle onto the cushy bedspread as though it was searing his hands.

"Do you want me to thump her for you?" Courtney asked, grinding her teeth.

Benoît's impulsive snort of laughter sliced through the awkward tension in the room like a warm ice-cream scoop. "Your offer is very kind, Courtney. But I snipped Monique from my life long ago like an infected hangnail."

"What did she do though? How did you know her?"

"She was my fiancée."

Courtney stiffened. "You had a fiancée?"

"A toxic, manipulative one but yes. She applied for a job at my winery…"

"Whoa, you had a winery?"

"I did. I had a small vineyard tucked away in the eighteenth *arrondissment* and a wine shop in *Montmartre* that was always hopping with both tourists and locals. My brand was a favorite among Parisian restaurants and I was something of a minor celebrity," Benoît ribbed.

"So you hired this Monique twat and she ran your business into the ground or something?"

"Well no," Benoît smirked at Courtney's conspicuous jealousy. "She lured me into her conniving web with those piercing green cat eyes. Monique had a mystique, a hypnotic effect on me. She had no experience when I interviewed her but I could tell she was smart. She was struggling to find work and I felt sorry for her. I thought if I gave her a chance…" Benoît lowered his head. "I try to find the good in everybody."

Courtney's heart squeezed like a tight fist.

"However," Benoît sighed, "I was looking so deeply… I suppose I saw only the qualities I wanted to see. There was no goodness in her. Just a deep, dark void."

Courtney's heart sank. "So she was what, using you?"

"I was right about one thing," Benoît nodded. "She was indeed smart. Like a crafty fox. She wanted my vineyard and my brand. Monique knows how to get what she wants... I thought she wanted me. But..."

"Holy smokes," Courtney said, inadvertently edging closer to Benoît. "So you're saying she conned you out of everything you worked for?"

"She slept with a good lawyer and well..."

Courtney's jaw dropped. "Dude. Is she even human or is she a mutation of the Herpes virus?"

Benoît squeezed his eyes, trying to suppress a laugh explosion. "Courtney," he squeaked, "your refreshing splash of vitriol is spoiling the heartbreaking seriousness of my story."

"Did you actually love that evil skank?"

"I..." Benoît hesitated. "...I wanted her love. I wanted it to be so."

Courtney's heart shattered into a million glassy shards when Benoît turned away to hide a tear.

"Was..." Courtney tried, "...was your wine any good?"

Benoît's downturned mouth curled up into a smile. "But of course!"

"Then..." Courtney tentatively handled the wine bottle, "... maybe we should try some?"

***

The balcony was cramped but the view was impressive. Courtney admired the sloping mountainscape as a scalding ball of orange nestled between the hills in an artistic sunset. The goatherds had lit up the village with lanterns for the festival and accordion music was echoing through the mountains.

"You know what would make this view even better?" Courtney asked, taking painfully small sips of wine. "If there were no satanic goats."

Benoît's face gleamed with amusement. "These particular goats mean you no harm," he jibed. "Trust me I am an expert on cloven hooved devils. I lived for three years with a satanic goat."

"Snap!" Courtney laughed, clinking glasses with Benoît. "Ten points, Benoît. Monique, one big rotund zero."

The wine, Courtney decided, was actually quite luscious and velvety. It was much tastier than she expected. From past experiences Courtney gathered that wine was vinegary with a tinfoil aftertaste. Benoît was a wine genius. Who knew? Courtney made a cognizant effort to pace herself. Each sip sent an exhilarating buzz directly to the pleasure sensors in her brain. She was already feeling giddier than usual and her tensions were unravelling like a loosely knit scarf.

"This stuff is good," Courtney said, failing miserably at sipping in a demure fashion.

Benoît blushed as his heart fluttered. "I am flattered. I poured my heart into that wine."

"Ha! Well, in case you were wondering, your heart is pretty damn scrumptious. Oh my god, did I say that out loud?" Courtney laughed. "I think I'm loopy."

Benoît joggled with a quiet chortle. He was preoccupied with the festival lights shimmering in Courtney's oceanic irises. Her smile was dazzling, her laugh infectious. Courtney had a frustrating habit of forbidding herself to smile. Tonight Benoît was in for a rare treat. He was determined to memorize every contour of her mouth as it illuminated with elation. He was not sure when his next opportunity would be to behold such a beauteous moment.

Bliss drained from Benoît's face when Courtney's cell phone rang. Courtney's smile morphed into a pin straight line when she glared at the phone. She threw the phone, cracking the screen.

"Why do they have to ruin every perfect moment..." Courtney sobbed.

"Courtney..."

"I can't answer that, Benoît. They're just going to tell me I can't... I don't deserve..."

"*Chérie...*"

"Why can't my family just be proud of me?"

"I... I am sure they are proud. In their way. Perhaps they express it by annoying you? Perhaps they cannot find the words. Or they are jealous."

"Why is it so exhausting just to squeeze one word of encouragement from the people who are supposed to love me *anyway?*"

Benoît was stumped. The only thing he could think to do was to offer Courtney more wine. Courtney took a desperate swig.

"I've got so much riding on this trip. Fashion Week. This event tomorrow. Oh God! What if we're wedged in this avalanche forever and I miss everything?"

Courtney passed her glass to Benoît to refill.

"I just wanted to make them proud. I know I'm kind of pathetic. They've made that clear. But I thought if I tried hard enough... But no matter how hard I... I'm such a loser... Unrefined and I don't seem to fit in anywhere. Maybe I don't deserve..."

Benoît watched Courtney as she chugged her wine. Then he carefully examined the wine in his own glass. "Funny thing about grapes," Benoît said observantly. "When you harvest them from the vineyard, the color of the grape can be deceiving. This is because color can change before the grape is fully ripe and ready to be plucked."

Courtney cocked an eyebrow.

"You must *taste* it," Benoît said, involuntarily licking his lips. "As the grape matures, the acidity decreases and it becomes sweeter. Benoît moved closer to Courtney. "Warmth makes the grapes grow sweeter but when grown in a cold climate the grape becomes a little tart."

Courtney sprayed wine in a fountain of laughter. "You said *little tart.*"

Benoît moved closer to Courtney. "Grapes with more *skin* will produce a *richer* more *velvety* texture and *intense* flavor."

Courtney's eyes met Benoît's and stuck there like an intense laser beam. Benoît put a glass to Courtney's lips. "Sip," he coaxed. "*Deep. Full-Bodied. Vigorous. Flavors stimulating every taste bud in your mouth. Cherry. Pepper. Tobacco. Leather and a hint of wood.*"

Courtney swallowed hard with beads of sweat forming under her hairline.

Benoît breathed. "So soft. Supple. Fleshy."

"Wow," Courtney croaked.

Benoît put a glass of wine beneath Courtney's nostrils. "It smells like desire, *oui?* Light, perfumed red. Tempting raspberries. Robust plums. Hints of damp earth…"

Courtney impulsively grabbed Benoît and kissed him passionately. She smushed her face so deeply into his, it caused them to both involuntarily grunt with ecstasy. Benoît tasted like oaky, peppery fruit. Yum. But dammit, what was she doing? Courtney pulled away abruptly. "I think I made a mistake," Courtney panicked.

"No, that was very good."

"That kiss didn't count."

"Didn't count?"

"It's this stupid, romantic mountain. It's making me lose control of my…" Courtney kissed Benoît even more passionately. "… actions. It's the ambiance. And the wine. And the lanterns. And accordion music. And that completely unfair crescent moon."

"Courtney…"

"I didn't come here to…" Courtney and Benoît kissed even more passionately. "… kiss a desirable…"

"I'm desirable?" Benoît dimpled proudly.

"Stop it! I'm drunk!"

"What if I want to kiss you again?"

"That would be..." Courtney grabbed Benoît's face with aggressive lust and pressed her lips desperately against his. "... dumb. I didn't come to France to find love. I came here to find my future."

Benoît was startled when Courtney farcically jumped him, causing them both to topple over clumsily. Benoît somehow ended up on top of Courtney.

"What am I doing?" Courtney wailed.

"Do I really need to explain?"

"I don't do things like this with foreigners!"

"Says the girl with the French guy on top of her."

"Just so we're clear, I get the bed tonight and you sleep in the bathtub."

CHAPTER THIRTY- FOUR:
(DAY 38)

Askew, Benoît and Courtney awkwardly lay in bed together, mangled in tangled sheets. Sunlight of a new day teased them through the sheer curtains.

"So um..." Courtney said after an awkward beat, "...so you made that wine yourself?"

"Did you enjoy it?"

"Yeah. It uh... it was really good *wine.*"

Another awkward beat.

"I should just..." Courtney said quickly, scrambling to wrap herself like a sheet taco, "... I need to be somewhere that's not here."

"Courtney, wait..."

"Dude, what we did is a serious faux pas."

"You have spoken French!" Benoît cheered. "Such is my girl! I am so proud of you!"

"Benoît, my God!"

"I was *that* good?" Benoît smirked proudly. "You are most welcome, Courtney."

"Benoît, we made a mistake. We were *drunk*. Can't you see that this never should have happened?" Courtney hid her face in a pillow. "I have a guy at home. What have I done?"

Benoît lolled his eyeballs downward in disappointment. "I regret nothing."

Courtney whimpered. "Benoît, I'm not trying to hurt your feelings. It's just... we can't do this."

"Why?" Benoît rasped.

"You don't want me. You have no idea what you'd be signing up for. Besides, Paul..."

"Have you spoken with him since you arrived in France?"

"Not really. I mean sort of. He was pixilated."

"You have not been talking to him at the end of every day? Eagerly telling him of all your adventures?"

"Not really."

"That is what I would be doing."

"Yes, because you're basically perfect. Not everybody can live up to your standards."

"Can we at least try..."

"You're not my type."

"You said I am basically perfect. Basically perfect is not your type?"

"No!"

"Forgive me, but you made the first move. I was innocently enjoying the scenery and describing my winemaking process when you jumped me like an amorous puma."

"I'm not exactly famous for my good judgement."

"Courtney, please be honest with me. Why did you ask me to drive you to Évian…"

"I told you. Because…"

"… when you are scared nearly to death of the consequences?"

"I needed a ride and you had nothing else to do for the rest of the summer…"

"And you let me show you around Paris. Why?"

"I have an unreliable sense of direction."

"You risked everything."

"I'm impulsive."

"If you tried hard enough you could have found another way to get to Évian. Why me?"

"Don't ask me…"

"Courtney…"

"I needed my Benoît fix," Courtney said quickly.

Benoît slithered closer to Courtney on the bed. Damn, these upgraded bedsheets were satiny. "So I am not so repulsive to you?"

"Don't' read into things. I needed someone familiar. I freak out less with you around. Now can you please put on some pants?"

Courtney's phone vibrated.

"Ah frig," Courtney panted as she noticed an incoming Skype call. "It's Paul. Hide."

Courtney shoved Benoît under the bedspread, covered her torso with a sheet and answered, trying not to sound frazzled. "Paul."

"You look like death," Paul said bluntly.

Courtney kicked Benoît under the blanket when he grunted at Paul's opening remark.

"Did you just grunt?" Paul asked.

"Yes," Courtney lied.

"Why do you look like that?"

"I had a bad dream. About goats."

Courtney kneed Benoît under the covers for snickering.

"I've been trying like mad to get in touch with you."

"I know, Paul. I'm sorry. I…"

"What's so important that you couldn't take my calls?"

"I've got stuff to do, Paul. I'm working."

"I need you to come home."

"I can't come home, Paul. Fashion Week…"

"That lasts what, like a week?"

"That's why they call it Fashion Week, Paul."

"We've got some important things to talk about, Babe. Long term plans."

"What about P…"

"I'm done with her. She served her purpose. She made me look good while I climbed the cheese ladder. My business has a good foundation now. I can support you."

"Why all of a sudden…"

"What's the deal with Bruce?"

"I don't want to talk about…"

"I don't like the idea of the two of you horsing around."

"We're not…"

"Have you been going around behind my back?"

"He tried to do nasty things to my jugs, Paul. It wasn't my fault."

"Did you tell him about me?"

"You…" Courtney chose her words carefully, being mindful of Benoît's presence. "You weren't around, Paul."

"Had I known someone else was trying to get his talons in you…"

"This isn't really a good time," Courtney tried not to laugh as Benoît was doing something under the sheets that tickled her feet.

"What is it with you? Do you think you're better than me because you spent some time in Paris? What, are you all cultured now? Too good for Colby Haven?"

"Paul, don't…"

"What about little Declan? And Dash? He was supposed to be the one that looks like you."

Courtney was suddenly pulled under the covers by a blanketed mound of Benoît. "Okay bye!" Courtney said rapidly as she slid under the blankets.

"Who are Declan and Dash?" Benoît asked. "And why does Dash look like you?"

"They're our kids, Paul's and mine."

"You have *kids?*"

"Hypothetical ones."

"You plan to make babies with such a..."

"Don't."

"Did you not hear the way he spoke to you?"

"He's a real person, Benoît. A normal guy. That's how normal guys talk."

"I am quite normal and I would never say such things to you..."

"Benoît..."

"... because you are perfect."

"Stop laying it on so thick, Benoît. You and I both know that's not true."

"So Paul, he is your *type?*"

"Can we not talk about this under a blanket fort? *Naked?*"

"You enjoy men who tell you that you look like the plague?"

"Death. He said I look like death. Get your facts straight."

"*Oh mon dieu.*"

"There's no need to swear."

"But you don't deserve…"

"Stop idealizing me, Benoît. You said yourself that you try to see the good in people even when the good is not there."

"This is not the same."

"I said no!" Courtney said a little louder than she intended as she swaddled herself in a sheet and stumbled out of the room.

CHAPTER THIRTY-FIVE

The mountain pass was dark at night and Courtney was grateful that she did not have to look at Benoît's expression as he drove. Her lungs heaved in relief when the hotel alerted them that the roads had been cleared enough to form a safe passageway through the rocks. Courtney had enough time to doll herself up in preparation and hop into the taxi – avoiding Benoît's yearning glances. They would arrive at the château with fifteen minutes to spare.

Benoît made sure he kept the remarks to a minimum when Courtney appeared in the taxi wearing a dress that complimented her dainty frame. He assumed that she made the dress herself. She made beautiful things. But for the sake of decorum, Benoît kept a mental inventory of all the flatteries he wanted to grant Courtney. But he held them privately like a winning hand of poker. The drive to the château was only forty-five minutes but the suffocating glop of silent awkwardness in the cab made it feel like several hours.

"*Château Lemieux,*" Benoît said with his usual panache, but quieter.

Courtney caught a glance of Benoît diverting his eyes from Courtney's well-prepared dazzle. She would be lying if she denied feeling a sinking sensation when her glance was not met with one of Benoît's doting, twinkly smiles. He inhaled deeply.

"Okay," Courtney exhaled, "so if you could just park..."

"Around at the back to avoid being seen."

"I might be late."

"I brought reading material," Benoît said, waving a rolled up newspaper.

Courtney nodded and let herself out of the cab. She traipsed up the walkway to the opulent château, looking back a few times at Benoît who had turned on a reading light in his dark taxi. Courtney silently wished that she had been granted a plus one to this shindig.

As Courtney approached the grand entrance of the château her feet froze to the stone walkway. Panic gripped her throat. Her breath sounded raspy and desperate. How could she have agreed to do something like this by herself? She lacked the social graces to mingle with people in high places. She did not splurge for a formal gown. What if she was embarrassingly underdressed? What if she passed out or barfed on Ralph Lauren? She felt like a fool for thinking she could handle herself in such a lofty situation and wished so badly that she had someone to put a calming hand on her shoulder to reassure her that she was not a completely hopeless dud.

She quickly glanced behind her but Benoît had already obediently parked out of sight.

"Bonsoir," a tuxedoed gent said, causing Courtney to spin around, gasp and gag on her own insecurities.

"Ugh..." Courtney choked.

"Bride or groom?" the cordial gent said, correctly guessing what language was fluent for Courtney.

"What do you mean?" Courtney said, stiffening like a starched shirt.

"Are you here for the bride or the groom?"

"I'm here for the…"

"Leroux, Hubert wedding?"

"What, no. I'm here for the fashion thing. I'm Courtney Stent."

The tuxedoed gent blinked.

"You don't know about the…" Courtney panicked. "Oh my god. Uh… am I at the *La Meow Castle*? Ralph Lauren is supposed to be here. And a bunch of others…"

"I am afraid none of that is happening, *Madame*."

"There must be some kind of a misunderstanding," Courtney said with her voice drifting away like a feather-light fairy floating to another realm. "This venue has been booked for a…"

"I am sorry. The misunderstanding is yours."

"No," Courtney quavered. "It can't be. I'm supposed to be here, I swear. Is this some kind of a practical joke?"

"Please do not make a scene. It is not fair to Lizette. This is her special day."

"Can… can I at least stay a while so my driver…"

"Private event," said the gent, closing the door in Courtney's face.

***

With the driver's seat reclined and with his legs crossed and lounging on the dash, Benoît unrolled his newspaper, preparing for a long, fork-in-the-eye-boring wait. He felt a sudden wave of nausea when he noticed a large photograph of Alexandria Fontrose on the front cover. Her hand was prominently staving the photographer away from her face to avoid recognition. But her flamboyant up-do, overly manicured fingers, gaudy jewelry and faux fur collar made her easy to recognize. Benoît gaped at the article, his eyeballs rapidly scanning each word. He startled when Courtney appeared like a flash storm in the front seat of the taxi. She heaved with uncontrollable sobs.

"Courtney..."

"Drive," Courtney sobbed.

"What happened?"

"I don't want to talk about it. Just drive me back to my sketchy hotel in Paris."

"Do you need to change or..."

"I just want to go. Please just go."

Benoît nodded, gaping at Courtney. His heart felt like a deep sinkhole. He wanted to do something comforting but he was not sure what the current rules were. As far as he could tell, any form of flattery, touch or empathy would be strictly forbidden. And yet here she was seated in the front of the taxi. Did she even realize she was sitting in the front seat with him?

"Why are you not probing me for details?" Courtney snuffed.

"I am allowed?"

"You're slipping," Courtney whimpered. "I figured you'd be all over this since you seem incapable of minding your own business."

"Are you okay?"

"I told you, I don't want to talk about it. But since you brought it up, no. No, I am not okay. I am the opposite of okay. This is the worst goddam night of my life. And that's all I'm going to say about the matter because it's private."

Benoît nodded.

"Except to say that I'm an idiot for thinking anyone would think I was special enough to make me the guest of honor at a nonexistent formal."

"Nonexistent?" Benoît did a double take.

"I actually believed Ralph Lauren wanted to meet me. How dunderheaded am I?"

"I am trying to understand, there was *no* formal gathering tonight at the château?"

"Lizette's wedding was there. But they wouldn't even let me stay for that at least, after I drove all the way from Paris and survived an avalanche to get there. Stupid Lizette. Stupid, selfish Lizette."

"The château was booked for a wedding. So no fashion goings-on whatsoever..."

"I am so humiliated. I just don't get it. Why would Dree send me all the way to Évian…"

"I am so sorry, Courtney. I take no pleasure in being right."

"Excuse me?"

"Courtney, she invented an elaborate lie and sent you on a long, redundant road trip with false transportation arrangements. Surely you can see…"

"I have to believe that this whole thing is just a massive misunderstanding. I just have no idea…"

Benoît tossed the newspaper to Courtney.

"What's this?" Courtney asked.

Benoît nudged towards the front page.

Courtney gaped at the article for a moment, color slowly draining from her face.

"They say she has not come up with an original idea in three years," Benoît said evenly. "She has resorted to reinventing her own stale designs from years past. Recycling them like old tuna cans."

"It's fake news," Courtney said hoarsely, stashing the paper in the glove box.

"She is not the designer she used to be, Courtney."

"So? She's in a slump. It happens to all kinds of artists."

"Forgive me, but do you not think it odd that such a big potato would have time for a humble contest? Stay in such a medium hotel? Take an interest in a fashion virgin?"

"Okay, first of all, it's none of your business what size potato Dree is. Secondly, don't say *virgin*. And why is it so hard to grasp that someone at her level would believe in me?"

"She is not who you think she is."

"She is my friend. Maybe my only friend."

Benoît bit his lip.

"Dree is literally the only person in the world who believes in me, Benoît."

Benoît pursed his lips and shook his head in disbelief. "What am I doing wrong?"

"What? Nothing. I mean I don't get why you refuse to pronounce the letter H..."

"How can I take this as anything but insulting?"

"What did I do now?"

"I have done nothing but try to be your friend. I am obsessed with your talent, Courtney. *Obsessed.* I have preserved your dignity like the world's very last jar of delicious, bergamot marmalade. Not once have I violated your trust and yet you blindly trust a woman who lies to you? Manipulates and deceives you? Abuses you?"

"That's not fair! Dree is always building me up..."

"... only to keep knocking you back down. She sucks you in with her plastic charm and her buttery compliments into her vortex of malice. Then she puts ideas of worthlessness into your mind."

Courtney deflated like a popped balloon. She noticed Benoît mashing a tear with a palm in his eye socket. "You…" she stammered. "…you're not… wrong."

"I just do not understand why you keep defending her."

"You called it, Benoît. You tried to warn me. But I… I just wanted… My family was right. I was naïve to think I could make it in Paris."

"Courtney, no."

"I can't believe I fell for this elaborate farce…"

"Courtney, of all the entrants, Alexandria picked *you*."

"She must have sensed my lack of street smarts."

"I do not believe that."

"Then you're just as naïve as I am."

"I do not think you are naïve," Benoît hesitated. "I just think that you need to be adored."

"That's lame."

"May I ask… Why Paul?"

"Good grief."

"Why do you gravitate towards people who…"

"Why are you changing the subject?"

"Actually, I am not. These subjects are one and the same. You seem drawn to people who verbally assault you…"

"That's not true."

"...when there is someone who genuinely..."

"Nope. You're reading into things."

"Can't you see what you are doing? You only trust people who hurt you."

"I don't do that."

"You do."

"I don't."

"Courtney..."

"I don't do things like that..." Courtney spat. *"Do I?"* she thought secretly.

"What about your monosyllabic, American boyfriend?" Benoît grunted.

"You can't know what a guy's like based on one Skype call you heard from under a blanket. Paul isn't always a jerk like that. Paul is nuanced."

Benoît hummed in disbelief.

"Paul is a pretty good catch. He's employable. He has cool eyelids. Decent taste in shirts. He once won me this huge, purple hippopotamus stuffy at the Curd Fair..."

"When is the last time you saw him?"

"What?"

"You are not formally together, are you."

"That is none of your..."

"Who is this other woman? What is a cheese ladder?"

"Yeesh. Okay, fine. Paul dumped me over a year ago..."

"I thought you said..."

"Let me finish. He and Paulette were... well, you know."

"While you were still together?"

"It happens. Anyhow, Paul has been trying to track me down..."

"Because of Bruce?"

"Yes. I mean no!"

"Who is Bruce?"

"The octopus who tried to steal my cookies."

"WHAT?"

"That's irrelevant. Now about Paul..."

"Did you give Bruce permission to..."

"Of course not. It was forceful. Bruce is a knuckle dragging savage with no scruples. Now Paul..."

"... is only interested in you because he thinks another man wants you."

"You're not paying attention..."

"Paul thinks of you as property. The idea of someone taking what is his..."

"You don't even know the guy. Now about Bruce... I mean Paul..."

"How do your parents feel about someone trying to forcefully pluck your geranium?"

"I... what?"

"Bruce."

"The parental units dig Bruce. They want us to get hitched."

"And Paul?"

"They think Paul is too good for me."

"*Oh mon dieu.*"

"You're not getting the context here. Back home I'm considered an old maid. Most girls get married straight after grad, or before if they get knocked up. I found myself a guy who digs me and it's time for me to consider settling down."

"You mean *settling.*"

"Paul and I had big plans. We were going to live in a craftsman bungalow on Hops Avenue with our brood of littles and a dog named Biff. Maybe a goldfish. Neither of us wanted to commit to that right away. We picked a property on the remote outskirts of Colby Haven, across the swamp to discourage my family from visiting. Everything was all planned – from our kitchen backsplash to our preferred family vehicle. Soul Red Mazda, in case you were wondering. We were well on our way to familial bliss until Paulette lured him away with her funky French cheese."

"Wait, Paulette is French?"

"Why do you think Paul couldn't resist her?"

Benoît smirked.

"Now about Paul. I wasn't very popular in school so when the captain of the curling club... shut up... when he asked me to the Squeaky Cheese Formal in the ninth grade..."

"Stop."

"This is the important part."

"Do you not see what you are doing? You are defending someone who treats you with disrespect. A person who causes you pain. Do you not see a pattern forming here?"

"No, no pattern. Paul is a good guy."

"He is emotionally abusive. He uses women to get what he wants."

"Look. My town is extremely small and the options are limited. Paul isn't perfect but I could have done a whole lot worse. Chad who talks to the radiator. Bartholomew with all the ferrets. Shane with the gasoline fume addiction. Bruce... "

"There is a whole world to explore, Courtney. You are not limited to the miscreants in your dysfunctional little village."

"It's... it's all I know."

Benoît closed his eyes empathetically.

"Benoît, is this your way of trying to hit on me?"

Benoît bit his lower lip hard. "Of course not. You have made your choice and I respect that."

Courtney formed a silent letter O with her lips, somewhat disappointed.

"All I want for you, Courtney, is to see yourself the way... the way others see you."

"People mostly think I'm a freak so..."

"That is only your perspective because you have lived your life surrounded by people who cannot see the beauty in things. Your family..."

"They are just trying to look out for me. They know me better than anyone and..."

"Do they though?"

"... they don't want me to be disappointed. They are honest with me. It hurts but at least I have people who worry about me. I'm not the easiest person to love. Now Chastity was always the easy one. I mean, uncomplicated. I'm not trying to say my sister is easy."

"You have a sister?"

"I mean it's obvious why Chastity is their favorite. She's successful, a mom, married sort of, lives under her own roof, makes pie. Really good pie, actually. And my folks keep reminding me that she's the pretty one. Which is weird because we're identical twins..."

"Are you jealous?"

"Me?" Courtney fake laughed. "Nah! Chastity is so boring. Beige. Annoying. Nothing excites her. Not even pie. I don't want to be snagged into a life like hers."

"Did it ever occur to you that your sister is the jealous one?"

"Of what? Me? Are you on glue?"

"Why not?" Benoît shrugged. "You are talented, funny, ambitious, adventurous, adorable…"

"Knock it off," Courtney blushed.

"I do not wish to, as you say, *knock it off,*" Benoît chuckled. "Meeting you this summer has been my favorite thing."

Courtney bit her lip. "Glad this summer's been working out for you because it has been a colossal poop storm for me." Courtney caught a disappointed gleam in Benoît's eye so she quickly recovered. "What with my dreams vaporizing, thrusting me into a mediocre life of being held against my will in an illegally renovated basement with asbestos in the walls."

"What do you mean?"

"This was my big break, Benoît. And it has been a colossal joke, one of which I am the butt. This whole experience has taught me that only the very lucky, the very rich and the very plastic can ever make it in this godawful industry. Chass was right. I don't fit in here."

Benoît squinted in scrutiny. "That is not the spitfire girl that I fell in…"

Courtney nearly gave herself whiplash as she rapidly turned her head towards Benoît who was now gaping at her.

"You are not a quitter," Benoît said, recovering. "You have tenacity. You have spunk. You are the feistiest girl I have ever met. You do not have it in you to give up on what you fall asleep thinking about every night and wake up inspired by each morning."

"It's a bust, Benoît. I'm out."

"*Mais non!*" Benoît said with wide eyes. "You did not come all the way here to turn back home in defeat."

"Dree…"

"She is meaningless. You did not come here because of her. You came here because your destiny led you here. You are prepared, Courtney. You have your beautiful garments into which you have poured your soul and essence."

Courtney exhaled. "So you're saying I should just go to Fashion Week."

"That is why you came to Paris in the first place, *non?* Courtney, this is your chance to show your family and Paul that you were born to be a designer. Nobody can take this from you."

"How am I supposed to…"

"You will figure it out."

"I have nothing appropriate to wear."

"What about the dress you are wearing now?"

"I can't wear this. It's not glamorous enough. I'll look like a spaz."

"You made that dress with your own hands. It is an original. It is…"

"I didn't think this through, wearing my own lousy designs. I thought this dress would do until I got here and saw how ostentatiously everyone in the industry dresses. I'll never be taken serious wearing this rag."

"You could buy a gown."

"With what? Dresses like that are expensive. Do you expect me to barter? Trade my soul? Offer the store clerk a handful of acorns and hope they accept it as currency?"

Benoît mused.

"I don't think I can do this," Courtney sighed.

Benoît disagreed.

CHAPTER THIRTY-SIX
(DAY 39 IN PARIS)

The sky was yellowing from the groggy sunrise when Benoît pulled the taxi up to the front entrance of Courtney's hotel. He blinked the drowsiness out of his eyes before turning to find Courtney sound asleep in the seat next to his. A long, drooly strand of hair was snagged in her open mouth. He nudged her.

"Courtney."

Courtney sleep-grunted.

"We have arrived."

Courtney dopily raised her head and squinted sleepily at Benoît. "Why am I in the front seat?" she said in a sleepy rasp.

Benoît shrugged.

"I think I'll be sleeping most of the day," Courtney said, stretching. "Take the day off or something."

Benoît looked down. "Okay."

"Thanks for the ride, man," Courtney yawned, lugging her bags out of the taxi and heading for the hotel.

***

The door was ajar.

Confused, Courtney edged her way into her hotel room, hoping to heck she had walked in on the cleaners. What she saw made her utter a guttural shriek. Her room had been ransacked and trashed. Curtain rods had been pulled down. The drawers were mindlessly thrown open. The mattress had been overturned and the television set was screen-down on the floor, smashed.

Panic-stricken, Courtney scoured the room, finding nothing but torn carpet, empty closet, empty drawers, empty medicine cabinet, empty toothbrush cup. Even the safe had been cracked open and was conspicuously missing Courtney's semi-valuables. An object had been thrown through the balcony window, leaving a terrifying shatter.

"Oh my god!"

***

"They took all my personal belongings!" Courtney said to a police officer. She was literally shaking. "Everything I brought with me, minus the one change of clothes I took with me to Évian. They took my jewelry, my facial creams that I spent a small fortune on, my cheese pencil. My lucky duck. They even took all my clothes. Why would they take my clothes?"

Jacques burst into the room, concern plastered to his face like extremely worried stucco. "What has happened?" he panted. "Is she okay?" Jacques made a beeline towards Courtney, placing his hands firmly on her arms and trying to make eye contact. "Are you okay?"

Courtney was too dazed to reply.

"Did you see anyone suspicious enter the building in the past twenty-four hours?" an officer asked Jacques.

"No, *Monsieur.*"

"Nobody at all?" the officer asked while scribbling something on a notepad. "Someone who should not have been here?"

"I promise," Jacques said, crossing his heart. "Everyone who has come through the door today and yesterday I knew by name."

"They took my passport," Courtney quavered. "Oh my god, and my credit cards. I put them in my purple chemise for safekeeping. I miss my purple chemise. I only have about thirty Euros that I brought with me on my road trip. I can't survive the next month on thirty Euros. Oh my god, this can't be happening!"

"*Madame,*" an officer said firmly, "you need to calm down."

"I was burgled!" Courtney blasted. "All my stuff's gone!"

"We are doing our best," the officer assured her.

"We need to cordon off the apartment for investigation. Jacques, you should call your insurance agents. This will take a while to repair. Courtney, do you have somewhere else to stay?"

Courtney turned imploringly to Jacques.

"Oh dear," Jacques said, running his fingers nervously through his hair. "We are booked solid for the next month. Fashion Week."

Anguish contorted Courtney's face into that of a Picasso character.

***

Courtney burst out of the hotel, sobbing and flailing with hot tears rolling vertically across her face from the frantic cross-breeze she was creating with her sprint. She did not know where she was running or what she was going to do. Her mind was fizzing with confusion and fear and her only lucid thought was of Benoît. She had to find him. When her lungs began to ache and constrict from too much exertion, Courtney stopped by a fig tree and rummaged through her purse. Panic clutched her throat when she could not find her phone.

"Oh god, no!" Courtney sobbed.

Courtney hailed a string of taxis, asking every driver if they knew Benoît. She was unsuccessful. She begged for metro money on the street. The whole city seemed to spin around her causing her to wobble and stagger down the streets without any sense of direction. If only she could find Benoît, his calming energy would make her heart stop dangerously speeding. Where did he live? Damn! Why did Courtney insist on keeping things so professional? Otherwise maybe Benoît would have mentioned his address or invited her over or...

Wait a minute. If Courtney could not find Benoît, there was always another option – and she knew exactly where to find him.

***

"Étienne!" Courtney wailed as she stumbled towards the open-air shop.

"Courtney?" Étienne startled.

"Where is Benoît?" Courtney cried. "I have to find Benoît!"

"He is not here," Étienne said sympathetically. "I spoke with him on the phone a couple of hours ago and he said he had something to do today."

"What?" Courtney spat. "What is he doing that's so important?"

"He did not say. Dear Courtney, are you okay?"

"NO!" Courtney was hysterical. "I was robbed! Everything's gone! All my nice clothes! My toothbrush! My lucky duck! Passport, credit cards, everything! I had to beg like a vagrant for a metro pass!"

"Oh, my fragile yet fragrant crêpe myrtle," Étienne said, folding Courtney's quivering body against his. "How you tremble! Come, let me comfort you in my firm arms."

"What am I going to do?" Courtney sobbed into his chest.

"Shhh," Étienne soothed. "Étienne will let no harm come to you."

"It's my own damn fault! The one time I put my guard down. The one time I trust..."

"Surely you do not blame my cousin for your misadventures."

"It was his idea to drive all the way to Évian despite the fact that Dree was clearly up to something... No wait, that was me. But still! If he didn't make me WANT him to drive me..."

"You are not thinking clearly. Benoît would never hurt you. This has nothing to do with him."

"Do you have a way to get in touch with Benoît? I need him... I mean I need his help."

Étienne held a finger up to assure Courtney that he would have Benoît on the phone momentarily. He bit the side of his mouth as the phone rang repeatedly. "He is not answering."

"I don't believe this."

Étienne left a message on Benoît's machine in French which frustrated Courtney. He shut off his phone, prompting a sigh of anxiety to waft out of Courtney. "I have told him to meet us here as soon as he picks up his messages."

Courtney put her face in her hands.

Étienne sat next to her on the sidewalk. "You can stay here until he arrives, okay?" He gave her anxious, balled-up fist a reassuring squeeze.

"You don't have to..."

"You are family, sweet Courtney."

"No I'm not."

"But of course you are," Étienne said, mussing Courtney's hair. "You have made my cousin happy."

"He's always happy."

"You have given him a great gift, Courtney. You have inspired him to love again. That is something I thought he would never have the courage to do. I love you for that. That makes you a Garnier from now on. Okay? At Christmastime remember that I take a size medium shirt."

"Benoît is lucky," Courtney swallowed.

"Indeed he is lucky to have such a beguiling woman in his company," Étienne winked.

"No, I mean... he has a nice... family. You guys are really close, aren't you? It must be wonderful."

Étienne's eyes glossed with sentiment right before he squeezed the bejesus out of Courtney. "Awww," he gushed. "Let me give you a big, cousinly squish!"

"That just sounds wrong," Courtney muffled from inside Étienne's hug.

* * *

Heads turned at the sound of an urgently slamming taxi door.

"Courtney!" Benoît yowled as he jogged towards Étienne's shop.

Courtney's heart slowed to a non-life-threatening pace and her eyes glowed with familiarity. "Where were you?" she asked in a tone that did not sound as angry as she had hoped. She impulsively hugged him, surprising Benoît with a lingering squeeze.

"I thought you gave me the day off. Étienne told me what happ…"

"Cousin!" Étienne gushed. "There is a spring in your step! Such a piquant gleam in your eye and the feverish flush of passion in your cheek! The rigid tendons in your neck have unraveled like a cheap sweater and your coy dimple tells a dirty, little secret."

Benoît and Courtney gaped at Étienne as though they had literally been caught in mid-dirty secret.

"Wow," Courtney managed. "That was graphic."

"Étienne, please…"

"I am so proud of you, Benoît!"

Courtney mouthed the words *Did you tell him?* Benoît shook his head rapidly.

"Courtney," Étienne said, winking at her, "you are now entitled to a discount I grant only to immediate family. Anyone who Benoît deflowers is like my sister."

"Is there any way you can un-say that?" Courtney said queasily.

Benoît put his arm around Courtney and guided her to his taxi. "Étienne told me about the robbery. You are staying with me."

Courtney wanted to protest but a fluttery sensation in her stomach overruled it.

"Please do not argue," Benoît said.

"She does not appear to be arguing, Cousin," Étienne winked.

"My space is small but we will make due," Benoît continued. "Thank you, Étienne, for entertaining her."

"It was my pleasure!" Étienne said. "She gave me some sage advice about my hideous inventory."

"She…" Benoît began.

"She is a smart cookie, Benoît," Étienne said confidentially. "Hold on to her. Tightly."

CHAPTER THIRTY-SEVEN

Courtney's stomach dipped as she followed Benoît into his apartment. Her eyes wandered the room, mesmerized by the otherwise underwhelming space. She scoured the living area. He did not have a couch. Everything was very clean and tidy but quite squishy for American standards. Even so, she felt safe. This little hovel felt like a haven to Courtney. Like walking into a hug.

Benoît spun around animatedly, spreading his arms. *"Voilà!"*

"It's nice," Courtney said, dropping her overnight bag containing her only remaining possessions. "This main room here looks kind of empty though. Why don't you have a couch?"

"I…" Benoît said, lolling his eyes, seemingly in search of an answer. "I… saw no need for one since I work such long hours. I come home and then plop right into bed. See? No couch."

Courtney nodded uncertainly.

"Are you okay?" Benoît asked, putting a hand on Courtney's shoulder.

"I'm not sure about this."

"You have nowhere else to stay. You have no money. I am most happy to…"

"What if we see each other naked?" Courtney blurted out.

Benoît pursed his lips mischievously, unsuccessfully forcing back a giggle that made Courtney blush. "Courtney, that ship has already sailed."

"Okay fine. But accommodations are only part of the issue. Those crooks stole my lucky duck." Courtney threw her arms up in defeat. "Great. No lucky duck. Now we're all going to die."

Benoît held the lucky duck out in the palm of his hand. *"Voilà.* You left him in my taxi. And also your phone."

"My... my duck and my... phone?" Courtney stammered emotionally. She was fighting back tears. "But what am I going to do about clothes for the next few weeks? I can't afford..."

"I can help you out with that."

"But...

"Oh!" Benoît chimed, "I almost forgot. I have been given instructions to give you something."

Courtney craned her neck to see what Benoît was bringing her from the other room.

"What's this?" Courtney asked, looking at a garment bag.

"It is part of your prize package. The contest organizers wanted you to have it before Fashion Week."

Courtney tentatively unzipped the garment bag and then let out a little gasp. Inside was a glittering, scarlet evening gown. It was an elegantly slender fit with a thigh-high slit and had an ethereal, frothy train. Courtney blinked at the sparkles. A pair of perfectly matched, glittery red shoes made her part her lips with wonder.

"Is it suitable?" Benoît asked eagerly.

"I… I could never wear this."

"But it is part of the prize package. You earned it, Courtney."

"I've never worn anything like that before."

"Imagine how wearing such a dress would make you feel."

"But Fashion Week…"

"You are going, *oui?* You must seize this opportunity."

"I can't."

"You have a dress so you are pretty much committed to it now."

"No, it's impossible to go…"

"Were your garments stolen in the robbery? The ones intended for your show?"

"Thankfully, no. Someone was sent to pick them up from me at my studio just before the road trip to Évian."

"Then?"

"I won't fit in. I'll be conspicuous. Everyone will know I don't belong there."

"You will never forgive yourself if you do not try. And clearly someone still believes in you if they sent you this dress for your big show."

"You think the contest organizers still think I can pull this off?"

"I do. And you now have this dress to prove your worthiness."

Courtney ran her fingers over the twinkly dress.

"You must be hungry after such a hellish day," Benoît said. "Do you like quiche?"

"You don't have to go to the trouble..."

"There is an incredible *boulangerie* at the street level of my building, which is why my flat is always filled with such mouthwatering aromas. I know, I know. You are envious."

Courtney had no idea what a *boulangerie* was but it sounded hot.

"I could eat quiche," Courtney said.

***

If Heaven had a flavor, Courtney guessed it would taste like the Quiche Lorraine that Benoît picked up from the *boulangerie* downstairs. It was so smooth, scintillating and eggy that it practically melted in her mouth and slid down her throat without needing to be chewed. She closed her eyes a few times, savoring forkfuls of the fluffy masterpiece. She and Benoît partook of their casual but delectable meal outside on the balcony. Courtney's heart sang when she discovered that Benoît had a view of the Eiffel Tower which was lit up brilliantly when the sun went down.

Courtney's gaze gravitated back and forth between the tower and Benoît, who was vivaciously telling stories of hilarious encounters with taxi riders. His face lit up with animation and he was practically buoyant, using his hands to tell the story with dramatic flourish. His eyes danced and his dimples flirted. Courtney was fixated on how Benoît smiled with his whole face and told stories using his whole body. He was a firecracker, fervently in love with life and he had an invigorating energy that made everyone around him smile. She never really understood what *joie de vivre* meant until she met Benoît.

Courtney's phone vibrated. She abruptly shut it off.

Benoît simpered coyly.

"That was good quiche," Courtney said, trying to swallow a yawn.

"You are tired," Benoît observed.

"No," Courtney lied. She secretly did not want this moment to end. Everything was perfect for once. Besides, the butterfly in her ribcage was reminding her of how complicated the bedtime arrangements would be.

"Please," Benoît said, getting up and putting a reassuring hand on Courtney's shoulder. "Take the bed. I will sleep on the floor in the other room."

"That doesn't seem fair," Courtney said smally. "These are your digs, after all."

The dishes clinked as Benoît collected them. "You are my guest."

Courtney's heart sank like a boot being sucked into marshy mud during a spring thaw. "I'd feel bad if you slept on the floor."

Benoît turned his head towards Courtney, perplexed.

"I mean, it's not like we've never been in a bed together," Courtney said uncertainly.

Benoît shook his head, stunned.

"And… I guess I could trust…"

"I will be on my best behavior," Benoît said, with a gentlemanly smile blossoming on his face like a happy day lily.

Courtney was unsure as to why she suddenly felt a surge of disappointment. "Yeah," she said awkwardly. "I know you will."

***

Alone, Courtney was tucked tightly under the blanket like a stiff envelope. The bed was much more comfortable than she imagined. Benoît had one of those divine, foamy mattresses. She felt her butt sink into a perfectly fitted, custom butt-mold. It was like sinking into a cozy cuddle. Benoît had great taste in blankets for a dude. They were simple but classy with black and white chevrons. And *damn* they were comfy. Courtney would not be surprised if she had dreams about being a warm, mushy burrito.

Reality walloped Courtney on the loaf. *She was in Benoît's bed. Like literally IN his actual bed.* Her heart fluttered and flapped like a swarm of frantic bats trying to escape a claustrophobic rafter. In a few brief moments, Benoît would be curled up beside her. Inches away. On purpose this time, not just a random, drunken accident. She could not decide if she was elated or terrified.

"Pajama party!" Benoît squealed as he ran boisterously into the room and did a cannonball on the bed, causing Courtney to catapult a few inches above the mattress.

Before Courtney could stop it from happening, she exploded into a sudden burst of laughter, covering her mouth in a futile attempt to be discreet.

"The hell?" Courtney tittered with girlish giddiness.

She ogled Benoît as he climbed across the bed.

"You have cartoon croissants on your pajama bottoms," Courtney observed. She chose not to state the obvious about Benoît being shirtless because that would make her voice squeak.

"I like things that are quirky," Benoît winked as he climbed under the chevron blanket and wriggled beneath with delight. Benoît turned to face Courtney, curling into a playful ball. "This will be so much fun, *oui?*"

Courtney gaped at Benoît. He generated so much warmth under the covers. It was dreamy. He was dreamy.

"Is something wrong, Courtney? Is the pillow not firm enough?"

"I smell," Courtney said faintly.

Benoît impulsively sprayed laughter spit nearly in Courtney's face, making her scrunch her nose.

"It's not funny, Benoît. I haven't showered in a couple of days. I'm funky. Don't lie there and tell me you don't smell me."

Benoît pursed his lips at the irony. Courtney's maddeningly perfect aroma distracted him on a daily basis. Even now he could faintly smell alluring, tropical guavas. "No, you're good," he smirked.

"So… how does this work?" Courtney asked nervously.

"We… lie here for a bit until we fall asleep?"

Courtney exhaled, "Right."

"Courtney, are you sure you would not prefer if I sleep in the other room? I get the feeling that you are anxious."

"No! I mean... I get cold easily. You're like a fricking radiator and it's kind of... not horrible."

"Not *horrible*?"

"Would it..." Courtney stammered. "... would it be against the rules if you..."

Benoît raised an eyebrow.

"I don't know," Courtney continued. "... moved a little closer?"

"You literally made up all the rules," Benoît laughed. "They are yours to break."

Courtney squirmed as Benoît wiggled closer to her. Her face felt like it was on fire.

"Better?" Benoît asked.

Courtney nodded vigorously.

"Benoît, I need you... to do me a favor."

"Mmm?"

"Will you please come to my Fashion Week show? As my plus one?"

Benoit gawked, utterly stunned.

CHAPTER THIRTY-EIGHT
(DAY 50 IN PARIS)

After waking up in the same place for eleven nights in row, Courtney was no longer startled to realize she was in Benoît's bed. It was a new kind of normal but also made her sad each day that inched closer to the day she would have to leave. Paris felt like *her place.* Benoît felt like *her person.* But it would all come to an end very soon.

Courtney's phone vibrated with a text. She rolled her eyes as she glanced at it. ***"You haven't answered your phone in nearly two weeks. What are you hiding, you little skank?... xoxo Gramma"***

Courtney grunted audibly and ignored the text. Sadly, the phone vibrated again. ***"If you don't respond, we're going to have to assume you have been sucked into an international crime circle. Or pole dancing to stay alive. Or dead. Jesus Christ, you're dead aren't you. Dammit, Courtney…. Gramma."***

Courtney fiddled with her phone, wondering if she should put her grandmother's mind at ease. Before she could finish her thought her phone alerted her of a Skype call. Courtney whimpered and quickly answered. "Make it quick, Gramma," she said to her grandmother's scowl on the screen.

"Would it kill you to answer your family's texts?"

"I'm fine, Gramma. Everything's fine. No need to alert the media."

"Where are you right now?"

"Hotel."

"Doesn't look like a hotel."

"It's a special hotel."

"You mean a brothel?"

"It's one of those full-service outfits."

"Lies."

"Gramma, can we not do this right now? My show is tonight and..."

Benoît sauntered out of the bathroom, freshly showered and wearing a towel around his waist. Courtney tried to shoo him back into the bathroom but Courtney's grandmother already saw him.

"Who is that?" Gramma snarled.

"Benoît," Courtney sighed.

Benoît cocked his head.

"Who the hell is Benoît?"

"My friend."

"You don't have friends."

"Gramma..."

"Why is he wearing a towel?"

"Because if he wasn't wearing a towel he would be naked."

Benoît buckled with laughter.

"Are you shacking up with some French pimp?"

"It's temporary. Benoît is helping me out."

"Why do you need help? What did you do?"

"Nothing."

"You can't trust him."

"I can, actually."

"What about Paul? You're engaged."

"No we're not."

"You would be if you'd get over yourself and take his calls. I tell ya, call display will lead to the fall of mankind. In my day you couldn't blow people off like you can with this witchcraft technology. Someone called, you answered the damn phone like a mofo."

"I don't love Paul."

Benoît raised an eyebrow.

"Don't be daft. Of course you do."

"No, Gramma. I don't."

"What about all those years you were together in the biblical sense?"

"I didn't know any better."

"What, are you enlightened now? Did they brainwash you over there? Have you been into the fricassée?"

"Cut me some slack, Gramma. Paul was one of like four guys in Colby Haven. I had nothing to compare him to. No frame of reference."

"Oh stop."

"I was so sheltered I didn't even realize what an ignorant redneck..."

"Paul has nice shirts!"

"I've never been treated like a grownup woman before."

"Because you're not..."

"I didn't even know... I had no idea I was... I can do better. I understand that now."

"You *have* been into the..."

"Fricassée is not a drug, Gramma. We've been over this."

"Get out of there, Courtney. Now. You are in grave danger. That seedy city is infested with French people."

"It's not infested with French people. This is their home. If anything, this place is infested with tourists."

"Now see here, girlie..."

Benoît swooped in and greeted Courtney's grandmother with his irresistible charm. *"Bonjour, Grand-maman! Ça va?"*

"Hey," Gramma grunted. "I remember you. You're the damn foreigner who kidnapped Courtney."

"I am afraid you are mistaken. I am not a foreigner. I was born here, in fact," Benoît said with a smile that went *"TING!"*

"Don't get fresh with me, Naked French Man."

"You can't talk to him that way!" Courtney spat.

"Dang! You spend a couple months with those churlish snobs and now you're absorbing all the rude..."

"He's not rude!" Courtney said, surprising herself with the angry volume of her voice.

"They're all rude!" Gramma barked. "Trying to sound all posh with their fake language..."

"Benoît is not rude, you ignorant bigot! He is literally the opposite of rude! And he's got *joie de vivre* coming out his butt! Don't you dare talk smack about him!"

Benoît blinked.

"You're speaking in riddles," Gramma snorted.

"The friends I've met on this trip are the most beautiful people on earth! They are warm and kind and open and generous and polite and have a zest for life that you wouldn't even believe!"

"You're right," Gramma said, crossing her arms. "I don't believe it."

"Well then I feel sorry for you, Gramma. Because you'll never understand how amazing it feels to know these people. The Parisians have made me a better person."

"That's not saying much," Gramma muttered.

"I don't have to put up with this," Courtney stated. "Not anymore."

Benoît smiled proudly.

"Good bye, Gramma. It's been real."

When Courtney shut her phone off, toweled Benoît slow clapped, segueing into an enthusiastic round of applause.

"Benoît, put on some pants."

***

The evening gown felt like butter when Courtney slipped it on. The Skype call she had with her grandmother was still under her skin and making her shake visibly. But she had to suck it up and go to her show, if nothing else than to stick it to her family. Courtney blew some stressed air that had been briefly stored in her cheeks and scrutinized herself in the mirror. She had never worn anything so dazzling and red. The contest administrators really guessed her measurements right. She almost felt like she belonged in this dress.

Courtney shyly stepped out of the bathroom with her hair pulled up and adorned with baby's breath buds. She wore a glossy cherry lipstick that matched her dress perfectly and shimmered along with the dress. The frothy train slid along behind her as she moved about self-consciously.

She cleared her throat.

Tuxedoed Benoît turned to see Courtney walk awkwardly out of the bathroom. His jaw dropped. *"Mon dieu,"* he breathed. A shimmer from Courtney's dress reflected on his wide eyes.

"So…" Courtney said self-consciously. "Do I look stupid?"

Benoît grasped for words.

"You clean up real nice," she offered.

"I have not worn this thing in many years. It is a little out of style."

"Is it?" Courtney played dumb. "Yeah, I wasn't going to say anything."

Benoît playfully cuffed Courtney before holding the door open for her. She pretended to say *"ow"* and goofily clocked him with her red, sparkly handbag, following him out the door.

CHAPTER THIRTY-NINE

The fashion show venue was abuzz with glamor and pretense. Alexandria Fontrose made an ostentatious entrance through a reception area, wearing a ludicrous, skin tight, yellow dress that literally looked like a banana peel. She fanned herself with fake modesty when she was approached by Gerald Featherstone, wearing one of his lofty scarves.

"Jealous!" Gerald fake-lisped when beholding the elegantly pompous Alexandria.

"My favorite deadly sin!" Alexandria said demurely, kissing the air on either side of Gerald's face.

"I have never seen you look so radiant," Gerald said, eyeballing Alexandria from top to bottom. "Explain yourself."

"Yellow is making a comeback," Alexandria bragged. "Didn't you get the memo?"

"Your design?"

"Naturally."

"Girl, you are on fire!" Gerald gushed. "And to think there were murmurings in Milan that you're a has-been. Shame on Milan!"

"That is simply obtuse."

"They say your ideas are redundant, your judgment foggy and your coffers empty."

"Pah-lease!" Alexandria smacked her lipstick. "Nobody says *coffers.*"

"Well," Gerald said confidentially, "I told Garth, Anatole, Crispin, Tristan H and Tristan W that you can *so* quit drinking whenever you want."

"Come ON!" Alexandria said, wondering how to hide her glass of Chianti. "I barely touch the stuff!"

"I told them also that you became a mentor out of the goodness of your heart. Not just to save your reputation."

Intense, Alexandria grabbed someone else's wine and swigged it.

✳✳✳

"VIP list," Courtney said with confidence she hoped was convincing. She offered her invitation to a security guard at the front entrance of the venue. "Courtney Stent. Alexandria Fontrose is expecting me."

Benoît chuffed.

"Ms. Fontrose didn't think you would make it tonight," the security guard said, studying the invitation with a sideways head."

"What?" Courtney asked, stumped.

"We are pleased you could make it," the security guard nodded. He then turned to Benoît with a sneer. "This is an exclusive event. Designers and media only."

"He's my plus one," Courtney insisted.

"Seriously?" the security guard said sardonically.

"Don't be a tool," Courtney responded to the guard, pulling Benoît into the venue.

Courtney and Benoît awkwardly walked around the room, looking quite out of place. Courtney spotted Alexandria's blinding dress from across the room.

"It's Dree," Courtney said, stiffening.

Benoît nodded, nudging Courtney to make her point.

"Well," Courtney explained, "she is the reason I'm here so…"

"Courtney…"

"You're right. I'm not here for her. I'm here for… me. Let's do this."

"My girl," Benoît said, squeezing her hand.

"This is ridiculous, Benoît. Everyone is looking at me."

"Only because you are stunning. Now take a deep breath, mind your posture and walk into that crowd like you own the place."

"Here goes nothing," Courtney inhaled as she sliced through the crowd.

Benoît got pulled aside by a waiter who handed him a tray.

"There you are," the waiter hissed, eyeing Benoît's tuxedo. "Take these little quiches. We're understaffed."

"I am not…" Benoît tried to explain, baffled.

"Don't spill on yourself!"

Confused, Benoît walked around the room with the tray. People took little quiches from him and stuffed Euros in his pockets.

Across the room, Alexandria was being interviewed by the media. "Then there was the time I spent in Tanzania," she said pretentiously into a microphone. "Designing clothes for orphans. Blind orphans. It was heart wrenching, really. They were always crying. Bumping into each other. All that filth made me realize…"

Alexandria noticed Courtney fumbling through the crowd and pulled her over. Confused, Courtney gaped dumbly at the camera.

"Speaking of my conscience," Alexandria gloated. "here is a fluffy, new baby chicken I took under my wing. She goes by the name of Courtney. Stent, to be more specific. My career exploded into a gorgeous display of firecrackers before I got around to having a daughter of my own. Excuse me, if you please."

Alexandria yanked Courtney aside, out of the view of the cameras. "I didn't think you would be here," she whispered to Courtney.

"Why does everyone keep saying that?" Courtney asked.

"You'd best make yourself scarce," Alexandria warned.

"Why? I earned the right to be here. What's going on?"

Alexandria swooped back around to face her public. "Crumpet," she said to Courtney. "Why don't you tell the nice people how the

Universe helped us find each other and all the valuable lessons I've taught you?"

"What the actual f..."

"Isn't she precious?" Alexandria said with her hands clasped together. "Like a little pearl in an oyster."

"Whoa," Courtney said loud enough to make Alexandria wince. "What are you wearing?"

"We're just like Da Vinci and Verrocchio, aren't we?" Alexandria swooned.

***

Still confused, Benoît continued to walk around with a platter. He turned his head when he heard a familiar voice called his name. Étienne approached Benoît with a sultry woman.

"*Cousin! Little quiches? Don't mind if I do.*"

"*Étienne, what are you doing here?*"

"*Look what I have! An underwear model. Say hello, Geneviève.*"

Geneviève gave Benoît the stink eye.

"*When did you become a waiter?*" Étienne asked with his mouth full of quiche.

"*I am not a waiter. I was mistaken for one when I came here with Courtney.*"

"You're still with Courtney? Thank God! What the two of you have is sacred. What a tragedy it would be if you stopped (insert cat noise) *—ing with her."*

Benoît did a double take when he noticed Étienne suddenly had his arm around another woman's waist.

"Who is that?" Benoît asked, dumbfounded.

"Oh this? It's Véronique. You may remember her from that billboard advertising lacy things. I found her moments ago by the sweet table, NOT eating profiteroles. Congratulate us, Benoît. I think it is love."

Benoît spotted Courtney across the room, flowing with a current of people into the auditorium. She looked nervous.

"Take this," Benoît said, giving the tray to Étienne and trying to slice through the crowd.

"Go get her!" Étienne called across the room to Benoît. *"Pursue her like a primal, Neolithic huntsman!"* Étienne turned to Véronique. *"I am so proud of him."*

***

Courtney nervously took her seat, surrounded by strangers, with a conspicuously empty seat next to hers. She sat slowly, trying not to let her dress ride up just as the lights began to dim.

Benoît discreetly slipped into the auditorium and stood at the back, surveying the room for Courtney.

Courtney looked intimidated as models strut down the catwalk, wearing outrageous styles. She turned to an aloof stranger sitting next to her. "Have you read the program?" she asked the stranger. "My designs are thirty-seventh in the running order."

"Is that supposed to mean something to me?" the stranger exhaled.

Courtney sighed, looked at the empty seat next to her then anxiously looked around for Benoît.

As Benoît apologetically searched for Courtney by checking each aisle, he heard a familiar cackle from the across the room. Benoît narrowed his eyes when he confirmed that the cackle was emitting from Alexandria.

Courtney was perplexed when a model strut down the catwalk wearing a yellow outfit.

"Oh god," Courtney quavered to herself.

An announcer nailed Courtney's darkest fear into her emotional coffin. "Catia is wearing a chiffon, sarong-style summer dress in a stunning canary yellow. With a cape. Capes have made an unexpected comeback this summer."

"What the hell's going on?" Courtney said, tugging on the aloof stranger's sleeve. "She's wearing my idea!"

The aloof stranger ignored Courtney.

"And you don't care," Courtney said, blowing the hair off of her forehead.

"Courtney!" Benoît panted as he reached for her arm. "Courtney?" he said again when he noticed how visibly distraught she was, quaking with trauma in her eyes.

"... the latest in the insurmountable summer collection of Alexandria Fontrose," the announcer boomed.

"What has happened, Courtney?" Benoît said, trying to stop her from getting up and leaving.

"Those are mine!" she bawled. "She can't do this! She just can't!"

"... thirty-seven years in the industry," the announcer continued mercilessly, "and Ms. Fontrose is still on top of her game."

Sobbing uncontrollably, Courtney struggled free from Benoît's embrace and scoured the room for an escape exit. She ran unceremoniously out of the auditorium with Benoît doing his best to keep up. She headed for the reception area, frantically looking for an exit when she stopped dead in her tracks at the sound of Alexandria's cackle. Alexandria was leaving the auditorium, deep in conversation with Gerald Featherstone. Courtney stomped across the room and interrupted.

"You lying piece of..."

"Shih Tzu Puppy!" Alexandria chimed innocently. "Although I'm always happy to see your sugar-sweet pie face, it still perplexes me as to why you showed up today."

"You invited me," Courtney seethed.

"Yes, Gummy Bear," Alexandria said, gesturing for Gerald to leave. "But after what happened at the hotel a few weeks ago, your automobile troubles, Évian... I thought you'd be on a plane to Wisconsin."

"It *was* you."

"Strudel…"

"Don't call me Strudel! I am not a Germanic pastry!"

Alexandria's eyes widened at the unexpected volume in Courtney's voice. "Love," she said maternally.

"You faux furred my taxi?" Courtney thundered, garnering attention from everyone around them. "You burgled my hotel room? You sent me on a wild goose chase to Évian and lied about Ralph Lauren? Only a complete psychopath would lie about Ralph Lauren!"

"Shhh. I was sparing your feelings."

"You stole my life's work!"

Alexandria fake laughed in the direction of a gawking onlooker. "A fan. Off balance. She's been *following* me since she was seven." Alexandria turned to Courtney and whispered harshly in her ear, "Think of it as a compliment."

Benoît found his way into the reception area and watched Courtney like a hawk.

"You liar!" Courtney shrieked like a hysterical pterodactyl.

Benoît winced.

"Pumpkin Seed," Alexandria said patiently, "I am a lot of things but I am not a liar."

"I trusted you!" Courtney wailed.

"I can't imagine why," Alexandria chuckled. "Didn't I tell you that trust sets you up for disappointment and pain? Consider this a lesson learned. You're welcome."

"You've ruined my life."

"Oh Cookie Crumb. You are so innocent. I just want to squeeze your cute, little chipmunk cheeks."

"You seriously think you can stand there in that banana peel and expect me to feel inferior to you?"

Some pretentious onlookers sniggered.

"If you are referring to the elegant dress I composed for the occasion..."

"What did the color yellow ever do to *you?*"

"I don't have to take this abuse."

"You better hope to hell there's no monkeys in here or you'll be a light afternoon snack, *bee-atch!*"

"You little urchin!" Alexandria snarled as she jumped Courtney, causing a nasty cat fight. Onlookers were both appalled and intrigued. Benoît was poised to lunge.

"After everything I've done for you!" Alexandria howled in a pile of dress and hair and claws.

"You are so dead!" Courtney roared.

Alexandria's ridiculous dress snagged and peeled off her body like a banana peel. The on-looking crowd collectively gasped, while horrified Alexandria stood, exposed in her unflattering undergarments. "Security!" Alexandria screamed.

Security guards rushed to the scene, making indecipherable faces at Alexandria's defrocked body.

"I want that horrible creature arrested for assault!" Alexandria whined.

"But she assaulted *me!*" Courtney insisted. "And not before she plagiarized my entire repertoire!"

"She is a talentless speck! What reason would I have to pilfer her meager designs?"

"Plus," Courtney added, "you should charge her for public drunkenness and indecent exposure!"

The security guard shrugged and put handcuffs on Alexandria.

"What in the name of Giorgio Armani are you doing?" Alexandria huffed.

"She raises a good point," the guard nodded. "You *are* naked. And it wouldn't be the first time we detained you for public intoxication."

"How would you like to tell him how *you* robbed and trashed my hotel room and nearly killed Benoît and I by sabotaging his car?"

"This is sacrilege!" Alexandria yowled. "I... would somebody please cover me with something?... It's her word against mine. And everyone in this room knows who I am so..."

The security guard sighed and raised his voice to be heard above the din of the crowd. "Can anybody here vouch for Courtney Stint?"

"Stent."

"Stent?"

"I can!" Benoît called, pushing his way to the front of the crowd.

"Who are you?" the guard grimaced.

"Her fiancé," Benoît gloated with a smile that could melt a million glaciers.

Courtney's heart stopped. Maybe literally. "Um.. what?"

"*Bijou,*" Benoît said dotingly, "you dropped this by the punch bowl."

Courtney gasped so intensely she nearly choked up a fur ball when Benoît put an engagement ring on her finger.

"What a shame it would have been if you had lost it," Benoît said bashfully.

"Is this for reals?" Courtney whispered breathlessly.

"If you want it to be," Benoît whispered back.

"But I can't..."

"Why on earth not, Silly Woman?"

"Because... because I don't deserve you."

Benoît cupped Courtney's face and looked her deep in the eyes. "Now you listen to me..."

"You're way too good for me."

"Courtney..."

"I don't want to hurt you."

"The only thing that would hurt me would be if you went back to Wisconsin."

Courtney pursed her lips with tears welling in her eyes. "But are you sure??"

"Yes."

"We only met like…"

"Does not matter."

"But I'm such a…"

"I do not think so."

"What if I screw…"

"You will not."

"How can you possibly know…"

"I just do."

"Can we just…"

"Yes, please."

They kissed for an awkward amount of time. The security guard wiped a tear from his eye. "I love Paris," the guard wept.

"OMFG!" Alexandria griped. "You're seriously going to listen to that oddly dressed piece of Euro-trash?"

"Watch it, Tramp!" Courtney barked. "That's the future father of my French babies!"

"He's not a reliable source!" Alexandria said, pointing an accusing, painted fingernail at Benoît. "He desecrated my favorite handbag with his stupid taxi!"

Benoît shook his head in disgust. "Vindictive demon."

Alexandria swerved around to point at Courtney. "That tarty little squirrel over here doesn't deserve to be here! She is not a designer!"

"Courtney is a brilliant designer," Benoît said coolly, putting Alexandria's finger away. "I have seen with my own eyes what she can create from pure, naturalistic inspiration. She brings nature to life. The trees. The sunshine. She is truly inspiring. I think it is clear why someone would want to lift her ideas."

"I might choke on my own sick," Alexandria gagged.

"Shhh!" the security guard hissed at Alexandria. "This is so beautiful."

"He's biased!" Alexandria snarled. "Love makes you stupid. Can anyone here definitively prove that Courtney has any link to the fashion industry at all?"

"I can!" Étienne piped up, pushing his way to the front of the crowd.

"*He* can," Alexandria said, going cross-eyed.

"Étienne Garnier," Étienne said in an overly professional manner. "Proprietor of one of the most frequented souvenir boutiques in Paris. Courtney Stent works for me."

"I do?" Courtney said, cocking her head.

"She does," Étienne nodded. "Courtney is the Goddess of sassy yet practical shoes. Comfortable enough to walk the cobblestones of Paris, but without making you look like a frumpy, sexless bag of potatoes."

Courtney gaped.

"I know her well," Étienne went on. "When I once sold hideous, rubber shoes in the shape of croissants, Courtney's keen eye and no-nonsense approach saved my business."

"She is very honest," Benoît smirked.

"Painfully honest," Étienne agreed. "Brutally honest. Just blurting out the truth all the time like a lunatic on a day pass."

"Too far," Benoît whispered.

"And how could she be anything but innocent with that girlish smile and statuesque derrière? Lucky for me, Garnier men share their women."

"No they do not," Benoît grunted.

"You cannot blame a guy for trying," Étienne smirked.

"Weird," the security guard said, scratching his head. "But good enough."

"I am a woman of influence!" Alexandria protested as the guard locked the handcuffs on her wrists.

"You are a woman of crapulence," the guard retorted.

As Alexandria was dragged away, blathering on about indignities and fancy lawyers, Benoît pulled Courtney aside, away from the chaos. He was about to whisper something coy in Courtney's ear but was inadvertently brushed aside when Étienne swarmed Courtney with a weepy hug.

"This is the happiest day of my life!" Étienne cartoonishly wept.

"Étienne..." Benoît said.

"I have always wanted a lady cousin to endow with my many flatteries, hug with abandon, mercilessly tease and with whom I can share my naughty secrets. You, Courtney have selected your man wisely. I highly endorse Benoît. He is perfection. Much like a delectable chocolate soufflé, sensually textured, deliciously tempting. And inside he is oozing with warm, irresistible sweetness."

"Pretty much," Courtney smirked. "Now if he only had a couch he'd basically be Jesus."

Benoît inhaled nervously.

"What is your meaning?" Étienne asked, narrowing a questioning, left eye. "Benoît has a beautiful, white leather couch…"

Benoît shook his head urgently at Étienne.

"… He spent an obscene amount of money on that couch," Étienne continued. "It is the only luxury he has ever allowed himself. That couch is his favorite worldly possess…ion."

The penny dropped. Courtney ran her hands down her perfect, red gown then goggled at the ring on her finger, which seemed to wink at her with an aptly timed sparkle. "Benoît…" she said faintly.

Benoît looked around modestly.

"Did you…" Courtney trailed off.

"It was only a couch," Benoît shrugged.

That weird syrupy emotion oozed over Courtney again. She gaped at Benoit, wondering if this is what acceptance and belonging felt like.

"I guess it doesn't matter anymore that my return airline ticket was stolen from the pocket of my purple chemise," Courtney said flirtatiously.

"But how will you survive Paris?" Benoît teased. "I threw Arthur H. Flummery's book out the window."

"Meh. I'll figure something out."

"You know," Benoît said, lifting Courtney's chin, "I have no intention of pronouncing the letter H."

"Yeah, I figured as much," Courtney smiled.

LOGGED IN

A Laugh Out Loud Romantic Comedy!

Allison McWood

LOVESICK LAKE

A Darkish Romantic Farce

Allison McWood

Allison McWood is an acclaimed, multi-published Canadian author, playwright and lyricist. Specializing in comedy, farce and satire, Allison's novels, plays, musicals and children's books all feature her signature quirkiness. Her writing has not only charmed readers and audiences across Canada, but her works have also been taught at Universities around the world from Vancouver to Lucknow, India. Holding a specialized Literature/Renaissance Drama degree from Toronto's York University, Allison is also a Shakespearean dramaturge, and Marlovian scholar.

When she is not writing, you can either find Allison in her red canoe, reading way too many books, playing air guitar, petting all the dogs or sipping cappuccino in a cute cafe.

www.instagram.com/annelidpress/